YOU MADE YOUR BED

Thank you –
[illegible]

YOU MADE YOUR BED

Joan Webb Basile

Library of Congress Control Number:		2007907550
ISBN:	Hardcover	978-1-4257-8580-2
	Softcover	978-1-4257-8556-7

This book was printed in the United States of America.

To order additional copies of this book, contact:
Xlibris Corporation
1-888-795-4274
www.Xlibris.com
Orders@Xlibris.com

42273

Dedication

This book is dedicated to my mom, Mary Ellen Bryant Webb. She was one of the strongest women I have ever known. She lived a hard life, exactly as she was told she should do it, raised her children the best way she knew how and if she didn't know how to hug us, at least she succumbed to my hugs, willingly, in her later years. I thank her for her determination, her honesty, her resilience and her example. They have served me well.

Acknowledgements

There are so many people who have come into my life as friends, mentors, and advisors, that the reader will have to bear with me while I mention them.

How does one say thank you for one's life? It is impossible to do, but I know that without the help of Ann and Ray David, and Dr George Soufleris, who were caring enough to take personal risks, I would not exist. Thank you from the bottom of my heart for everything you did.

My childhood buddies, especially Donna Delahunt, Carol Davis, Sammy Riccelli, George Wright, Ronnie Wallace, Arena Webb, Ginny Riccelli and Mable Winn, will always occupy a very special place in my heart. My high school friends, Elet Vollmer, Barry Goldsmith, Ruby Hinman, Neal Brown, Bud Hemmings, Paul Pierce, Paul Murphy, Joanne Lay, Roger Russell, Ed Tyler, Dave Sheldon, Sue, Joyce and Bud Oatman, and a host of others, are right up there, as well.

A special thanks to Linda, for being my sweet sister.

My adult friends are too numerous to mention, except for those who spent hours reading the book and making suggestions. They are Sandy Huffer, Lynn Morrow, Jan Joyce, Jennifer Keyes, Karen Norcross, Norma Hook and Bill Molesky . Thanks to them for all their help, support and love.

Lynn Prichard gave me the confidence in my teaching ability to allow me to reach out and go for the Big Time. If it hadn't been for Lynn, I probably wouldn't have.

Thanks to Bill Goss who was a great supporter all through the process with wonderful suggestions and Bill Kleis, who patiently educated me in the physical ramifications of the problems I faced, along with Dr. Marvin Brown who birthed my children, provided a lifetime of excellent care and kept my secret.

A very special thank you goes to Bennet Pomerantz, without whom I would never have lengthened a short audio script into a full-length book

No one could be as lucky as I, in acquiring a new family. Jeannine, Anne and Vicky are three of the greatest women in the world. Their father, the love of my life, Mr. Florine Basile, JR, is one of the world's best dads. Watching them together is a delight.

My beautiful daughters, Tracy and Suzanne, have been an inspiration to me all of their lives, although they probably don't realize it. I just can't imagine a life without them and without them I would not have had the courage to survive. Thank you for letting me be your mom.

My wonderful husband, Flory, has stuck with me and encouraged me throughout the fifteen plus years of what feels like hundreds of re-writes. Your patience and understanding speak your love for me in volumes.

For all of you, I am blessed.

Joan

Foreword

by Bennet Pomerantz

I have a pet peeve regarding most book forewords, especially those from so-called experts in the field who never met the author but imply they have by seeming to be buddy-buddy with the author In their foreword, they agree with the author point by point and won't disagree with anything unless they write their own book on the subject. Many times the author of the foreword is a first-time writer as well and tends to promote his own book from the foreword.

I also dislike the book forewords from those persons who love every single word the author has written—and it is the author's first book. Then there are the special media personas who have had a family member who was affected by something similar to what the book expresses. These celebrities tend to address their foundation or charities while mentioning the author's work.

So when Joan asked me to write this foreword for her first book, I was very happy to do it. You see, I was one of the lucky ones who read the beginnings of her book fifteen years ago, when it was in the format of an audio script. When I first read her words, I encouraged her to write the book you now hold in your hands.

Joan has told me a few times that she is very grateful and appreciative for everything I have done for her. Well, Joan, I have BAD news for you. I set you up. I hooked you into writing your first book. Hopefully, the second one will be easier to write, and I cannot wait to read the next one as I savored this one.

Now the audience has this work in their hands. My job as a media critic is easy to do. I get to review what an author has done and tell them what

I think. However, the book audience is a harsher critic than I ever will be. I know I could write the most glowing review for this book; however, the readers are the true judges of the book's merit. The reason that they are harsher is because they do it with their own money.

Now let's talk a little about the book. I read it and was overwhelmed. This personal biography is touching and hard-hitting. Joan opened a vein of her life and placed it on the page. Is this book strong in content and message? Yes. Is this book hard-hitting? Yes. Is the text very honestly told? You better believe it!

What makes this publication worth your time is the human factor. In this book, Joan takes the reader where they may not be comfortable. In her written words, she makes you care about her personal story—because she lived it!

I do not want to reveal too much about this book. If I did, it could spoil the reader of any justice in their enjoyment and/or discomfort in reading this engaging text. All I can say is this—you will be haunted by this text long after you finish reading the words.

Bennet Pomerantz
Writer/Author/Media Critic for Amazon.com and AUDIOWORLD
September 2007

Prologue

December 21, 1965

Something was terribly wrong. Why were they so quiet? Suddenly, a reason that she didn't want to consider burst unbidden into her reluctant psyche. Fear exploded inside her and began drizzling unwanted adrenaline through her already jangled nervous system. Did they know?

She cast a furtive glance across their faces, trying to read what was there. Had they found out? She could usually read them like a book, but she was too frightened and too distracted to concentrate. If they knew, then this evening that they had worked so hard to accomplish, could end in tragedy.

During the past few weeks, she had finally been able to relax a little. Police and sheriff's cars no longer sent her into unbridled panic. Suddenly a vision of herself rising up out of a steamy hot bathtub, the flesh on her legs and abdomen scalding red, exploded into her consciousness. Her stomach churned. She wanted to pace. Every muscle in her body cried out for that simple release of tension, but she couldn't let them know her fears. This evening was something she had longed for, for most of her twenty-eight years, but now she wondered if the haste of wanting it so badly had caused her to make a wrong decision.

"Look at them," she thought to herself. "They're too quiet." They should have been climbing the walls with pent-up nervousness, but instead they just sat there calmly.

Despite her fear, she couldn't help the little flip-flop her heart did as she looked at them all, decked out in their dressiest black-and-white finery and best hairdos. Their mom's jewelry and dad's cufflinks; just sitting, chatting quietly as if they were waiting for another routine rehearsal to begin. They were disguising their feelings, she could tell. They must know!

Maybe she was imagining things, she prayed. They'd sounded fine during warm-ups. Pitch was good, vocal quality never better. They seemed ready to perform and ready to remember everything she had taught them over the semester. But something was missing. There was no spark, no intensity, only this strange calm. At rehearsal that afternoon, she had scarcely been able to control them; they were so excited. What had happened to dampen their enthusiasm? She was afraid of the answer.

The awful suspicion began to surface again, but she pushed it back down and tried to return to exploring more acceptable possibilities. But she couldn't avoid the fact that they had been talking boisterously as she was coming up the stairs. They'd been loudly discussing something when she burst happily into the room. Steve shushed them quickly as if he didn't want her to hear what they had been talking about. A hush had fallen over them, and they immediately began to check out their shoes, consult their music, or commune with the softly falling snow outside the steamy windows. Anything to avoid looking her in the eyes, she thought.

She groped for reasons for their strange behavior. The last group she had brought to concert had been a junior-high choir. Perhaps the greater maturity of the high-school student was the explanation for the calm. But even as her mind said it, her heart knew it wasn't true. Every choral professor she had worked with in college had warned about the importance of harnessing the preconcert jitters and redirecting the energy toward the performance. She had hung on every word, taking copious notes in order to remember everything that would make her future high-school chorus a success. Nothing she had heard would explain this behavior. She was just kidding herself that there was nothing wrong.

An overwhelming sadness crept over her that this night of nights could be in jeopardy because of something she had done. It made no difference that she'd had no choice. It now threatened her career and family. She also knew that if she didn't start thinking clearly and logically, she could ruin all the hard work they had accomplished.

It just didn't make sense that after all this time someone would have found out and spread the word. It had only been a few hours since she had left them that afternoon. Even in Camden, New York, gossip couldn't travel that fast. She hoped.

She forced herself to think calmly instead of reacting to imagined threats. The fact that this was her big debut as a high-school choral conductor was probably eliciting this kind of jitters and causing this overreaction. Her ability at this level was relatively untested. Tonight's performance was a demanding one. There were several difficult cues, any one of which would cause a musical disaster if she missed. This probably accounted for a lot of her unrealistic fear.

There was that one spot in the fourth movement that was particularly tricky. If she managed to get them through that, everything else would fall into place, providing their odd behavior was not the result of their having found out.

The normally soothing fragrance of Christmas pine wafted its way up the staircase from the auditorium below, but it did little to relieve her apprehension. She heard the first crisp tones of the band playing, "The Carol of the Bells." It echoed up the stairway and into the warm-up room.

Her first Christmas concert had begun.

She swallowed hard, wondering what the outcome of the evening would be. She knew without a doubt that the possible threat of the loss of her career would be minuscule compared to the real threat she'd been living with for months. The two were inextricably woven together, though, because she knew that without a job, she couldn't support the twins, and even if she were lucky enough to avoid being arrested, if her secret were found out, she would lose them anyway—to their father or the authorities.

She had been going through this for months, and just when she thought it was behind her, here it was, raising its ugly presence again. They'd never let her keep the girls. She knew their father could never raise them in an emotionally stable environment, but the pressure his mother would put to bear in order to save face would oblige him to seek their custody.

She knew there wasn't much in this world she couldn't live without for their sakes, but to live without them would be impossible. It was even difficult for her to imagine that she had thought her life was complete before they came into it. The love that had erupted from somewhere inside of her when they brought "Baby A" to her in the hospital was almost overwhelming. Baby A, Tracy, was breathtaking. She had beautiful blue eyes, platinum blond hair—what there was of it, and the very nose that Joan had been trying to disavow every day of her life but now kissed thankfully. The baby had ten fingers and ten toes, two ears, and she was five pounds, eight ounces of pure love.

It would be awhile before "Baby B" would be able to leave the nursery. Stubborn from the beginning, Suzanne apparently just wasn't ready to be born yet, but the doctors didn't agree. She remembered them on top of her, pushing to dislodge the baby from under her ribs. She tried to persuade them to let things take their own course, but they pushed on her abdomen for four hours, forcing the baby into the birth canal. Joan had put up such a struggle that they had finally put a mask over her mouth, which she struggled against to no avail. She had felt herself being sucked down into unconsciousness.

When she awoke, she was told that because of the difficult birth, Suzanne might have a major defect such as mental retardation, blindness, or hearing disorders. No, she wasn't allowed to go to the nursery to see the baby. She was too weak. She had lost too much blood during the delivery. She would have to wait. She didn't want to.

She waited until the nurses were busy and climbed down off the bed. They couldn't keep her away from her own baby. But when her feet hit the floor, it seemed to slowly come up to meet her, and she folded down into a heap beside it on the floor. She was scolded for disobeying orders, but they finally agreed to bring her baby to her.

Suzanne was suddenly in her arms, and Joan panicked. What if she hurt her? What if she made a mistake? But when their eyes met, the world stopped. Joan knew there was nothing wrong with her child that her love couldn't fix. She would take care of this little one. Eyes so dark and fetching, two more little ears to kiss, another life to cherish. Nothing could stop them now, she thought. Both of her precious babies would grow strong and flourish. They would do it together, she promised.

The first time all three of them were together alone, Joan felt her heart melt and puddle around them protectively.

This night would be their first Christmas concert too, she thought. They had been so excited, getting ready with their brand new red-and-green plaid taffeta dresses. She hoped that two four-year-olds wouldn't be too much for their grandmother. She hoped they were sitting still for the band.

Suddenly, a horrible image erupted into her mind. She saw herself, dripping with the sweat of exertion, ramming a heavy glass vase into her abdomen over and over again. The violence of the scene shocked her so that it made her gasp with surprise. She sat, momentarily paralyzed by the sight.

She looked quickly around to see if anyone had noticed. Apparently they hadn't—their manner was the same; they were still sitting there too quietly. She managed a few silent deep breaths and attempted to calm herself down.

She welcomed the sounds of the band coming up through the stairway and forced herself to picture Lynn in his well-worn but very acceptable black suit. She imagined him standing on the podium in front of the band, arms outstretched, directing in his long-practiced, easy style. She envisioned the pine boughs and garlands that he and his students had spent the entire afternoon hanging. They had also decorated two huge Christmas trees that now framed the stage.

His warm, self-effacing sense of humor endeared him to his students. A subtle joviality perpetually sparkled its way through the thick lenses of his wire-rimmed glasses. He had the knack of being just serious enough to get the job done, but it never occurred to him that anything he did in his lessons or rehearsals was momentous enough to really make a difference. Little did he know the depth of love and respect his students and fellow teachers accorded him. He was a real hometown hero.

When they'd entered the building together earlier, he hadn't been the least bit nervous. She envied his self-assurance and yearned for the day she would feel the same confidence.

She glanced nervously around the room again, studying the young faces, intensely trying to understand their calm. Could it be that they didn't even care? In light of their past enthusiasm, that didn't seem possible. Did they know her secret?

Maybe they were beginning to resent her again, on this evening of their first concert without their beloved Allan Allen. She had taken a huge chance after he announced he was leaving for greener pastures, insisting that she be given the opportunity to take over his high-school chorus. But it was all she had ever wanted for as long as she could remember. She knew that the chances of finding another high school job within commuting distance was next to impossible, and because of the divorce, she didn't want to move the twins just yet. This was her only chance to fulfill her dream.

Allan had hired her two years earlier to teach elementary vocal music. Maybe she should have been content with that. She could hear her mother's voice. *"You're never satisfied with what you have. You're never happy to have what everyone else has. Always has to be something special or you're not satisfied!"*

She knew she was lucky to have any kind of job at all that was within commuting distance of their little lakefront house. School districts were very few and far between in the area. Maybe her mother was right this time. Maybe she had been too ambitious.

At first, all she could think of was that she was finally going to have her choir. Her *very own*! Somehow she would do it. She would prove to them that she would make them as good as Mr. Allen had. Now she was concerned that the high-profile nature of this position might have caused her secret to come out into the open.

There were few opportunities for cultural enrichment in this small rural community so the high-school band and chorus took on an importance unheard of in larger, more sophisticated areas. Concerts in this school were always sold out, especially at Christmas. The fact that she directed that chorus had probably created a curiosity about her that was usually reserved for someone who had achieved a degree of celebrity. Could that misguided interest have caused the type of scrutiny that would have revealed her tragic actions? If so, this would probably be her first and last high-school concert.

Taking over the chorus had been even more difficult than she had ever imagined. Allan had been more popular and well-loved than she had realized. She should have realized this right from the start because she had loved and respected him as her boss.

The students actually resented her being there at first as if it were her fault that Mr. Allen had left in the first place. She was so busy disciplining them that she didn't have a chance to be herself with them. They had no idea who she was, what she was capable of, or even that she had a sense of humor.

In the first few weeks, everything she did backfired. There was no music library to draw from because Mr. Allen was so disorganized that the music disappeared before it ever got filed. She couldn't very well tell them this, so she just tried to make do with the few scraps of things she *did* have. Unfortunately the only things left were songs they had recently done with him, so she had to make do with those. They posed a problem of their own because there was an ongoing argument over how they should be performed so that they would sound like they did when Mr. Allen was there.

Finally, she realized she had to do something drastic and took home some masters for the mimeograph machine. She worked all weekend on an arrangement of "Moon River," which was currently very popular. After finishing the arrangement, it took several hours to draw the five lines and four spaces required for notating the notes. It was an extremely trying and tiresome process and took so long that she felt guilty because she had neglected the twins. It took the whole weekend, but she had to have something new to work on in rehearsal, or she knew they would do her in.

She was so excited by the prospect of introducing the piece that she was at school two hours early to run off the copies, collate, and staple them. She impatiently taught her morning elementary classes, jumped into her car, and sped to the high school, taking the three flights of stairs two at a time. Dispensing with attendance, she quickly handed out the music and enthusiastically introduced it to them. They looked at her as if she were crazy. They had never seen a handwritten piece of music before. No matter how well it is done, it is much more difficult to read than a published piece. They scoffed at it as if it were a piece of trivia.

She went berserk!

Sitting there in that chorus room, waiting for her part of the concert to begin, she still wasn't quite sure what had transpired that day. She knew she had snapped. She totally lost control. She could remember only bits and pieces of what had transpired, but she knew that she had come unglued. She had shouted at them that she was sorry Mr. Allen had left them. She shouted that she was sorry she had wasted her entire weekend on something she thought they would enjoy, and all they did was ridicule it. She shouted louder that she was sick and tired of not being good enough for them. She was very sorry that she was so inferior to Mr. Allen, but she was all they had, and if they knew what was best for them, they had damned well better start cooperating with her, or they were going to look like fools at the Christmas concert. She stomped out of the room and slammed the door.

She had no idea it would happen, but in those few minutes of naked, honest truth, something had transpired that made them realize that she really cared about them. Apparently, that was all they wanted to know. After several very tense minutes of waiting, Steve, the chorus president, had come out in the hall and apologized and asked her to please come back in. From that time on, they had been wonderful. As her confidence in them grew, so did an idea she had been nurturing since college.

One of her music professors had introduced a simplified version of Handel's *Messiah* in one of her choral literature classes. As was his intention, it had become a matter of great discussion and not a few down and out esoteric arguments. Some felt it was a sacrilege to presume to simplify such a classic, and the others felt that it was a legitimate thing to do if that were the only way a small, unsophisticated group could ever be exposed to the great masters. She knew this was the perfect way to take advantage of the group's newfound respect for her. It would be different and challenging for them, something even Mr. Allen hadn't done.

Holding her breath, she introduced the idea, telling them that it would be the most difficult thing they had ever done, but if they continued to work as hard as they had been lately, she knew they could do it. They had risen to the occasion, and after weeks of grueling hard work, both before and after school, they were all here, ready to perform it.

She heard distant applause, and the band struck up its third piece. She thought dejectedly that maybe her students had changed their minds again. Perhaps they had only been humoring her to get some peace and quiet and they still resented her. But they had seemed so genuine that that scenario was hard to believe. They had almost demanded after-school work because they were afraid they wouldn't be ready. They had even tolerated sight-singing exercises because she'd finally convinced them that they would be able to learn the notes faster.

The enthusiasm they had displayed over the music was a wonder to her. She began to realize that in the past, the only success they had experienced was through Mr. Allen's gregarious, vivacious personality. He would stand in front of the crowd and he, not they, would entertain. He, not they, received the accolades. It was only how well he "played" them that mattered.

As they began to mature musically, getting more familiar with the music and with her, she became aware that a metamorphosis had begun. They were taking charge of their own responsibility to the group. They were not relying on her for their impetus but were becoming their own inspiration. The music became the important focal point. The success would not be measured by her ability alone, nor theirs, but the ability of all of them working together to reproduce the masterpiece that was so profoundly affecting their lives.

They had been her salvation throughout that semester, which had been the very worst of her life. They had been the hard work that had seen her through the wrenching days and nights of terror. She had gone from the heights of celebration over their acceptance of her and down through the depths of despair that had taken the edge off the joy she felt over her work with them. They and the twins had sustained her throughout the ordeal.

Their discovery of her secret was the only thing that would explain their peculiar behavior. Somehow the unimaginable had happened. Someone from Camden had gained access to the records in Syracuse.

Somehow, someone must have found out, and they were just waiting until after the concert to let her know.

After everything they had all been through together, they would be terribly disappointed in her, but they might also be thinking about salvaging enough of their hard work to make a go of the concert tonight. If that were the case, the performance would be perfunctory, at best. At the worst, total disaster. It would be impossible to focus as they needed to focus, to feel as they needed to feel, and care as they needed to care, in order for it to happen. The piece was much too difficult to perform if they were distracted in any way. She realized that before the second movement was over with, she would have her answer as to how much they knew.

As for the school officials, if they'd found out, they would let the concert go on, and then after it was over and Christmas vacation had started, they would dismiss her. Actually, a mere dismissal would be a blessing.

She heard applause. Her heart started to pound. The band was beginning its fifth number. One more to go. It was time to line up. It wouldn't be long now and she would know. She was sure of one thing—these kids were not sophisticated enough to bring off a difficult performance like this one with anything else but the music on their minds.

She was also disappointed because she had thought that there was the slight possibility of a very special thing happening that would never happen if they knew. It was something that could occur between conductor and performer, be they young, old, amateur, professional, choral or instrumental, for which there was no name that she had ever heard successfully coined. It was a deep, almost innate understanding, a reading of the mind and some small sliver of the soul. Without that mutual empathy, there could only be mediocrity. With it, it was possible to achieve the soaring joy that could inexplicably take over a group of performers, propel them to an excellence far beyond their individual capability, and unite them in a bond of indescribable musical rapture and shared human glory. Most people, performers included, lived a lifetime and never experienced it. It had happened to Joan just once.

She wondered if she would ever achieve the level of excellence that would allow one of her groups to experience that mysterious happenstance. There was one instance in rehearsal that they had been close, but the bell rang and shattered the moment. It certainly wouldn't happen tonight if they had any suspicion at all of what she had done. Total trust was the foundation upon which the phenomenon depended.

She sighed quietly and motioned for them to line up. As they began to separate into sections, she wondered if this would be the last time she would lead them. What an experience it had been. No matter what, she knew that their lives had been made better by having done it. It was impossible to live through this kind of extraordinary musical experience and not have one's life changed in some way. It had the possibility of becoming one of the most significant moments in their young lives.

The music itself was so powerful that at its premier before the king of England, King George had become so overwhelmed by its magnificence that he stood in reverence and admiration for the composer during the entire last movement, which was "The Hallelujah Chorus." Since that time, it had become customary for all audiences to stand in recognition of excellence whenever a successful performance of the work was presented.

She wondered if they knew that in Camden, New York. She wondered what else they knew in Camden, New York.

Her reverie was broken when the heel of her shoe became caught in the hem of her skirt, and she almost stumbled as she began to move with them.

At least I look great," she thought as she extricated the heel. She was very happy she had spent the money for the matching black-velvet jacket, floor-length skirt, and white lace blouse. It was so striking that it had elicited a couple of admiring under-the-breath but respectful whistles from three of the boys as she had entered the building with Lynn earlier. It said she cared. If this were to be the last high-school concert she conducted, she was going down with grace, beauty, dignity, and her head held high.

Her natural blond hair was done up in one of the new "beehive" styles, which she thought was quite becoming on her. Her light blue eyes were highlighted by the outfit, and the shoes she had chosen added at least an inch to her five-foot-two frame. It had taken several months after the birth of her twins to get her figure back, but her hard work had paid off nicely.

Her makeup was designed to add age to her features because at twenty-eight-years old, she was tired of being mistaken for one of her students. The reaction of the boys earlier had convinced her that she had succeeded in looking pretty darned good!

Her hands shook as she buttoned her jacket and motioned them along. As they prepared to make their way into the auditorium, through the audience and up onto the stage, they seemed to move in that slow motion that overtakes one sometimes when the spirit perceives itself to be in imminent danger. As they moved, her heart was throbbing violently in real time as her hands continued to shake. It would be a very long walk from the wings, across the stage, and all the way across to the podium.

Chapter 1

Wednesday, October 17, 1965 Early Evening

Joan stood on the dank, cold sidewalk, pondering the fate that awaited her across the street. She stared at the Hotel Syracuse, wondering how many other women had stood there in fear of what awaited them. Fear gripped her as she reluctantly crossed the street. Her eyes swept over the elaborate facade, and she counted up four floors.

"Room four-twenty-eight, room four-twenty-eight," she had rehearsed in her mind as she had struggled to memorize it in her panic. What awaited her there? What awful thing was going to happen to her there?

She entered the elegant old hotel, realizing that the most terrifying thoughts she had harbored, in what she had thought was her overactive imagination, couldn't begin to compare with her present reality. Terror streaked through her veins, pounding into her temples and spilling out through her moist, cold palms. She entered the slowly revolving glass doors and glanced quickly around the surrounding area. The regal red-velvet staircase rose between two wide side foyers that framed it as it made its graceful invitation upward. She had always wanted to be here, always wondered what it would feel like to have the luxury of being a frequent guest here, but now her sense of foreboding erased all those pleasant wonderings.

She knew that the foyers, which led to posh restaurants and retail stores, could be concealing anyone. The authorities could be watching her every move, her every hesitation. She swallowed hard as she tried to rehearse what she might say if she ran into someone she knew. What possible excuse could she use to explain her presence in this place, so far beyond her means to afford?

She forced her weakening legs to begin the ascent, trying to conceal her dependence on the lush banisters as she moved reluctantly upward, hanging on for dear life. When she reached the top, the lobby opened up into a resplendent large room of gold leaf, potted palms, and richly mirrored paneling. Was anyone watching her? It was impossible to know for sure.

Red-fezzed men were everywhere. A convention. Good. That made it easier to be invisible. They swarmed. They stood in groups. They laughed. They dominated everything. They could hide her. They could hide anyone who was watching her.

It was obvious from the tone of the two phone calls she had received that every precaution had been taken to secure the secrecy that was so necessary, but that had been two long months ago, plenty of time for leaks to emerge. She had begged for more information but was given none. She was completely ignorant of any detail of what was about to happen to her.

She wished that David were there to ride up the elevator with her. It would have made everything so much easier, but they said no to that as well. No need to have anyone else implicated, in case something went wrong. He had been so sweet to come see how the new elevator worked. They had specifically said to take the automatic one. With no operator, there would be less people to identify her.

The bank of elevators stood across an endless red-carpeted space, and even with all the commotion, she really didn't know how she could possibly traverse it without drawing attention to herself. Actually, she didn't feel like her legs would hold out long enough to do it, but she knew she had to. Somehow she had to put one foot in front of the other and make them move.

Suddenly she wanted to rush wildly for the door to get it over with, but she realized the absurdity of that action and attempted to calm herself down. Why hadn't she thought to bring a suitcase or shopping bags with her so she would seem like just another hotel guest in town for a little shopping? She glanced at her watch and realized that time was becoming critical. This made it easier to begin, and she started to make her reluctant way toward the bank of elevators.

She was just approaching the furthest car to the left, as per her instructions, when the door slid open, spilling several ladies out into the lobby. They were obviously good friends and enjoying themselves. She envied them their camaraderie.

She had been told to avoid entering the elevator if there were anyone on it. The place was so busy she doubted if that would be possible, but suddenly the two ladies standing in the rear realized that they had been left behind and quickly moved to catch up with the others. She slipped inside, relieved to be alone, and breathed a sigh of relief when the door began to close behind her.

She stared uncertainly at the row of buttons, going over in her mind the instructions of her anonymous caller. Even though her goal was the fourth floor, she was to push the button for the tenth floor, then when she reached it, she was to wait a few minutes and push the down button. How long were a few minutes, she wondered. How would she know precisely how long to wait?

"Just stand there and wait," she had been told by the formless voice, across unseen lines, from a place with no name.

She was to push all of the floor buttons so that the elevator would stop on each floor as it descended. She was to exit on 4 on the way back down. She did as she had been told and pressed the tenth-floor button. The elevator began its ascent.

As she passed the second floor, she could hear the rowdiness of a very large party going on. Then she realized that the elevator was slowing. How could that be? She had pushed 10. Why was it stopping on 3? What was she going to do? This wasn't part of the plan!

The elevator opened, and she gasped as she saw five conventioneers, obviously drunk, standing there. One of them giggled, and another addressed her.

"Hi there, sweet thing. Going my way?"

They all thought that was hysterical and guffawed loudly.

She opened her mouth to reply, but they all crowded in around her. The stench of alcohol filled her nostrils, making her feel queasy. She struggled to get to the relative safety in the back of the car as they all attempted to analyze this new invention. Each man took a stab at getting them down to the party on the second floor, but since she had already pushed the button for the tenth floor, the elevator made its unrelenting way to the top.

Several of the men began to curse. They got louder and louder as the elevator rose steadily higher, their frustration mounting. One of them began pounding the door with his fist.

"Get us out of here!"

"Somebody help, we've been kidnapped by this fucking thing," yelled another.

They were all shouting at the top of their lungs when the door opened, and she pushed her way past them and out into the hallway.

Immediately their anger turned to celebration, and within seconds, they were bantering about who had been the most scared, who had yelled the loudest, and who had outdrunk the rest. They began indiscriminately pushing buttons as the door began to close.

She looked at her watch and realized she was running out of time. She was to knock on the door of room 428 at 7:20, no earlier and no later. If she were not timely, the door would not be opened. She pushed the Down button, hoping against hope that no one else was going to push another one. Who knew how long it would take those idiots to figure out what to do and for her to get the elevator back. She began pacing nervously as the boisterous voices of her elevator companions grew increasingly weaker. She pushed the down button again, not understanding the way it worked but hoping it would turn back immediately.

Chapter 2

Actually, it wasn't so bad up here alone, she thought. She was beginning to relax a little when she heard something in the distance. She listened carefully, wondering what it could be. Her senses were so acute from all of the adrenaline that she thought she would be able to hear the sigh of a hummingbird from fifty yards away. There it was again.

Someone was coming! But there wasn't supposed to be anyone on this floor. It was the banquet floor. It was supposed to be safe! Whoever it was was getting closer. She didn't know what to do. Even if the elevator came back, she couldn't get on right this minute—she'd be early. Maybe whoever it was would go somewhere else besides here.

Keys, she could hear the jingle of keys. It must be a janitor. Then she saw him. He was large, his hair was an unruly mop, and he was not someone she wished to be having a conversation with at that particular moment.

"Hey, lady, ya lost or something? There's nothin' here tonight. The meetin' was over two hours ago."

He sauntered toward her in his starched green uniform.

"Ah, no," she hesitated, "I'm not lost. I . . . ah . . . lost an earring earlier and thought I'd look around."

Her mind wandered back over one of the warnings they had given her about avoiding hotel employees.

"I didn't find it, but that's okay . . . it was just a cheap one, anyway," she faltered.

"Housekeeping came and went a long time ago, but I can call 'em and see if they have it," he offered.

"No . . . really! It isn't important . . . I'll just forget about it," she stammered.

"Won't hear of it," he said. "You thought it was important enough to come back for, didn't you? It'll only take a second to call Clara, the house phone's right here."

"Okay, call her," she said quickly, not wanting an argument with him. "I have to get going though . . . I . . . ah . . . I'm late . . ."

He stopped middial, "Hey! If you don't want me to call, I won't call. I was just trying to be helpful, but if you don't want my help . . ."

"No, please . . . call!" she said, not wanting to aggravate him further. "I really appreciate everything you're trying to do. It's very kind of you, very kind."

Resuming the dialing he went on rather defensively, "Well, okay, if you're sure."

Then into the phone, "Yeah, yeah, is Clara there? Tell her it's Louie. He wants to talk to her."

There was a pause and then, "Yeah, Doll. Look, there's this nice chick here on 10 wants to know, did any a yer gals find an earring after the meetin? Yeah, okay, go check."

He tapped his foot impatiently, "Yeah, I know Myrtie. She's a sweetlittleass! Hah-hah. Where is she? Yeah, go ask."

He looked at Joan with sudden concern and covered the receiver with his huge hand.

"Hey, lady, you okay? You look a little green around the gills!" Gathering every ounce of self-control she could muster, she answered quickly, "No . . . ah . . . yes . . . I'm fine. Just fine! Just in a little hurry, that's all. I really appreciate all the time you're taking . . ."

Interrupting, he said suspiciously into the phone, "Okay, Clara, ya sure? She wouldn't just be pocketin' it, would she?"

Not wanting any more problems with employees, Joan overreacted, "No, Louie, it was old. Not worth the effort to steal. Any woman would know that. Don't bother Clara anymore. Please, Louie, forget it ever happened."

She realized she was virtually pleading with him.

"Awright, awright," he said peevishly. "Jesus, lady, make up yer mind! First yer snoopin' around, lookin' fer an earring, then it don't matter!"

To Clara, he said, "Awright, she says it wasn't worth much. Thanks, sweetie."

With a hint of lust, he added, "See ya later, alligator."

He hung up the phone, smiling. Forgetting his previous anger, he apologized, "Sorry, lady. No luck."

She heard the elevator approaching from the floor below. She had to get away from him but had to do it politely.

"That's perfectly all right. You can't imagine how helpful you've been."

She knew she had to push the button or it might not come up all the way. She wished again that she knew more about the way they operated. She pushed it frantically several times.

"You've been just great. Thank you again for your time." She could hear the elevator moving. When would it open up?

He started toward her, and from the expression on his face, she began to think she had been a little too liberal with her thanks. He observed her as if for the first time. He addressed her in a low, husky voice, "Well, I'm never too busy to help a sweet young lady find a lost earring. Why, sometimes I think this whole—" The elevator stopped. He continued toward her—"world is in too much of a hurry—"

The door opened—"for its own good."

Just as he reached out to touch her face, she whirled around and dashed into the elevator. She began blindly pushing buttons.

He stood there, obviously startled, and as the door began to close, she heard his voice fading away, "Well, I'll be a son of a bitch."

"Thank you for all your help," she called as she continued to push buttons.

She had eluded him, but she wasn't sure which buttons she had pushed. She began pressing them deliberately as the elevator began its slow descent to whatever awaited her.

She started to panic when the elevator began to stop on the ninth floor, then she remembered that it was supposed to do that. It would stop on every floor until she exited from it on the fourth floor. She panicked again when she looked at her watch, thinking she was going to be late. If she were late, they wouldn't do anything. What were they going to do, anyway?

Eighth floor . . . open . . . wait . . . close

Seventh floor . . . open . . . wait . . . close

Sixth floor . . . open . . . wait . . . close

Fifth floor . . . open . . . wait . . . A WOMAN!

The woman smiled sweetly, "Hello, dear, are you going up?"

"No, I'm going down," Joan almost shouted as she backed defensively into the corner like a caged threatened animal. She prayed the door would close before someone else came along. It seemed to take forever, but it finally closed with a whoosh.

She took several slow deep breaths, willing herself to calm down. She knew there was only one more floor to go. She checked her watch and realized with astonishment that she was actually early. How had that happened? A minute ago, on the tenth floor, she thought she was going to be late. Now what? She couldn't just stand around in the hallway.

Then she saw a button that looked like it was designed to hold the door open. She decided that she would just push on it for a couple of minutes until it was time to go. She was pleased with herself for making this calm decision. She pushed.

Abruptly, a bell began clanging loudly, wildly coursing through what seemed like the entire length and breadth of the hotel. She jumped, releasing her hold on the button. The sound stopped as quickly as it had begun. Then the door began to close, threatening to entrap her and send her unwillingly to another floor. That would make her late! She reached desperately for the door, not knowing if it would stop or crush her to death. Feeling she had nothing to lose, she hung on, frantically trying to keep it open.

Finally it stopped, and she stumbled into the hallway, fighting the fear that was threatening to paralyze her. Leaning on the wall, she gasped in relief as the doors slowly began to close.

She stood there breathing deeply for a few moments, then suddenly the absurdity of what had just transpired began to unroll slowly before her eyes. Borne out of the ignorance of the operation of the elevator, she had created a scene that could have been a storyline for a Lucille Ball comedy.

She closed her eyes, reviewing the whole thing, from the entrance of the conventioneers to the maintenance man to the warning bell, and she began to snicker. Just a little at first, but the more she thought about the ridiculous fiasco, the funnier it became. The harder she tried to squelch the laughter, the more helpless she became to control it. It engulfed her in waves of unleashed giggles and snorts until she was powerless to stop the tears from running down her face. She slipped down the wall to the floor, legs spread-eagled in front of her, and roared with reckless abandon.

It was just like those times in elementary school when for little reason or no reason at all her classmates would start giggling, and the more they feared a reproach, the more uncontrollable it became. Like the time Mable Winn brought her dog, Ferdie, to school.

The image slowly spread into her mind. The church, the Grange Hall, and the school were all down the hill and around a slight bend from the rest of the town. The only thing that separated them all from the lake was State Route 49. Behind them all was the town cemetery, which was part of their play yard.

There was an iron fence around the entire schoolyard, but it didn't make anything secure because there were no gates left, and it was falling down in several places. There was a sidewalk, which split the front lawn and led up two steps to the porch, which had benches on either side, and above it was the bell tower.

The entryway housed the girl's room on the left and the boy's room on the right. Directly ahead were the entrances to the two classrooms with the "little room" on the right and the "big room" on the left. The rooms were mirror images, with plenty of windows and large blackboards covering the entire front walls, which were back-to-back. Each had a potbelly stove and a small "sink room," which had the only running water in the school.

Mrs. Clarence didn't want to let Ferdie in that day, but it was raining and very cold, so they finally persuaded her.

Ferdie was no ordinary dog. He was too dumb to be ordinary. He was also ugly. He was so ugly that if anyone had seen him as a full-grown dog before they picked him out as a puppy, he never would have lived to grow up!

His hair was short and brown, with spots and splotches all over him. He had a long tail that just sort of hung there with no purpose in mind. His ears were short and were supposed to stand up straight, but they never quite made it. As if that weren't enough, he had droopy, watery eyes and a real bad runny nose. On top of all that, he drooled. He was the ugliest dog in town, and they all loved him.

He was with them whenever they weren't in school. When they were little, they rode him horseback or hitched him up to Mable's little red wagon. He helped with all of their bird funerals, pulling the caskets as they sang "Nearer My God To Thee." He never made a fuss and did exactly as he was told, at least until that crazy day at school.

Now Mrs. Clarence was a nice lady. She was very heavy, with a large square face and gray hair. She tried very hard to do her job, which was almost impossible. There were about thirty kids in her room, who were in the fifth to eighth grades. First through fourth grades were next door, in the "little room."

Some of the eighth graders were twelve, and some of them were fifteen. Not many of them were sixteen because that's when the state let them quit school. The only reason they obeyed the state was because if they didn't, the family didn't get the welfare check.

Whether they passed or not, they were promoted, or at least allowed to sit in the eighth-grade row. It would have looked a little funny to see six-footers sitting with the fifth graders! They must have been a chore for Mrs. Clarence because they didn't really give a darn about anything in school. They were there, never giving the rest of them any hassles except for their poor personal habits.

By the end of March each year, it was obvious that some of the kids had no running water in their homes. A lot of them wore what they referred to as union suits. They were one-piece long johns with a trapdoor in the back for doing personal duties. They put them on in the late fall and took them off in the spring. As the cuffs got dirty, they just cut them off.

The whole school was rife with odors. The drinking water came from a well that was sulphur water. It smelled like rotten eggs. They held their noses when they had to drink it. The only restrooms were nothing more than outhouses that weren't out. They weren't in the same room as the students, of course, but they were so close that at times they may as well have been. During warm weather, they were another reason for holding noses.

Mrs. Clarence didn't help matters, either. She had what was referred to on the radio as B.O., which stood for body odor. That's what Lifebuoy soap called it on their radio ads. They could never figure it out. She was clean and kept herself neat, but she had this problem. In their fifth-grade wisdom, they decided it must have something to do with her weight, which was considerable.

There were three things that would set them off into peals of laughter. The first was when someone whose diet was on the beany side would make an indiscrete noise. Another was when someone would ask for help with seatwork, and she'd go over to help. Everyone knew that if she stayed long it got hard to breathe.

The funniest thing that happened was when she'd sit down at her desk. The desk had a high back and arms that curved down from the middle of the back to the seat. It was old, and the arms weren't quite wide enough for her enormous behind, so when she sat down in it and the arms reluctantly spread apart, the result was a long, drawn-out loud squawk.

This particular rainy day, Ferdie was also at his smelliest. He was soaking wet, and due to the fact that he hadn't had a bath in months, he really reeked.

One of the requirements for his staying indoors was that he had to spend the day under Mrs. Clarence's desk so that his presence wouldn't interrupt the "learning process." The kids thought that was pretty funny because they didn't know they had "a learning process." They didn't expect the rule to stick but agreed anyway, and Mable made him go under there.

They started out with the usual pledge and the singing of "The Star-Spangled Banner," then Mrs. Clarence said to get busy with their seatwork, which they did. She wandered around the room for a while, making sure everyone had something to do, and after awhile, she went to her desk and sat down.

The usual snicker or two rose up at the noise made by the chair, but nothing else happened, and everyone settled down to work. They worked in peace for a while, but then Ferdie did something really strange. Sounding like he was trying to be very careful and quiet, he cleared his throat! They'd never heard anything like that! They didn't even know a dog could clear its throat, and here he was, trying to be quiet about it! It was like he was trying not to make a ruckus and get thrown out in the rain. They knew it had to be pretty cozy under there with Mrs. Clarence's B.O. and Ferdie's own stench.

Joan looked at Donna and saw her eyes filling up with tears. That was a sure sign Donna was losing it. Carol was twisting her braids, trying hard not to laugh. Mable looked like she was going to cry, and the rest sat paralyzed in their seats, waiting to see what happened next.

A few seconds passed without incident, and just as they were beginning to breath easy, he did it again, only louder.

Then he let out several rapid-fire coughs. Joan tried not to look up, knowing if she did, it would be all over. She sat staring at her papers, trying to keep control. Finally, she stole a glance at George to see if the boys thought there was anything funny. He was sitting there, staring at the ceiling all innocentlike, pretending to whistle. She looked over at Sammy. He was sitting there, with his hands folded neatly in front of him, which he always did when he knew there was going to be trouble, but this time he had his eyes crossed.

She looked at Donna. Donna looked at her. They both inhaled at the same time, trying to hold it in. Then, when nothing in the world could have kept it harnessed, that dammed-up flood of laughter burst forth as Ferdie let out one long, drawn-out soulful howl and crawled out from under the desk on his belly, combat-style, coughing his brains out. His skinny hip bones were sticking straight out, and his ears were plastered back against his head. Then, with a hearty harrrrrruuuumph, he stood up, weaving, spitting, sneezing, and shaking his head.

What followed was total bedlam. The more he coughed those great retching coughs, the more he shook his head. The more he shook his head, the more moisture from his eyes, nose, and mouth went spraying all over the front-row seats and Mrs. Clarence. Everyone started diving for cover toward the back of the room.

They were all laughing so hard by then that there was no holding it back. Ferdie freaked out and started running around in circles, barking. Mable was chasing him and hollering at him to stop. No one could help because they were laughing too hard, but they started following her so she wouldn't feel alone. They had a pretty good parade started there for a while. By then, the near-sixteen-year-olds were getting into it, trailing along behind, and just when total pandemonium was imminent, Mrs. Clarence let out a bloodcurdling screech that would have stopped a tiger in its tracks, and everyone froze.

She stood there in silence, looking from one to the other of them, trying to get control. She rested her hand on her upper chest and patted as if she were trying to calm herself down. She fingered the necklace she found there and then started talking. She was quiet at first, almost whispering, saying something to the effect that she had never seen anything like that before in her entire teaching career. The pitch, volume, and speed of her voice slowly began to elevate as she talked on, getting increasingly angry. Then she really got loud as she screamed at the top of her lungs,

"GETOUTOFHEREANDDON'TCOMEBACKUNTIL YOUHEARTHEBELL!!"

By then they were on their way, and she slammed the door behind them. They raced out as fast as they could, and just as they were about to erupt in laughter again, she whipped the door open and screeched, **"AND GET RID OF THAT GODDAMNED DOG!" Slam!**

Chapter 3

As suddenly as the frivolity had begun, reality thundered down on Joan to erase any thoughts of long ago and happier times. She was sitting on the floor in a hotel hallway, about to take the most desperate action she had taken in all of her twenty-eight years. The haze of the past dropped away as she realized that in real time, the lapse had only lasted several seconds, but it was threatening to make her late. She couldn't afford to be late.

It occurred to her briefly that the sudden mood swing might be an indication that she was skating dangerously on the edge of hysteria and that she had better calm down and get on with it.

She reminded herself that she had to find room 428 as she struggled to get up. She began to feel a little calmer, now that the room was closer at hand. All she had to do was find the little arrows that indicated how the room numbers ran, but there didn't seem to be any! She decided to walk a couple of doors down the hall and check the way the numbers ran.

"Don't panic," she said to herself half aloud as she moved slowly down the hallway searching for room numbers.

"Oh, please, God, help me," she murmured, thinking it would probably be wrong for God to help her do this thing. Sudden anger welled.

"How did you let this happen to me?" she demanded inside her head.

"Am I so rotten that you let this happen?" she frightened herself even further.

All of a sudden, she had to get out of there! Press the Down button and get out! She simply couldn't take any more. She had to end it! She turned and started to run back toward the elevators, but as she passed the last door on the right, she realized that it was room 428. She stopped abruptly, and coming back to her senses, she looked around, wondering how she had missed it in the first place.

"All right, get control of yourself. You're going to calm down now."

She forced herself to take a long, slow breath. She checked her watch. It was precisely 7:20. It was now or never. She thought of the twins and reminded herself that this was an absolute necessity. She had no choice. It was the only way she could rescue her life, her career, and keep her precious babies. She dragged her courage up from the bottoms of her feet and into her hand as she raised it to knock.

"What are they going to do to me in there?" she wondered.

"I am not afraid! Will it hurt? I am not going to be sick. Just don't cry. Don't cry!" she willed herself.

"I can knock on this door. I won't panic. Only weak people panic. I am strong. Everyone says how strong I am," she thought.

"God, I am so angry that you let this happen to me!" she scolded.

She drew herself up straight and squared her shoulders.

"Oh, God, please help me!"

The minister said all they had to do was ask, and help would be there. She had been promised that there was never a reason to panic if they had enough faith.

"Church smells great today. Must be all the spring flowers."

Her mommy had brought most of them, but Haddy Gleason had brought some, too. She knew her mommy didn't like Haddy very much. She didn't like having to take turns being in charge of the church suppers. She always complained about how Haddy ran hers. Nothin' was right the way Haddy did it, according to her mommy.

"Nothing is right the way I do it, either," she thought. "Maybe Haddy and I ought to get together." That would really make her mommy mad, she knew.

Her mommy was mad anyway because they had arrived a little late for services, which was also her fault, and now some perfect strangers were sitting in their pew. She couldn't remember ever having to sit in a different place, but there they were, on the other side of the church, in the front row where nobody wanted to sit! She had wanted to march right up to those strangers and ask them to move, but her daddy had said that it wouldn't be the Christian thing to do.

She knew it would soon be time for her to sing her solo. She liked to sing in church. Everyone always said how beautiful she sounded. Her mommy liked it, too. That was the one thing her mommy didn't complain about. She had been doing it for as long as she could remember. Everyone always said that they could remember her singing "Jesus Loves Me" when she was only two years old.

She thought that church was fun sometimes, especially when something happened that wasn't supposed to happen. Last week, the minister had been talking about faith and the fact that if they had enough faith, there was never a reason to panic. He must have been trying to make them understand this when he told a story that didn't come out exactly the way he had planned.

It seemed that there was this man who was rowing a boat down a river. Suddenly he heard a roaring sound. Sure enough, the more he listened, the louder it got. Pretty soon, he realized that he was heading for some rapids that ended in a huge waterfall. He started rowing like crazy, and in his panic, he lost an oar. Now he was really getting scared! He struggled and struggled with that one oar till he got his boat almost to shore. He jumped out and pulled the boat to safety and dropped dead of a fart attack.

She had howled! Her mother's elbow was so swift ramming into her ribs that she was sure her mother had wanted to laugh as well but jabbed her instead, in order to keep from laughing The minister just kept going on about how useless it was to lose control and panic.

He extorted, "We should all have enough faith that panic becomes unnecessary. It does no good to panic!"

Suddenly she realized that she was one minute late! Late! Should she knock? Should she run? No, she knew she shouldn't run; she had already worked that out. She should stay here and face it. Face what? What were they going to do to her?

They *had* to let her in, late or not! She had done everything they had asked her to do. She had taken the pills for two days. She had come alone. She hadn't told anyone but Anne and David. It wasn't her fault that the lack of arrows slowed her down. They should have looked themselves, and they would have seen there were no arrows, then they would know why she was late!

She wondered what she should do if they didn't answer the door. She would have to run away, but she didn't have any money! The next check from school wouldn't come for another three weeks. She wished that she hadn't paid all the bills last week, but it was too late now. She could write a few bad checks before they caught on to what she had done, but how could she manage with the twins? How would she feed them, much less afford a place to live? She would have no one she trusted to take care of them while she worked.

She wouldn't make enough money to support them anyway. She certainly wouldn't be able to teach anymore, and the only other profession that paid anything was nursing, and she wasn't trained for that.

If she packed all of the food in the house, it would only last a little while, and she'd need to buy gas. The money she had left after paying the bills wouldn't last a week on the road. Besides, if she ran away, the twins would never know their grandparents or cousins.

She wondered which would be worse for them—growing up without their grandparents or without her. It definitely would be worse without her. Otherwise they would be brought up just the way she had been. The only important thing in life would be, "What would the neighbors think?"

"What would they think now, Mom?" she thought bitterly.

"The only thing you would feel was embarrassment for the disgrace I caused. What would the minister think? What would the Ladies Aid Society think? They'd probably love it—enough gossip to last through several meetings. You'd have to go to every meeting just so they wouldn't be able to talk about me!"

She realized that she shouldn't dwell on that now. She had to go through with this. It had to be done. There was no choice. She could not let someone else bring her babies up. She could not leave them to their father because his mother would end up raising them. She couldn't leave them for a foster home or her mother. Each choice would be as bad as the other. There was just no other way!

Suddenly she realized that the door was already open a crack. She jumped back a step in shock. She stared at it as if it were a living thing. She wondered why they would have left it open. She took a tentative, frightened step forward as terror streaked through her like an electric shock, turning her knees into oatmeal.

Didn't they know she was a minute late? Maybe they didn't really care. Maybe it was just a scare tactic, or maybe they knew about the arrows and made allowances for them.

"It doesn't matter why," she thought. "The door is open. I've gotten this far. I'm going in!"

She cautiously leaned her back against the doorframe and carefully turned her head to peer in. There was a television playing loudly inside, which lent a sense of the bizarre to the inexplicable scene. As she looked, she realized that it was almost dark inside. The only light she saw was the neonlike flicker from the television set.

Her heart was doing some sort of wild hammering dance as it slapped itself against her rib cage. She strained her eyes, waiting for them to adjust to the relative darkness. Then, with a whimper of fright, she saw him.

He stood silhouetted in the doorway to the bathroom. Fear clawed at her heart again. He looked so weird. He had a hat on his head! She wondered why he had a hat on his head. It was a bowler hat, no less. He looked grotesque, like a throwback to a gruesomely macabre Charlie Chaplin movie. It was absurd. It was so hot and stuffy in the room that she could hardly get a decent breath, and he stood there with a bowler hat on his head!

Then, close to hysterics, she realized the reason. It was a disguise, a ludicrous, ridiculous disguise!

"What did he think I was going to do?" she wondered. "Pick him out of a lineup?" She wondered if that meant he had been in trouble with the police

Her mind raced, considering all of the unthinkable possibilities. She wondered if he were a real doctor as they had promised. Maybe he was just another back-alley butcher hiding out in the safety of an elegant hotel room.

Then her mind did a terrified somersault as she realized that he was in a position to do anything he wanted to her, and she had no options. Was he going to rape her before he did whatever it was he was going to do? She knew without question that she was defenseless. She couldn't call the police on him, and she knew that he knew it! Her blood ran cold as he stepped forward and motioned her into the room.

Chapter 4

She took a hesitant step forward. The room emanated an eerie, surrealistic quality. Walking toward her, he spoke over the sound of the television set in a clipped, impersonal tone.

"First of all, I would like you to tell me why you are here."

She stopped dead in her tracks and looked at him. Was he kidding?

"What do you mean, tell you why I'm here? Don't you know why I'm here?"

She tried to swallow the nausea that threatened.

Coldly, he replied, "I know why you are here, but I want to hear it from you. I want you to tell me why."

He seemed to be keeping his face slightly averted, making it difficult for her to look him directly in the eye.

"Why am I doing this?" she asked incredulously. "You have the nerve to ask me why I'm doing this?" The more she talked, the shakier she became.

She felt like screaming. She shouldn't scream, she thought. It would make him nervous if she screamed. She just wished he would turn off the damned television. She knew that she had to stay calm and answer the question. Her mind dashed about wildly. She had to think of a logical beginning.

"Don't scream!" she ordered herself, fiercely.

She wondered if she could cry. Yes, she probably could, but then she wouldn't be able to talk because her throat always got choked up when she cried, and she couldn't get the words out right. She had to stay calm and try to explain. She was glad now that he was attempting to avoid looking her straight in the eye.

"Why am I doing this?" she began quietly, tears threatening, "I'm doing this because I have no other choice. The father is a married man, and I'm a divorced woman! If I don't do this, they'll take my babies away from me." she said, getting increasingly upset and beginning to cry.

"I'm a teacher! They'll take away my high-school students, my junior-high students, my elementary students. They'll take away my music!"

Hysteria raised its ugly head again and ricocheted around inside of her.

"I'll lose everything I love. My highly respected Christian family will be totally disgraced if I don't do this. My church will never forgive me if I don't do this. Do you think they want an adulterer in their midst? The people I work with would never be able to look me in the face again. If I don't do this, I'll live the rest of my life in disgrace!"

She was shouting now, and he was becoming noticeably uncomfortable. So she whispered venomously, "If I don't do this, what will the neighbors think?"

He made a move toward her as if he were going to try to calm her down. She backed away and slapped her hands over her mouth, trying to curb any further outburst. The television was still blaring, and she had everything she could do to keep herself from bolting through the door in uncontrolled panic. Her eyes darted around the room, searching for something to focus on, something familiar that would help her settle down. Then for the first time she saw the lamp. It had a piece of red material thrown over the shade in an obvious attempt to dim the light. The curiosity of the whole thing caught her attention.

She stood there, looking from him to the lamp. Then another horror occurred to her, and she implored uncertainly, "Is this a test? If I didn't answer right, are you going to refuse to do it? Did I answer right?"

He replied coolly, "Please calm down and get up onto the bed."

She stood there, stunned, wondering what to do.

"Get up on the bed, please," he repeated without ceremony.

Suddenly the words echoed through the halls of time and space to another place, another bed of disgrace, and she heard her mother's voice.

"You get yourself up on that bed, young lady!" she snarled, "I'll show you what happens to big five-year-olds who wet their pants!

Crack!

The sharp blow from the palm of Ellen's hand seared Joan's upper thigh, and she began to cry. She hadn't meant to do it. She had just been playing. She just hadn't wanted to take the time to go into the house to the bathroom. She tried to explain, but her mother wouldn't listen.

"They get put into diapers like their baby sister, that's what happens!"

Crack!

She looked at her mother in disbelief as she realized that she was actually going to try to put the diaper on her. Her mother's expression was menacing as she wrestled roughly with the underpants, deliberately trying to cause more hurt as she pulled them off.

"Look at that! You're so big, the diaper doesn't even fit around you!"

Crack.

"You big galoot, I don't know why I even bother with you. I don't even want to look at you. Get out of my sight before I—"

"I'll show her!" Joan thought as she slid quickly off the bed. "I won't cry! I'll stop. I'll show her. She can hurt me all she wants, but she won't make me cry anymore, and I don't care if she doesn't want to bother with me. She'll never, never make me cry again!"

Joan came back to reality as the doctor was politely asking her to remove her stockings and panties. She did as he asked, wondering with alarm if she had anything to worry about. She could feel sweat breaking out on her upper lip, but she was shaking so violently that she didn't dare wipe it off. Was he going to do it, or was he going to rape her first? For the first time, she was glad the television was so loud. He wouldn't be able to hear the persistent pounding of her heart.

"Now put your knees up and spread your legs as if you were at the doctor's office."

His manner was almost overly casual, and she wondered if it were deliberate.

"Oh, God! What is he going to do to me?" she thought as she lay there in that incredibly vulnerable and humiliating position.

"Do you see this reed?" he asked as he glibly held a vicious-looking object up for her to see. It looked like an eight-inch reed with a ball on the end of it.

She nodded, terror stricken.

"I'm going to insert this through your vagina and into your uterus."

She sucked in her breath in horror.

Quickly, he added, "Don't worry, it will be absolutely painless. It will be prevented from falling out by this little ball on the end. Do you see? It must stay in place until you feel contractions and the abortion begins, in about twelve to forty-eight hours from now."

"WHAT?" she screamed, bolting upright and staring at him in disbelief. She prayed she had misunderstood him. What she was hearing just wasn't possible!

"What do you mean, twelve to forty-eight hours? Are you saying this is not going to be over with when I leave this room tonight?"

"Certainly not," he replied without emotion. "I would not wish to be present."

"You would not wish to be present?' she asked, astonished. "You would not wish to be present?" Her voice inadvertently began to rise.

"But what about me? What did I pay you all of that money for? I don't know what to do! I've never done anything like this before in all my life. I'll need help, I can't do this all alone!"

"I'm afraid you will have to, my dear," he said firmly. "Unless you have someone you trust who is willing to take the chance, and if you don't calm down, I will pack my things and be out of here. You are putting us both in jeopardy!"

She knew he was right. She had to get control of herself. She hadn't come this far to lose it all now. Somehow she would figure out what to do. She sighed a resigned sigh and apologized, promising to calm down.

"Good," he said. "Because I have important instructions, and I must know that you understand them. They are not going to be easy, but they are necessary. You were never told that this was a simple process. Now are you going to listen quietly while I explain?"

She would not let him make her cry, she told herself. He could hurt her all he wanted, but she would not let him make her cry.

"Yes", she said, biting the inside of her cheek to stop the tears from welling up.

"After you leave here, you must keep a three-pound coffee can or something similar with you at all times. Anything smaller will not do—you are too far along. You must catch it all, so be sure you have the right receptacle."

He stopped, giving her time to absorb all that he was implying, but she was so overwhelmed that she just lay there, staring at him.

"Be sure you do not attempt to flush the remains down a toilet. It will clog up, and plumbers are required by law to report to the police any suspicious material they find in the sewer lines. The only safe way to dispose of the remains is to bury them. You must dig a hole deep enough so that the neighborhood dogs don't dig them up. Now, shall we get on with it? I'll get my things."

He left to rummage around in the bathroom.

"Oh, my God," she thought helplessly. This was much worse than anything she had imagined. She never thought it would be this bad.

How would she get through it? She had already been through more fear and self-loathing than any one person should have to endure for a lifetime. For months, she had thought that nothing could be as bad as the not knowing, but this knowing was worse.

In the beginning, she had read everything she could get her hands on concerning pregnancy. Maybe if she learned enough, she would learn how to end it.

One night, she had pounded herself in the abdomen with anything she could get her hands on. There was a heavy cranberry-colored hobnail vase that she had received as a wedding gift that sat on the shelf in the living room. Using it like a battering ram, she hit herself in her abdomen with it time and time again. This just couldn't be true. It couldn't be true.

She rammed the handle of her umbrella into her stomach, over and over, and when that didn't work, she tried every pot and pan in the kitchen. It couldn't be happening, not to her! She tried heavy books, cans of vegetables, and a hammer.

When she had been pregnant with the twins, Dr. Brown had told her not to go horseback riding, so she started doing fifty to a hundred jumping jacks every night. When she finished with the jumping jacks, she would soak in a scalding-hot tub night after night, waiting for the blood that would indicate the start of her period.

One night, she added hot water over and over again, convinced that if she got it hot enough, the flow of blood would start. She scalded the whole lower part of her body doing it. She was in pain the whole next week from her garter belt chafing her burned flesh.

Every time she went to the bathroom, she had herself convinced that there would be blood and everything would finally be all right. Standing in the classroom, she would imagine that she felt a trickle and race, after class, to the teachers room to check. The answer was always the same. She would return to her room time after time on the verge of tears, knowing full well that if she were to be found out, her students would be lost to her forever. Her only avenue of professional fulfillment and success would vanish in a heartbeat.

She had been keeping it all from David. She wasn't sure how he would react, but the time had come when she had to tell him. Dear, sweet, loving David. She had been afraid he wouldn't believe the baby was his. They hadn't known each other for very long. Would he even believe her?

Chapter 5

When the night finally arrived and the inevitable couldn't be avoided any longer, she was awash with conflicting emotions. She hadn't seen him in a whole week, and she had missed him very much. When he arrived and embraced her, her eyes involuntarily filled with tears of relief at having someone to lean on. It had been so difficult all of those long, sleepless nights. Now here he was, and even though he didn't know anything was wrong, his strength helped her face the facts that she knew she had to tell him.

She decided to wait until after dinner and a few drinks to bring it up. It was a long drive to the restaurant they had decided on. The view along the north shore of Oneida Lake would be pretty, and so would the hills along the New York State Thruway. If she brought it up in the car, she risked the chance of ruining what otherwise promised to be a wonderful time together. She wanted to enjoy him while she had the chance, rather than discussing something that could quite possibly end their relationship altogether.

She glanced over at him, and her heart did a few little flutters as it usually did when she saw him after a long separation. She admired his quiet confidence. He was much different than the coaches she had taught with. They tended to be self-important and full of themselves. He was gentle and kind, and he lavished her with loving attention. She hadn't quite known what to do the first time he had opened a car door for her, and the first time he had held out a chair for her, she had caught her toe on the corner of the leg and almost ended up falling into it.

His beautiful eyes were a wonderful honey brown. They were deep and full of expression, which he never tried to disguise. He wore his emotions openly, never apologizing for them. It would be impossible for him to be disingenuous because his eyes would give him away. His light brown wavy hair was the exact same color, as if he had been color-coordinated by a body designer. He could have almost been too tall for her except that somehow, when they embraced or danced, he had a way of holding her that made it seem as if she were three inches taller than her five-foot-two build.

Their conversation was easy as usual. They caught up on the little things that had happened to each of them during the past week. The few phone calls he had been able to make were hardly enough to touch the high points, so it seemed like quite a luxury to have enough time to really share the details. Every once in a while, the unhappy circumstance would push at her consciousness, but she succeeded in keeping it harnessed.

The drive went by so swiftly that she was surprised when they arrived at the restaurant. She had always wanted to go Trinkaus Manor, but it had seemed like one of those things that would remain out of her reach. The restaurant was a beautiful old mansion that had been restored and turned into one of the most sophisticated places in the area. There were white tablecloths and glistening stemware, something she had dreamed about but never expected to actually enjoy. It was so like David to bring her to a place like this. In spite of the looming conversation, she felt almost giddy with happiness, and for a few minutes, she actually toyed with the idea of not telling him.

The music that wafted from the grand piano and across the elegant dining room lent an aura of all of those nineteen-fifties romantic movies she had watched enviously as a teenager. She half expected to see Cary Grant and Grace Kelly gliding gracefully across the room. When dinner was over with, and David asked her to dance, she fairly floated onto the dance floor and into his waiting arms. By the end of their second dance, however, tears were seeping unbidden from her eyes as she tried unsuccessfully to hide them from David.

He led her quickly back to their table and held the chair for her, which made her all the more sorry she had to do what she could no longer avoid doing. She sat down and tented her knuckles to her forehead, trying to hide the tears, but she couldn't hold them back any longer.

"My darling, what's wrong? You were so happy a few minutes ago. Did I say something to hurt you?"

"No, it isn't you. You're wonderful. I just have something to tell you which is very difficult. And I don't know where to begin."

Her throat was constricting around the very words she knew she must speak.

"Sweetheart, please try. It can't be all that bad. I won't let anything hurt you, I promise. Please tell me what's wrong."

"Okay, all right, I'll tell you," she stammered. "But first, I have to go to the ladies' room."

She bolted from her chair and across the nearly empty dining room. She virtually threw herself down the stairs, through the ladies room door, and into a stall. She didn't want anyone to see her. She stood, panting, with her back against the door. She felt trapped. She had nowhere to go. There was no good way out of this. If she told him, he'd leave her; if she didn't tell him, she didn't know what would happen, but she knew it wouldn't be good.

She took several deep breaths, calmed herself down, blew her nose, sniffed, and decided. She had to tell him. There was no other way to do it. If she lost him, she would have to deal with it somehow. The decision having been made, she sat down to relieve herself before going back upstairs. When she finished, she automatically checked the tissue as she had been doing for weeks. It was still a habit even after she had accepted the inevitable.

It was spotted! There was blood! Beautiful . . . Red . . . BLOOD!

Waves of relief swept over her making her feel light-headed and giddy. The knots left her stomach. The constriction in her chest let go. She smiled and chuckled a little. There was blood, red, sweet, blood. Her body must have created this whole thing out of fear and guilt. She was not pregnant! She was safe! Her babies were safe! Her life was safe! She hurriedly rummaged through her purse for the tampon she had been hoping to use for weeks. She applied it and rushed towards the stairs.

When she arrived at the top, she had to deliberately stop herself from running over to the table and throwing her arms around David. It would have been unseemly in the expensive, subdued atmosphere. She had to behave herself, but it was difficult to contain her happiness.

She had no idea of what she looked like when she returned to the table. She had toyed with the idea of not telling him anything, but the incredulity in his expression made that impossible. It was only fair to give him a complete explanation.

"What on earth is going on, honey? First you leave me in hysterical tears, and then you return looking like you've just won a million bucks! Tell me what's happening!"

She sat down and took his hands in hers. She cleared her throat to give herself a minute to decide where to start, and before she knew it, she was spilling the whole story out in every gruesome detail through tears and gulps of relief.

He was astounded. He was also angry. Astounded that she would go through all of that alone and angry because she hadn't trusted him enough to confide in him. Her love for him at that moment was total and unequivocal. If she hadn't been before, she was now hopelessly, helplessly in love with him. The circumstances no longer mattered. This was someone she could trust with her deepest, most carefully guarded inner being, someone with whom she could share her very self.

He reached across the table and took her hand tenderly in his. He lifted it to his lips and gently kissed her fingertips. Then, holding her hand in both of his, he said, "There is something I want you to promise me."

"I will promise you anything," she said, weeping softly with joy and relief. "You may have anything and everything I have to offer." The intimacy of the moment was so intense that she wasn't sure she could hold herself together.

"All I want is your promise that you will never keep anything from me again. Promise me that no matter how much you think something will hurt or bother me, you will have enough faith and confidence in us to share it with me," he said softly.

"I promise," she whispered.

She felt closer to him at that moment than she had ever allowed herself to be with another human being except her babies.

As they drove the long route home that evening, she was overwhelmed by a sense of warmth and security. At last she had someone she could truly trust. She didn't have to be alone anymore. She didn't have to be 100 percent responsible for everything anymore. She could relax and enjoy her life and not be constantly on guard anymore. She could love without reservation because she had someone in whom she had found complete trust—and she wasn't pregnant!

When they arrived back at her little house on the lake, it was so late, because of their long but wonderfully rewarding conversation, that he was forced to leave her without their making love. She was disappointed. She would have liked the opportunity to really solidify their new commitment to one another, but at the same time, she was so happy that she realized it really wasn't necessary.

He was hers, despite his wife and family, and she was his. She went to sleep with a relief seldom experienced in her twenty-eight years. Little did she know how short-lived that relief would be.

Chapter 6

The following day, Saturday, was a nightmare relived. Her tampon was clean. There was no blood. Apparently, she had just spotted or imagined the whole thing. There was no denying the pregnancy now. One good thing had come out of last night's reprieve, however—she knew without a shadow of a doubt that David would stand beside her. She prayed he would be able to call her soon.

She was grateful that the twins were with their father for the weekend, which meant that Sally was gone as well. They wouldn't be home until after seven. By then, she was sure David would have already called, and she wouldn't have to worry about their conversation being overheard. On weekends, he usually called from school during a break in football practice.

In some ways, it was wonderful having a live-in babysitter. Joan didn't have to be concerned about the quality of care the girls were given, but the house was so small there wasn't much privacy. Sally's bedroom was the only room upstairs, and although she usually went up right after dinner each night, it still felt cramped. The fact that Sally's mother lived in Rome and was close enough for her to visit every weekend was a real blessing.

Joan was lucky to have found her. The county funds Sally's foster family had received were stopped when she graduated from high school. They couldn't afford to keep her without the money, and she had been unable to find a job. Sally's guidance counselor had put them together. Her personal references from all of her teachers had been excellent, so Joan saw no reason not to hire her.

She never knew why it had been necessary to remove Sally from her own family. Sally had never offered the information, and Joan had been reluctant to quiz her about it. Joan thought that she must have had a decent relationship with her mother or she wouldn't go visit her so often. She also had a very close relationship with her foster family.

She was a strange girl in some respects. She was very overweight, and Joan suspected that she had probably been teased a lot as a child.

Because of her size, her clothes were a problem. She was forced to wear men's shirts because it was difficult to find women's blouses that fit her. Her shoulder-length hair was a curly brown, which needed no more care than a simple shampooing. Joan felt that was probably a good thing because she didn't seem to care much about her appearance. She was pleasant to have around, though, and she was very happy to have a solution to her financial problem.

The arrangement had been good for all of them. Sally had a roof over her head, good food, and a little spending money. She actually had more spending money than Joan had ever had. She had no necessities to buy at all, so anything she *did* spend was on things she wanted rather than needed. In turn, Joan had someone reliable to care for the twins while she made a living for them all.

Joan busied herself with the usual chores, nervously waiting. It wasn't the same clawing nervousness she had felt before last night, but it was still pretty close to it. One minute she felt assured that everything would work out, but the next minute, she was filled with doubts again. The phone startled her, and she jumped. Her hand was shaking as she lifted the receiver.

"Hi, Toots," he said cheerfully. She hadn't thought about the fact that he would be happier than she was, so it took her by surprise.

"Hello," she said uncertainly, "I was mistaken."

The rest of the words tumbled one after the other into the phone lines between them.

He told her that he would come. He would somehow get away and come to her. Maybe everything would work out after all. Maybe they would survive this after all was said and done.

He arrived around four o'clock. They held hands and cried, he as hard as she. They talked about possibilities and realized that the only thing that made any sense was an abortion. She couldn't bear the responsibility of breaking up his family, and she knew that it would be impossible to keep this child and the twins. The hard reality was obvious, but how would they go about finding out what to do? There were people, but where were they? How would they contact them?

The first thing to do, they decided, was to make an appointment for a pregnancy test. They knew what the results would be but thought she should have one anyway. Maybe the doctor could help.

She didn't dare go to Dr. Brown, who had cared for her all of her life. He had nursed her through the flu, measles, chicken pox, mumps, whooping cough, and the birth of the twins. She trusted him completely, but there were too many possibilities of results leaking out from office files or from secretaries or nurses. It was in that home/office in Cleveland that he had discovered that she was carrying twins. Everyone was so excited that by the time she made the two-mile trip back to her mother's in Bernhards Bay, Dr. Brown's wife had been on the phone to her mother. Joan had been a little annoyed that she'd been deprived of making the announcement herself, but she was so happy that the resentment never really took hold. No, she couldn't go to Dr. Brown for this.

The city doctor she selected turned out to be very good for her. Dr. George was the first gynecologist she had ever been to. She reluctantly told him everything and all of the circumstances. She had expected him to be judgmental when he learned that the father was married to someone else, but he wasn't. He understood completely and sympathized greatly. However, his positive diagnosis felt like a sentence of death. It wasn't surprising, but she had been secretly praying for a fibrous tumor or uterine cancer, anything but pregnancy!

She asked him if he could help in any way. He said that he couldn't. State law forbade him from making any suggestions at all. He would lose his license to practice and possibly be found guilty of conspiracy to murder. He explained the legal chances she might risk if she decided to terminate the pregnancy. She could also face charges up to and including murder.

She explained that it didn't much matter what the consequences were, she couldn't go through with the pregnancy. He understood and didn't try to talk her out of it or moralize in any way. She was most grateful for that.

Dr. George explained that even though he couldn't make any suggestions, he could give her some important advice. He told her that if any instruments were going to be inserted inside of her to make sure they were sterilized and to make sure that the hands of anyone touching her were sterile as well. He very firmly stated that if she should begin to run a fever after having a procedure, even a slight one, she was to call him immediately, any time of the day or night. He reiterated sympathetically that he wished he could do more. When she left, he patted her on the shoulder and reminded her to call if she ran into any problems at all.

At that time, she hadn't expected that it would be possible to run into any problems that would be worse, but now she realized that lying on that hotel bed with her legs spread apart and a perfect stranger about to ram an eight-inch reed into her uterus definitely qualified as worse! Much worse! It was worse than anything she had envisioned in all of her nightmares!

He started coming toward her from the bathroom, and she felt a scream begin to bump against her throat. She tried to tell herself to be calm and not make any noise. If she screamed, he would run away, and then what would she do? Then, as if the idea would save her, she gave herself permission to cry. She knew she had to do something, so she let the tears well up and spill over.

"When we're through here, I'm going to give you a prescription," he said distractedly.

"But you already did," she said weakly, talking through the tears. "I thought I was supposed to start taking it yesterday. Did I do something wrong?"

"Calm down," he said with obvious annoyance. "That was to curb infection. This is to assist in the actual abortion process."

"How will it assist?" she asked, not wanting to hear the answer.

"That isn't important for you to know, and it's time-consuming to explain. What is important for you to know is that you must use a different name on this one than you did the other one. Check the bottle to make sure of the name and change it, even if you fill it in another community. Is that clear?"

"Yes," she murmured, too frightened to care.

"These two drugs together will send up a red flag to the authorities. All the druggists in the state are required to report any suspicious medications such as this combination. The reason these arrangements have taken so long is that they are beginning to suspect our network exists. They are looking for any thread they can tie together to track us down. If they catch you, they will have a much better chance of finding us."

She realized that he didn't give a damn about her, he just didn't want anything to happen that could implicate him.

"I think I'm going to be sick," she said weakly, placing her hands on her abdomen.

"No, you aren't! Now let's get started. I have to get back to Roch . . . ah . . . home. Now please calm down. I told you that this wouldn't hurt. It will be like having a cancer smear or wearing a tampon."

She told herself that it would be all right. She would be brave. She realized he was getting ready to insert the reed, which he had handled with his unwashed hands while he was explaining it to her.

"Wait!" she shouted, "Dr. George said to make sure everything was sterile. You haven't even washed your hands! He said you had to scrub your hands!"

He froze in place, looking surprised and threatened.

"What? Who did you discuss this with? Who have you told? I should refuse to do this . . ."

"No one," she explained urgently, "it was before . . . a long time ago, when I first found out I was pregnant!"

Her mind was racing so fast she was almost incoherent.

"Please don't stop! No one knows I'm here except the baby's father and his friend who made the arrangements and my friend who got the prescription filled. Please, please, don't stop. Just get it over with!"

Coldly, he replied, "Very well, spread your legs."

She obeyed.

"I'll let him make me cry," she thought desperately. "I have to let him make me cry, or I'll scream!"

His touched her, probed inside of her as he inserted the reed into her uterus.

"It's so ugly! So Ugly!" she shrieked inside her head.

"Think of David. Concentrate on David. David . . . David . . ."

Chapter 7

Shaky knees or not, going down in the elevator was easier than going up had been. Regardless of the ultimate consequences, at least she would have some idea of what to expect from then on, however vague he had been about the details.

Her mind was reeling with emotions as her body attempted to compensate for the overload of adrenaline. Her heart was still thrashing wildly around in her chest.

She kept telling herself that there wasn't anyone in the hotel watching her. If there had been, surely they would have broken into that room to stop the procedure, wouldn't they? If they were there and on the lookout, they would have made themselves known by now, wouldn't they?

She felt fairly secure about using the elevators now, so that was no longer a consideration. She was tormented by all the unanswered questions swirling around in her head, though. What was going to happen next? When would this thing begin? When would it end? Would she feel pain? Would she have contractions, like a normal childbirth? Would they be as severe? Where would she be when they started? Would Sally and the twins be home?

She had thought it would all be over by now. She felt hopeless and threatened.

If this damned thing wouldn't stop on every floor, she'd be out of here by now, she complained to herself.

Maybe going down wasn't any easier than going up, after all. Maybe it was even worse, like climbing one of her dad's lumber piles. Going up was always fun. You didn't have to look back. You just kept climbing upward toward the top without the slightest fear of what would happen when you were ready to go down again. Then, when you decided to go down, the first thing you did was to look over the edge, and it hit you that it wasn't going to be as easy as you had thought.

They had seemed like skyscrapers rising into the sky. They were scattered all over the large lumberyard so there was always a choice of views. Sometimes the ones in the back of the yard were so tall it was possible to see bits and pieces of the lake between the trees that lined the shore.

They were piled without heed to the length of the individual boards, so that one end of the pile lined up perfectly, and the other end would have uneven lengths which protruded out, providing steps that were perfect for climbing.

"I'll get slivers in my fingers," Donna grumbled, trying to hold onto her sandwich bag and the boards at the same time.

"So what?" Joan chided breathlessly. "You can pull 'em out when we get up there. I'll bet we'll be able to see your house from the top. Maybe even the lake!"

"What've you got to eat?" Donna panted, her brown paper bag swinging lazily back and forth in her fist as she climbed hand over hand up the lumber pile.

"Peanut butter and mayonnaise," Joan replied, her mouth watering.

"How can you stand that stuff?" Donna groused. "I like peanut butter and jelly. Peanut butter and mayonnaise sounds awful. Yuk!"

"Well, I made it up, and I like it," Joan replied defensively.

The day before, she hadn't been able to find the jelly, and not wanting to waste any time hunting for it, she slathered on some mayonnaise. She was surprised how good the combination was. She also made ketchup sandwiches with lots of butter sometimes, but she wasn't going to tell Donna.

"There! I beat you," Donna said, puffing triumphantly and crawling to safety toward the middle of the lumber pile.

"Well, you didn't have to carry the milk jar. You could hold onto the boards better," Joan grouched, not wanting to admit defeat.

"Look, we're higher than the sawdust pile, and I can see my house and the lake," Donna said excitedly.

"Here's some milk." Joan said, forgiving her friend for outmaneuvering her. "Wanna go swimming after we eat?"

"Yeah, but we have to wait an hour first."

They sat down cross-legged on their lumber mountain and prepared to eat.

"Mommy says that maybe I can go way out to the end of the dock this year. Can you?" Donna asked.

"Nah, but I like it where we go now," Joan murmured, not wanting Donna to know that her mother wouldn't allow her that privilege. "Besides, I like to jump in the shallow end, and I like the pollywogs and tadpoles on the other side of the boats in there."

"You and your pollywogs. They're ugly!" Donna said disgustedly.

"What's the matter with pollywogs? They grow up to be frogs, you know," she replied as if Donna had no idea.

She knew Donna and Carol didn't care for such things as much as she did. Sometimes Joan resented the time Donna spent playing with Carol. They were cousins, but she was still a little jealous.

"You and your frogs and toads, I hate 'em!" Donna reiterated.

"Well, I like 'em, so there!" Joan said sarcastically.

"Well, maybe I'll just go swimming with Carol then. She doesn't like 'em either!" Donna said nastily.

"Ok, see if I care!" Joan challenged. "Sammy likes 'em. I'll go swimming with Sammy!"

"Ok!"

"Ok!" Joan replied, chewing on her peanut butter and mayonnaise.

"I'm getting down," Donna announced haughtily.

"Go ahead!" Joan hurtled back.

Donna stomped over to the edge of the log pile, sat down hard, and slung her legs over the side. "Wow, it's a long ways when you look straight down!" she said, fear creeping into her voice and face, "I didn't know we came up that far!"

Joan had felt that same fright many times, and knowing her experience was more extensive than Donna's, she was prepared to forgive the pollywog incident in favor of being able to take charge of their descent.

"Let's finish lunch, and I'll tell you what to do," Joan suggested.

They both calmed down and settled into eating their sandwiches.

"It's just like the short piles," Joan explained. "You shouldn't look down on the straight end or the sides." She was enjoying being parental. "It always looks worse."

"The jagged edge shows you how the boards are all different lengths. Some stick out farther than the others, and they make steps to climb down on. That's how we got up, remember?" she said reassuringly.

"You have to go one board at a time and only look at the next board stickin' out underneath. Then after you do that, you can find the next one that sticks out and put your foot on that. It's easy," Joan bragged.

"Don't look all the way to the bottom. It's too scary. Just look at one board at a time and take one step at a time."

The elevator crept gently down through its vertical tunnel.

"If I don't look all the way down, if I go one board at a time, maybe I can get through this," she resolved.

But she was very disheartened. She had thought that it would all be over with by now, but the reality was that it was only the beginning. A dull weariness began to envelop her.

A three-pound coffee can, she thought with dread. Where would she get one? She had never bought three pounds of coffee at the same time in her life. Would Sally find it strange?

Suddenly, she wished Sally didn't live with them. How would she explain it? She'd have to keep lots of towels around everywhere, in every room.

She didn't know where or when it might . . . what? What would happen?

Would it all come out at once, or in pieces?

What would it look like?

Would she be able to tell if it had been a boy or a girl?

Would there be a lot of blood?

How many towels should she keep in each room?

Where would she put them all so Sally wouldn't suspect something?

She'd have to wear her long housecoat all the time so she could stick some between her legs in order to stop Sally or the kids from seeing anything until she could run into another room.

Where? Where would I run? she thought with mounting alarm.

"Don't look all the way to the bottom," she told herself. "If I take one board at a time, I can do it."

She had to get to David and Bob. They were waiting for her next door at the Hackney House. She had to stay calm going back through the lobby. It was so big and so public! Checking her watch, she couldn't believe how late it was. They had been waiting a very long time. She realized that they were probably worried sick.

What would they have done without Bob, she wondered. He and David were longtime friends who had known one another since they were freshmen in college and had roomed together until they graduated. After going their separate ways to do their obligatory stint in the service, they had ended up as rival coaches in neighboring towns. Bob had been David's best man, but because he had remained single, he had not been able to reciprocate. Even with teaching and coaching, he had lots of time on his hands, so he became a part-time bartender. It was through the contacts in the bar business that he had been able to direct Joan and David to the right people.

As bad as everything was, she knew it could have been worse. She had David, without whose support she never could have afforded this. Without Bob's support, they wouldn't have known where to turn. She would be forever grateful to both of them, but what would she tell them about what happened to her? Would they be able to imagine what she had been through? Could they possibly know the terror she had experienced? How would she explain without feeling totally humiliated?

"One step at a time," she affirmed.

"Don't look all the way down."

Chapter 8

The Hackney House was as sedate and well-appointed as she had imagined it would be. Music, tinkling ice, and the faint smell of rich leather mingled in the air in opposition to the heaviness she felt in her soul.

She spotted them just as David looked up. He rose quickly from his seat and met her halfway.

He looked at her urgently and questioned, "Are you all right? You look like you've been crying. Are you okay?"

"Yes, fine, fine. I'm okay, fine," she stammered. "I'd really like a drink."

Bob, overhearing as they approached, stood quickly and offered his services. "What would you like?" he said sympathetically.

"A Seven and Seven, if you don't mind," she said weakly.

"Be right back," he said, concern sounding in his voice.

Joan sank wearily into the plush booth, fatigue threatening to swallow her up. She leaned into David's welcoming security, grateful to have him near.

"You're wonderful," he said simply. "You've been through so much."

He took both her hands in his and gently whispered, "Can you tell me what happened? Do you feel better now that it's over?"

"It isn't over," she said flatly, tears threatening to constrict her throat again.

He looked at her incredulously, "It isn't over! What do you mean it isn't over?"

"There's an eight-inch reed stuck in my uterus," she replied, wondering how she had ever had the guts to let that bowler hat put it there.

"What? Right now?" he gasped, appalled.

"Yes, right now."

"Why? Why is that necessary?"

"I don't know. It's the way they do it, I guess."

He was getting more furious and more protective with each question. "How long does it have to stay there?"

"I don't know. Anywhere from twelve to forty-eight hours."

His face was beginning to redden as the rage increased.

"Do you mean he just left it in there?"

She felt as if all of her emotions had been spent and there were none left to express.

Bob returned to the table with the drinks and began serving them. David looked at him accusingly and hissed, "That butcher left an eight-inch reed stuck in her uterus. Did you know he was going to do that?"

Bob went white. "Good God, no! I didn't know!"

"Does it hurt?" The concern he felt was obvious in his face.

"Not really, but I can tell it's there," she said, caught between having to be candid and being embarrassed.

"No one told me any details," he continued. "I feel terrible! Why did he do that?"

"So they wouldn't have to deal with anything that would mess up their hotel room, I guess," she answered sarcastically.

"I don't think the girls who helped with the arrangements knew, either," he said. "The only thing they told me was to make sure you took the antibiotics."

David stood abruptly, knocking an empty glass to the floor.

"If I could get my hands on that bastard, I'd beat the . . ."

Joan reached for his hand and pulled him gently back toward the seat. "No, it wouldn't do any good now. I'm sure he's already on his way back to Rochester."

Bob agreed. "David, we've gotten this far, and I think Joan can handle it."

"Thanks, Bob," she said, grateful for his confidence but not knowing for sure if she deserved it.

"I think I can handle it, but I'm getting very tired, and I promised Ann I would stop and see her on the way home. She wanted to come with me, but her babysitter was busy, so she couldn't. She wants to know that I'm okay. If you don't mind, I'm anxious to see her, and then I can get the long drive home over with. You understand, don't you?"

"Of course," they replied in unison.

David reached for her coat. Concern was obvious in his every gesture.

"After what you've been through, you do exactly as you want. Are you sure you can drive? Will you be all right? I don't want anything more to happen to you tonight."

"Yes, I'm fine, just emotionally bled dry," she confided. "I'm still a little shaky, but it won't take long to get to Ann's, and if there's a problem, I'll have her to help me. Don't worry."

He looked at her with so much love in his eyes she almost melted.

"You know I'll worry," he said. "I'm selfish that way."

Bob got up and gave her a brotherly hug, saying, "I just wish this were over for you."

"So do I," she agreed. "I'll deal with it somehow."

She let David help her on with her coat.

"Bye for now, Bob, and thank you for everything you've done. We couldn't have asked for a better friend. I can't imagine how difficult this would have been without you."

David took her hand and, putting his arm around her shoulder, steered her toward the door. When they arrived at her car, she could tell he was in as much turmoil as she was. She had had more time to become accustomed to it. They hugged a gentle hug goodnight. Words were unnecessary and seemed somehow inappropriate.

As she turned the corner out of the parking lot she checked the rearview mirror and saw Bob approaching David. It was comforting to know he wasn't alone as she started for Ann's and the long drive home.

Chapter 9

She wondered how many times she had driven this road. How many happy times? How many sad times? Millions of times. At least twice a day for her entire high-school career, she thought as she watched the short white lines flit under the front of the fast-moving car.

It had been a long bus ride, taking around an hour with all the starts and stops. The kids from Central Square, where the district high school was located, considered themselves a cut above the others. Joan and her friends were considered real hicks because they lived "way down on the North Shore" which, although undesignated on the map as such, was the name of the area that encompassed the three tiny towns of Constantia, Bernhards Bay, and Cleveland.

The North Shore kids had thought the Central Square kids were silly for being proud of the fact that they lived in a place that had such a ridiculous name. The North Shore kids told them that "Central Square" sounded like it should be part of a city or something, not a one-horse town that didn't even have a real square in it. It only had a little triangular-shaped thing where five roads came together in the middle of town and was just big enough for a water fountain.

How they had kidded one another about those insignificant trivialities! How much fun it all had been, she thought as she drove her weary way home.

She'd walked this road many times also, going home from cheerleading practice or some other after-school activity. They never had to walk the whole twelve miles, though. They had devised a rather ingenious system for getting home safely.

Half of the girls would walk a few hundred feet behind the others, and when a car went by, the first group would check out the contents. If it contained women or men they knew, they would scream and yell an okay to the group up front, who would flag the car down and get in, leaving the others behind.

The remaining group would then split again and repeat the process. If the car approaching were familiar, the rear group had the advantage and would flag it down, leaving the front group behind. When the numbers were low, they refused any ride that would leave less than three of them.

The boys were lucky. There was a team bus that took them home. The girls weren't allowed to ride it because it was only for players. Coach said that girls were a bad influence on the guys, so they had to be kept separated. The girls could never figure out what he thought they did all the rest of the time.

He said the girls would contaminate his precious players and affect their playing ability, but even if that were true, they could see no reason why they shouldn't be allowed to ride the bus after a practice session when there wasn't even any game!

The girls also knew that Coach Hoepple put them down in front of the guys at practice all the time. Some of the boys actually confided to their girl friends about it. The girls always forgave him though because he was a great coach. They won the championship every year in all three major sports, but the girls didn't like him much personally, because of his attitude. *They loved his wife, though. She was one of their favorite teachers. They often wondered how he treated her.*

Most of the time, they didn't mind not being able to ride the bus, but it was really infuriating when the bus went by while they were hitchhiking, and the boys would all hang out the windows and jeer at them on the way past. Big strong men!

She especially remembered the walk along this road the year their cheerleading squad started falling apart right in the middle of football season. The majority of the squad was from the North Shore, so they had had plenty of time to discuss things and gossip while they walked.

They had been totally shocked when they found out that Evie, their fellow junior cheerleader, had been foolish enough to get pregnant! They hadn't even realized she was "that kind of girl." They knew she was going steady, but they didn't know she would go "all the way" when she wasn't even married!

"My, my," Joan thought to herself as she drove along. "How circumstances change. Here we are, eleven short years later, and look at the predicament I'm in!"

They knew they would probably never see much of Evie again. She'd have to get married, and they certainly wouldn't let her return to school after having a baby! She would have to accept the disgrace and try to make the most of it.

You just didn't do those things when you were a sophomore in high school—there was too much at stake. At least Evie hadn't wanted to go to college. That would have been really devastating. It was bad enough as it was. Her whole life would be lived under a cloud, with manufactured anniversaries and birthdays so that the child would be protected from the awful truth.

They just couldn't believe she'd done it! Every girl knew you didn't let a boy get that excited. Girls knew it was up to them to keep control of the situation. Heaven knew the boys wouldn't! They were told that if they didn't maintain that control, they would get just what they deserved.

They had just finished making all of the adjustments in the cheers for Evie's absence when Dorothy told them she was pregnant, too! They decided those Central Square girls didn't have any morals at all!

Looking back on it from this perspective, it seemed like a century instead of just over a decade. Not much had changed in the way that people looked at unwed pregnancy, though.

Imagine what her mother would say if she knew what was going on inside her right at that minute, she thought as she made her way toward home. No doubt it would be, "You made your bed, young lady. Now you can lie in it!"

Her mother always called her "young lady" when she was really disgusted with her, and Joan had no doubt that she would be disgusted if she knew.

Ellen Webb was a mystery to her daughter. She was small and wiry and weighed only ninety-eight pounds. Her shoe size was a mere 5. Joan wondered if her lack of physical stature was what made her so defensive and ornery.

She wasn't ornery all of the time though. She would volunteer to head up the Bernhards Bay Methodist church suppers and spend hundreds of hours planning, assigning jobs and donations, preparing and cooking the food, and when it was over with balance all of the books and settle up all of the accounts. She would accomplish all of this with joy and satisfaction, and then the next week, she would seem to be perpetually unhappy again.

She loved a big project around the house also, like spring and fall cleaning or painting the entire house and everything in it, including the living room piano and dining room table. They were extremely strenuous jobs, but she would tackle them with enthusiasm. But most of the time when she was home, she complained incessantly about problems such as heartburn, tiredness, feeling nervous and jumpy and unappreciated. Joan didn't like spending time alone with her. She had given up trying to understand her and just decided to avoid her as much as possible.

Ann had been her usually-concerned self when Joan had stopped in awhile ago. She had wanted her to stay, but Joan had promised the twins that she would be home when they woke up in the morning. She didn't want to disappoint them. How many times had she driven this road with Ann?

Amazing how they had become so close, so fast, that first year in high school. They were a perfect match. Ann played the piano, Joan sang. Ann was a pragmatist; Joan was a would-be daredevil and was always in the thick of things, a had-to-jump-off-the-railroad-bridge-into-the-river-because-the-boys-did type. Ann couldn't have cared less about what the boys did. She had more important things to be concerned with, like schoolwork and getting into college.

She didn't seem interested in dating, but Joan knew that she was a little self-conscious about her weight and had always wondered if that were why she didn't participate as enthusiastically as the other girls did in "boy-talk." Joan had always wanted to tell her how pretty her face was and how attractive her light brown hair was, what a wonderful person she was and that she should make herself more available to be flirted with, but she never got up the courage to do it, fearing she would hurt Ann's feelings.

Ann was very happily married now, though, so it was evident that she could take care of her own well-being. She had a beautiful daughter and a loving husband, which pleased Joan very much. Joan still couldn't get over how quickly she had not only volunteered but actually insisted upon getting the second prescription filled.

Joan knew that her friend recognized full well that it could get her into deep trouble if she were to get caught, and they weren't over that threat by a long shot. She had also insisted on bringing the medication out to the lake house tomorrow.

Joan owed Ann for more than just this incident. If it hadn't been for her, Joan would still be stuck in a marriage that would ultimately have been as destructive as this abortion. Her marriage, had it lasted, would have had many more long-lasting and detrimental effects for her babies than this could ever have—unless she were caught, of course.

She could never have functioned well as a parent to them because she was too busy being a parent to their father. If he had only been able to make a decision, one easy decision somewhere along the line, she might have taken a chance on sticking it out. She would have been more than happy to try as long as he was willing to stay in therapy.

The night he announced that he was quitting Dr. Reed, she knew the marriage was doomed. She even told him that in so many words. She wanted to be sure he understood so she explicitly and carefully said, "If you don't go back to the psychologist, we are through. It is your choice. If you decide not to go back, this marriage is over. I refuse to live this way, Gene. I can't deal with a life in which the only consideration for happiness is the maintaining of the status quo. We haven't made love in over a year. Doesn't that mean anything to you? Do you want to spend the rest of your life like this? Always pretending that we have a marriage?"

She had even gone on further. "I want my life to count for something. I want to be happy, not just pretend to be. I want the children and me to be the most important things in your life. I want something to be important to you. Something besides protecting yourself from change."

"There is a world out there. It means something, but you only want to hide from it. I want to be married to someone who stands for something, who thinks for himself, who allows himself to feel things, who laughs out loud instead of with smirks. Someone who will take a stand on something, who is not afraid to express an opinion."

"I want a husband who will be himself and not what someone else wants him to be. I want to be a wife who is herself and herself alone. Not herself and you at the same time. It's hard enough just to be me. I don't want to be you any longer!"

"If you don't go back to Dr. Reed, you will never know who you are. You have to find yourself. I've been in therapy for months longer than you have. I've found out what my problems are. Now it's your turn. When we both know what our problems are, we can face them together, but we have to be willing to face some problems before the problems overtake us."

"I've been able to get over the negativity of my upbringing. I know I won't inflict those things on the girls. I want to know you are able to do the same thing. For once in your life, I want you to take responsibility for yourself and not leave our lives solely in my hands. Whether you save this marriage or not is completely up to you. If you don't go back to Dr. Reed, we are through. The decision is yours and yours alone."

His departure for his mother's house to fix her storm windows had sealed the fate of the marriage, she thought. He never went back to Dr. Reed, and they never discussed their problem again. They had separated a few months later.

She knew now that she had had hints of this emotional disability as early as their first year of marriage. It took her the whole year to get up enough nerve to tell him about her college voice teacher, who made an outrageous pass at her a few weeks before their wedding. He had looked at her as if to ask why on earth she was telling him about it!

"What do you want me to do about it?" he had said. "What difference does it make now, anyway?"

So then she was not only embarrassed about the fact that it had happened, she was embarrassed for having told him that it had happened. She should have known then that he was an emotional cripple.

"Thank you, Ann," she said silently. "You made that first appointment with Dr. Reed for me. You knew better than to leave it up to me to call him. I would have put it off and caused all kinds of unnecessary further damage."

Joan slowed a little to avoid hitting a rabbit and then continued rehashing her divorce. It didn't seem possible that two years had passed since all of that unhappiness. Things had settled down nicely. The girls had enjoyed getting Daddy's apartment ready. They had handled it all very well, she felt, for the sake of the twins. His new job was a perfect reason for him to move fifty miles away and take his own place "so he wouldn't have to commute on weekdays." The weekends that he spent home were uncomfortable, but they allowed time for the girls to get accustomed to his not being there full-time.

The first weekend he took them to his place alone was wrenching for her, but they thought it was great fun. She knew she had made the right decision. It would be much easier at two or three years old than twelve. She felt that adjustments were easy when you were that young.

For her, the adjustment to being single had been easy. She had had all of the responsibility anyway. It was being divorced that was hard. Being divorced was lonely. She didn't get invitations anymore. It was like all of a sudden, she had become a threat to all of the married couples she knew. Divorce was like a disease that friends had to be wary of catching. Even the teachers that she had worked with for two years didn't invite her to their parties anymore, and her life was so busy with the twins and school that she didn't have time for making outside friends.

That was why David had become so important to her so fast. She had looked forward to graduate school for some time. It would give her a chance for a change of pace, but she certainly hadn't anticipated what happened.

"I've never let my emotions run away with me like that," she thought regretfully.

She had been a nervous wreck at the beginning of summer school at a new college, and he had really helped her calm down. She had known of him slightly for many years, so conversation hadn't been difficult. They had even taught briefly in the same district at one point. She was in the junior-high music department, and he was in the senior high, teaching physical education. She didn't know much about him personally, nor did he know anything about her in that regard. She knew the students thought highly of him and his coaching abilities. Eventually he went to Glensville, and she went to Camden.

He was aware of her teaching reputation also and made her feel capable and intelligent with his admiration of it. She didn't have to prove anything to him. He accepted her and admired her for herself! No one had ever done that before. Her worth had always been attached to another entity, like the boss's daughter or Gene's wife.

"When he looked at me, he saw me, and when I looked at him, I liked what I saw," she thought, smiling to herself.

They had gone out casually several times as friends in a new community would, just for a drink, without any intentions of its going further. That had changed fast, though, because by the time she realized he was married, she was already committed. She couldn't have walked away if she had tried.

What difference would it have made anyway? She knew there had been many other women in his life, which was why she had thought he was single. It wasn't as if she were ruining something that was intact. He told her that he was staying in the marriage only for the sake of his kids, and she couldn't argue with that.

"I'm beginning to believe he really does love me as much as he says he does," she thought happily. There was no other reason he would be going through this. He didn't have to believe her that he was part of this nightmare. He could have easily walked away.

She knew they couldn't have made love more than a few times before the conception. She wondered how on earth she could have misjudged the timing so completely. How could she have been that stupid? This kind of thing happened to other people, not to her! It happens to people who were foolish, not to her! Not to the bright, up-and-coming choral teacher who was going to set the music world on its ear!

One thing was for sure—when this was over with, she was going to ask Dr. George for a prescription for the new birth control pills she'd heard about. Because she was single, he probably wouldn't be able to give them to her, but at least she intended to try.

How could she have fallen so hard and so fast for someone she had known only by reputation? She shouldn't have let herself get so impressed by the way he treated her, like opening doors and such. She'd never had anyone do that! He would actually get angry if she forgot and opened the car door herself. It had made her nervous when he held a chair out for her in a restaurant, but she liked it! She liked being loved and cherished!

She wished he were with her now. She wished she hadn't had to leave him standing there with Bob. She wished she didn't feel so alone, but she knew this was something she had to do all by herself, whether she liked it or not. It was her problem and hers alone, really. The others could be helpful, but it was not their bodies and souls going through this. All of a sudden, the real implications of her total aloneness became terrifyingly clear.

Chapter 10

Awaking from her musings, she wondered how many times she had driven through this little town called West Monroe. Funny, she couldn't remember ever hearing of a Monroe, or East Monroe, or North Monroe. She wondered why the "West."

How many times in her twenty-eight years had she driven through here on her way home? Constantia was next, and then the old hometown, Bernhards Bay or "Buzzards Bay," as the kids from the Square called it teasingly. There was Bernhards Bay, then Cleveland, and then their little waterfront cottage in North Bay, and most importantly, her babies.

How many times had she driven this way home by herself? Well, never with an eight-inch reed stuck in her uterus, that was for sure!

She wondered what memories would be jogged free as she drove through her peaceful little hometown tonight. Something about the beautiful little white church with the pretty steeple, whose miniature beauty belied the hateful hypocrisy it exuded?

She was sure there would be a mixture of emotions for a life that was wonderful, easygoing, carefree, fun-feeling, secure, but at the same time there would be the relief of being out from under the thumb of her mother's constant judgment, distrust of the world, and her gnawing anger at unknown injustices done to her by unknown people.

Her mother was getting a little better now, or at least she was beginning to understand her mother better. She seemed to be softening around the edges since she'd gotten over the shock of Joan's father's death. She had also improved after Joan told her to lay off the guilt trips she tried to inflict on Joan following the divorce.

Regardless, she couldn't let her find out about this! She couldn't even begin to imagine what her mother would do or how she would react. At the very least, she would be hysterical. Knowing her, she would probably call the police herself just to make sure Joan would be sufficiently punished. She could imagine her mother's snide comment ringing in her ears, "You made your bed, young lady . . ."

Finally she was in Constantia. It was bigger than Bernhards Bay but not as pretty, of course. Home of the famous Oneida Lake Pike Hatchery. This was about where she had been that horrible day in 1963, with a bus full of seventh- and eighth graders returning from a Syracuse Symphony concert.

The entire rear of the bus erupted in a scream for quiet. An unseen current seemed to run from the back of the bus to the front where she sat. She heard Walter Cronkite's familiar, usually soothing voice over the bus radio, saying those dreadful words, "Ladies and gentlemen, the President of the United States, John Fitzgerald Kennedy, is dead."

Then came the silence and the awful quiet of disbelief; the searching in the mind for the right set of thoughts that would make the words real.

"The President of the United States is dead."

The sudden, lasting absence of sound had spoken volumes of disbelief. They rode the entire forty minutes back to school in a quiet that had been unimaginable in their naïve, exuberant lives. As the quiet had begun, their innocence had taken flight.

When they arrived back at school, she had gotten off the bus first so she could look at each one of them as they disembarked. She wanted to make sure they were all right. She also wanted to touch each one of them for some reason, like a small touch of reassurance. It had been important for her to do that in order to make sure that they were all right and to let them know she cared about their grief and fear.

As they stepped to the ground the ominous questions had begun softly. Some were silent, some audible.

"Was it the Russians?"

"Will we . . . be bombed?"

"Do the rest of the kids know?"

"Can I call my mother before I go back to class?"

Then, a few weeks after the presidential burial, the other dreadful words came, over the phone this time. It was her sister-in-law, Keitha.

"I have bad news to tell you . . . your father has had a heart attack."

"How bad is it?"

"Very bad."

"Will he . . . survive?"

"No."

"Is he already . . . gone?"

"Yes, he's gone."

There was the same searching for thoughts to go with the words. Those words became an angry, oozing sore in the pit of her heart.

As she approached Bernhards Bay, she spotted the lumber company up ahead. His lumber company. Now it was all her brother's. There had been an unspoken agreement that if she intended to make anything of herself by having a career, she needn't consider the lumber company. There was no room for a woman. She could have been a secretary or a bookkeeper but couldn't expect anything important or to make any decisions. That was men's territory. It was man's work, and women didn't have any real part in it or in the rest of the world of business. No matter. She had wanted to be a music teacher since she had been in fourth grade, and she had become a successful one, thank you very much!

The lumber company . . . she decided to turn in. She hadn't been near it since her dad died. Strange, it just didn't seem possible that he could be gone and it could still be here. It was so much a part of him that it, too, should have slipped away, disappearing off the face of the earth as that gentle heart went to sleep. How could he have done that, just gone away with no warning?

He had been getting better. His smile was even healed. It had embarrassed him so to have his face distorted, but it was only a little bit, for a little while. The stroke was mild, and he was on the mend. They all said so, but they also said that he should quit smoking. She had known he wouldn't. It was one of the few pleasures he had. How could she have pestered him and insisted?

Now she wished she had! She wished she had taken the rotten things away from him and stomped on every last one of them or ripped them apart with her bare hands! Maybe then he would have realized how important it was. But he enjoyed smoking so much that it almost seemed selfish to demand that from him, and everyone was reluctant to upset him—even her mother had ceased her bickering. At least he had changed to a mild filter. That was better than nothing, or at least that's what they had thought.

She hadn't done a very good job at the funeral. Linda had been angry with her, but it wasn't Joan's fault that Linda had married a funeral director and considered it a personal insult to her that Joan wouldn't go in to view the body. She could see Linda's point, though. Their family had spent so much time wondering about what other people would think, she was practically programmed to feel that way. Well, Joan didn't care what people thought. She did feel bad about Linda's disapproval, but she hoped her sister would forgive her. Besides, she knew that their father was shy, and the last thing in the world he would have wanted was a bunch of people ogling him!

Joan had done her bit, she felt. She stood in the vestibule and greeted and said good-bye to people, but that wasn't enough, according to public opinion. She wouldn't do the obligatory thing and look at the body. She was selfish and not thinking about anything or anyone but herself. Damned right, she was! She was selfishly nurturing her grief. It was bad enough that he was gone. She saw no reason why she had to comply with some societal expectation just to please *the neighbors!*

She just couldn't go in there, couldn't say good-bye. He never said good-bye, he always made them say so long. *Never say good-bye. She couldn't say* so long *either, it was almost worse. She couldn't look at him dead, with no breath in him and no twinkle, with nothing there. That's it! There was nothing there—not even him!*

That should have made it easier, but it didn't. There were too many things that she hadn't said that couldn't be said to that thing in there. She hated that shell for representing itself as him. It wasn't him, and it had no business being there, and she would not look at it!

She couldn't tell that lifeless form that she was sorry for the way she had treated him that night soon after he came home from the hospital and he had wanted to go bowling. Why did she react that way? She couldn't tell it that she was sorry for speaking to him that way. She was sorry for telling him that she wouldn't go with him if he were the last person on earth to go with.

She was afraid bowling wouldn't be good for him, but she didn't say so because that would have shown loving concern, and they weren't supposed to do that. Concern implied weakness—or worse, softness. They were supposed to be tough and not let things bother them or be overly protective about one another, and because she wasn't allowed to show these things she misspoke, not knowing what else to say or how to say it. She tried to explain later, to apologize, but that seemed to make it worse. She couldn't tell it how much it had hurt her to have hurt him.

She also couldn't thank that shell. It wouldn't know how he would play boogeyman every night when he came home from work and how she would run screaming to hide in the closet under the stairs to be inevitably caught, then simultaneously terrified and elated to be in her daddy's arms.

She couldn't thank that lifeless form for taking her to Sylvan Beach and buying her endless strings of tickets for the merry-go-round and then sitting there and waving every time her horse and she went by. It would never be able to understand how proud she was that her daddy waved!

She couldn't thank an impersonal corpse for the times he would comb out her long fine hair after her mother rinsed it with fresh unstrained lemon juice because someone told her it would keep her hair platinum-blond and how, unlike her mother, he would patiently comb tiny little strands at a time so it wouldn't hurt.

That shell wouldn't even know about baseball, so how could she thank it for taking her to all those Syracuse Chiefs games with him and for sometimes not going with the men because she begged him so to go. Or if the men did *go, for letting her sit in the backseat (if she could be quiet) so they could talk man-talk up front. She would have ridden in the trunk if it had been necessary. She couldn't thank it for teaching her to keep score on a real major-league scorecard and for spending night after night in front of the radio, cheering on the team when they were on the road.*

That empty body had never been for a walk in the woods, so what good would it do to thank it for teaching her to appreciate the moist green moss, the pinecones, finding animal droppings and wondering how long before they discovered them the animals had left them there. For the wonder she felt one time when he walked up to a tree and patted it reverently, saying in a mysterious soft voice, "This is mine. This is my tree." For teaching her that nature was something to be loved and respected, not just used up for no good reason.

She couldn't thank that shell for the love he instilled in her for the lake or for the hours they spent fishing. For teaching her to drive the boat and eventually trusting her to do it alone, for showing her where the best spots were, how the fishing was better at buoy marker 127 right after it rained, how the Pancake Shoals way out in the middle of the lake where it should be very deep, would rise up within two feet of the surface, providing a beautiful look at the bottom. How to fish at night with a gas lantern hanging over the side to attract the pike and especially for not getting angry with her the night she dropped his brand-new pole in the water and they had to watch it sink into the shadowy depths, forever lost.

That cold thing in there could never understand how much fun it was the summer she was carrying the twins, to go fishing almost every night. It had been one of the nicest summers of her adult life, living in the spacious warm basement of her parent's brand-new lakefront home while their new house was being built. That body in there couldn't accept her thanks for the building lot her father gave to them, qualifying them for a mortgage.

That empty body would never understand how proud she'd felt for the job she'd done in giving him beautiful twin granddaughters, how happy it made her to make him happy through them. She couldn't tell it how she would want to hug him for letting Suzanne jump, jump, jump or Tracy giggle, giggle, giggle on his lap until he was exhausted.

She never dared hug him. They just didn't do that sort of thing. No one hugged. She couldn't tell it she had wanted a hug! Or that more than anything, she had wanted him to stick around long enough for her babies to have a Gramps to remember. It wouldn't know how sad she felt for them, that they never really had a chance to get to know and love him.

Chapter 11

Well, the funeral had come and gone now. She had thought it was the worst thing that had ever happened to her, but the period following the funeral was even harder. Her grief seemed to be all encompassing. There was nowhere to go to avoid it.

She would take the twins down to her mother's to try to cheer her mother up, but it didn't help her. Thanksgiving was dreadful, but Christmas was the depths of despair. Normally, getting her elementary students ready for their concerts left her a madwoman with all the last-minute details, but that year, it just didn't matter. Who cared? She went through the motions. That was about all.

This pregnancy had been that kind of a nightmare, too. The last few weeks had been as hard to endure as the funeral was. Then, as now, she would cry herself to sleep night after night and, after falling exhausted into oblivion, would awake in the morning under a blanket of unnamed despair, knowing that when she came fully awake, she would have to deal with unspeakable sorrow but not quite realizing the cause. Then it would descend on her with a force equal to all the silent grief in the universe, ripping at her soul with wrenching hopelessness, and she would be awake.

After her father's death, she felt like her life was coming apart at the seams, but she didn't know what to do about it. She knew her grief was probably having an adverse effect on the children but felt helpless to change anything. But unlike this time, a miracle happened. Not a sort-of miracle or an almost-miracle, but a real, full-blown, honest-to-goodness miracle! One that logic could not explain.

It was time for her biannual hair perm, so like the automaton she had become, she made an appointment. What greeted her was not her usual good-natured hairdresser but a person who, not knowing the circumstances, guessed there was something drastically wrong with her. She took one look at Joan's hair and asked what she had been doing to herself.

Joan explained that her father had died in November, right after President Kennedy, and she was having a hard time dealing with it. The hairdresser's response was to tell her that she had better find a way to come to terms with it because judging from the condition of her hair, she could be causing irreparable harm to her health. It was decided the perm was not a good idea and that she should wait until she straightened her life around. Another blow that she didn't know how to deal with. How could she just decide to get over it and expect it to happen?

She went to bed that night in the same depressed state that she had been in, but unlike other nights, she fell asleep quickly, and there, lo and behold, there was her dad! It was not a dream. She was not hallucinating. He was real. She spoke to him, he answered. They walked together. He held her hand. She knew it was him because his hands were the same rough, thick-skinned lumberman's hands she had known all her life.

He comforted her and let her cry. He hugged her and patted her and told her that he loved her. He explained that he had learned a lot since he had left, and that now he realized how important it was not only to love but also to express that love to one another. He said he was happy and content except for her uncontrolled grief, and that because of it, he was being prevented from growing and doing the things he was supposed to be doing.

He said he understood everything she had been going through and that he knew about all her guilt feelings and that they were uncalled-for because he already understood. He asked her forgiveness for some of the ways he had treated her, and she told him how unnecessary it was for him to apologize to her because she understood, too.

Then he told her something very shocking. He said that the universe and reality were not what they seemed. They were not the hard, solid things that people perceived them to be. Instead, they were extremely pliable and changing all the while. He said that time, as we know it, didn't really exist but was only a convenience for them while they were there on earth.

He told her that if she wanted him to, he could even come back to life, and that it would seem to everyone that he had never died! The incident would not exist in their world, and he would be there with them as if nothing had ever happened. He wouldn't even remember it himself, except as a dream.

Then he warned her that if she decided that she wanted him to come back that someday she would have to go through the grief again. He was older than she was, so it only made sense that he would probably die before she did. Then she'd have to start all over dealing with it again, at a later time.

He promised her that he would not mind either way, that the decision was solely up to her. She thought long and hard, not only about herself but her mother, Linda, and Jack. They were all grieving, too. She finally decided that as long as he was already gone, it made more sense for him to stay there. He said he agreed with that and that it was time for him to be getting back. They had hugged some more, and then she was awake.

It was a glorious wakeing! The sun was shining, the lake was gleaming brightly with newly fallen diamonds on its cover of snow, and the blanket of despair was lifted. She felt whole for the first time in months. She could take a deep breath of relief and not feel it would disappear. At last she could look forward to the future without sadness in her heart, knowing he was happy and content and that he loved her and would be watching over her.

She felt completely protected and enveloped in a tremendous sense of awe, which she was completely unable to explain. She had believed in all the old "Church" miracles all her life, but this one had happened to her right there in her own bedroom in the middle of the twentieth century!

The grief wasn't gone, but it was tempered. It was livable. It was grief that she could deal with. She could get on with her life and get over his death to the point that someday she would be able to remember things about him without remembering the pain of loss. She was almost there now, and she could smile about some of the things he used to do.

"Ok, Webb Lumber Company, I don't want you to slide into oblivion," she thought.

She wanted the company to go on as a living, breathing monument to him. After all, it had been a large part of the lives of them all, not just her dad's, and he'd probably prefer it to continue.

Even as a little child, she had been fascinated by the lumber company. It was so different then. It was very small, with only a few men working. She knew all of them. They were so good to her. She remembered sitting for hours on the logs that had been dumped on the sloped ramp that led down to the log carriage inside the open-walled sawmill.

From the ramp, the men used peeves to roll the logs onto the carriage in the open-sided sawmill. Once they were there, the men would secure them with three downward spikes that slid up and down on steel posts that were attached to the carriage. Three men would grab hold of the handle of the spikes, lift up on them, then slam them downward where they became embedded securely in the log. This would keep the log from rolling as the carriage began its ride toward the swiftly spinning saw.

The sawyer, Tom, who was in charge of the operation, would decide how wide the cut should be. Then he would pull a steel handle that went down into the carriage apparatus to make the adjustment. The log would move back and forth, toward or away from him, as he pulled. Joan loved the sound of the carriage beginning to move and the change in pitch the saw made as it bit into the log on its way down the track.

When the slice was completed, two other men would remove the piece to get ready for the next one. In the meantime, the carriage would race quickly back to the original position.

Then they would turn the log with the peeves to expose another side of bark, which had to be removed. The first few slices were put aside as slab wood for burning in fireplaces and furnaces. Then the carriage would be ready for its next commands from Tom, and they would begin sawing the real lumber.

The sounds were almost symphonic. Once the rhythm got going, it was predictable enough for her to tell exactly where they were in the procedure even with her eyes closed. She would sit by the hour and watch and listen.

One day when she was four or five years old, she was sitting there in her favorite pink pinafore and pigtails. She had her eyes closed and was just listening when a tremendous shout went up. The men all started screaming. One of them grabbed her and whisked her away from the area, depositing her on a short lumber pile and then running back to the carriage.

She couldn't imagine what she had done to cause this reaction. She had just been sitting there quietly as usual. What could be wrong? Then she noticed that the men all looked liked they were dancing. They were jumping up and down and hollering, but now they were waving their arms about as if trying to fly or something. It was a really funny scene. She decided that she wasn't going to be left out, so she started to walk back over toward them.

Then she saw the problem. Hundreds of them. Bees! Everywhere! They were crawling all over the outside of the log like maggots and flying in big black clouds all around the open-walled mill shed. She decided that she didn't need to stick around, so when one of the men shouted for her to get out of there, she did! She ran all the way to the mill office without so much as slowing down.

That night, they had sticky, gooey, drizzly, real honest-to-goodness honeycomb for dessert. The little octagon-shaped cells were fascinating. There wasn't much flavor to them. It was almost like they were made of superthin wax. But no matter, the honey was scrumptious. Luckily, no one was stung too badly, and the men all got to take some honey home, too.

She reminisced about the biggest thing she was always grateful to the lumber company for, and that was the opportunity it provided for making extra money. She remembered stacking slab wood into cords so it would dry properly. It was a by-product of the industry and a source of inexpensive heat. The people who couldn't afford to burn coal burned slab wood.

She remembered watching as the slabs of bark came off the saw and were taken to another building where they would be cut into chunks just long enough to fit in a stove or fireplace. Then they would be dumped unceremoniously in piles in the section of the yard where she sat right now. In fact, the supply looked a little low, but she guessed there weren't many people heating with wood anymore or, for that matter, with coal either.

Whenever they wanted to make some extra money, all they had to do was stack the piles of wood into cords. A cord was exactly four feet long, four feet high, and four feet thick. In that section of the yard, there were always several stakes, measured exactly four feet apart and four feet high so that the cords were automatically measured as they were stacked. The wood was cut in approximately two-foot lengths, so it was necessary to make the stacks a double thickness.

They earned a dime a cord, which was pretty good pay for a ten-year-old in 1947, but there was a catch. They had to wait a week before they collected. This was to guarantee that they hadn't been careless. Her dad said that if it stayed up for a week, chances were that it was piled properly, and they were paid.

The summer of 1952, her sophomore year, was very profitable. Until that year, all lumber piling and moving had to be done by hand. After the forklift was invented, it only had to be piled once on a pallet, and the forklift did the rest. The pallets provided her with the most lucrative job she'd had up until that point.

She was paid fifty cents each to build them, and since the lumber was already cut to the right lengths, all she had to do was nail them together. She could work as long as she pleased and didn't have to wait to see if they would fall apart! Eventually she became so fast at it that they had to slow her down. She could build them faster than they could use them. She thought she was absolutely rich and quite the carpenter!

The very best thing about this piecework was that she was the only kid in town who had access to a boat, so when anyone wanted to go swimming or on a water picnic or just for a ride, she got lots of help.

"Gee, I can't leave till I get these pallets built. Do you want to help, so we can get going faster?" It never failed!

The other summers she worked there weren't nearly as lucrative she reflected since she had to go on the time clock and had the privilege of paying New York State and the Feds what seemed like an enormous portion of her hard-earned money. What a shock that first deduction was! Becoming a taxpayer was not fun! Most of the subsequent summers, except for one, were spent in the office doing paperwork. Boring.

Sitting in this place now, looking back, she remembered that her romance with cars had begun in this very yard. This was where she had her first taste of the freedom that a car could provide.

Jack had bought an army surplus jeep that had been left over from the war. It was used in the yard and was just left there with the keys in the ignition whenever no one was using it. By the time she was thirteen, she could resist no longer, but by then, it only had two gears left—low and reverse. Eventually the low gear gave out also, so she basically learned to drive in reverse.

No one else wanted it in that condition, so she had it pretty much to herself. There wasn't much room to drive around in between the lumber piles, but she stayed at it by the hour all the same. Most days, her neck would ache from craning it around to see where she was going. She could never understand why no one ever bothered her about it. She guessed they felt that as long as it only went in reverse that she couldn't do any harm to anyone. About the only thing she could back into was a lumber pile. She was in heaven.

But the next year, the excitement of going backwards eventually wore off, and that's when they stole the family car. "Borrowed" might be a better word. They didn't intend to keep it, after all, but that didn't seem to matter. Donna tried to warn her, but she wouldn't listen.

Her mother never came home from the lumber company office except for lunch. She was glued there all day long, every day, waiting on customers and doing bookwork. It had been that way for as long as Joan could remember, and she saw no reason why it should change on this particular day. The house was next to the lumber company, so if they needed anything, they would just go over to see her mother at the office. Consequently, there was no reason for her mother to go home—usually.

She was scared, but not enough to stop her. She had to find out what it was like to drive a real car. It was a warm early spring day, really beautiful. Laura, Donna, and Joan got in the car, started it, and excitedly headed slowly down the road that went between the mill and the house, down to the lake. Wow, this was a cinch. Driving forward was fun!

When they got to the grove where the trees started and the road turned, they realized they might have a problem. The ground was still very soft from the spring melt, and the last part of the road that led to the summer camps was underwater. They needed to turn around. Did they dare pull into one of the driveways and risk getting stuck? They were just dirt, not gravel like the road, so chances were that the wheels would sink in.

What should they do? Of course! They could just back up the road. After all, it wasn't as if she had no experience at it. She had spent her entire driving career going backwards! No problem! At least until, looking out the back window, she saw a tiny figure in the distance, walking quickly down the road from her house. Oh, oh . . . now they were in for it! It was her mother! Why did she have to go home, today of all days?

Joan could tell by her walk how angry her mother was, and she was fuming! What should she do? She couldn't go forward; that was a dead end. She couldn't continue backward because her mother was coming. TRAPPED! Nothing to do but keep backing up and face the consequences. How could they have been so stupid? Stealing the car right there in broad daylight, right next to the mill! Her mother probably even watched them pull out!

For some reason, sitting there in the lumberyard that night, Joan had no recollection of being punished for that episode. There was no doubt in her mind that she *had* been punished, but she didn't remember it. She did remember sometime later asking to drive the car back down to the grove and being absolutely astounded when her mother replied that she could, if she promised to be careful. It was all downhill after that.

Joan asked if she could drive down to the grove and, instead of turning around and coming back, take the right turn that led around behind the apple orchard before turning around. Yes to that, too! They were all gravel roads. They were rarely traveled—more like driveways, really. No one would have minded even if they had come along.

It was sometime during the summer when she was fifteen years old that one of the kids told the story that when her father was a kid, they were allowed to drive on any road without a license as long as the road didn't have a white line down the middle. This sounded like a pretty interesting idea to her, so after much deliberation and hours of mustering up courage, she managed to broach the idea to her mother—at the office, of course, when she was very busy.

"Mom?" she'd said.

"What?" her mother said distractedly.

"You know what Pat Pellon's father said the other day?"

"No, what did he say," still distracted, working on payroll.

"Well, he says that you don't need a license to drive a car as long as you stay on the small county roads that don't have a white line down the middle."

No response.

"Mom?"

"What?

With gathering courage, Joan said, "We could go from here down to the grove, then around the orchard and up to Route 49. From there we could just sort of hurry across that because it has a white line, then we'd be on Shacksbush Road, which is gravel and certainly doesn't have a white line, and from there, we could go to lots of places. Don't you think?"

Silence.

Cautiously, "Mom?"

Losing patience, "What?"

"Don't you think?"

Irritably, "I suppose so. Now leave me alone, I'm busy!"

They had done just that! They had left her alone so fast, she probably hadn't known what hit her.

To this very day, Joan thought, she didn't know if the affirmative reply was in response to the idea of its being okay to take the car or simply in response to the idea that if they were allowed to do it, they could get to lots of places. She smiled, thinking about their escape from the office. They hadn't waited around to find out, either. Away they went, down to the grove, a right turn behind the orchard, another right to complete the U, quickly but cautiously across Route 49, and on to FREEDOM! If her mother ever realized what transpired that day, she had never let on. It became accepted routine for them to take the car.

They knew every back road in Oswego County and could get anywhere they wanted to go except to Central Square and Brewerton where several of their friends lived. There were too many roads with white lines down the middle, and try as they might, they couldn't figure a way to do it.

It was paradise just to drive around. They didn't need a destination to be in seventh heaven. They could go to Constantia, Cleveland, even Camden if they wanted to. Most of the time, they just went to the dam at the fish hatchery to go swimming when the lake was dirty. The lake was dirty a lot that summer, or so her mother thought. Her mother didn't get down there much, so whenever it looked the least bit dirty, of course they had to take the car.

Oneida Lake had the habit of "cleaning itself" as the old timers called it. It would spew forth all of its algae several times a summer, usually when the heat was at its worst, and this horrible green slime, the color of pea soup, would cover the entire surface. Once this began, it usually took several days to go back to normal. The stench was unbearable, and most of the natives around the lake believed it was very unhealthy when in this condition.

Unhealthy or not, it was definitely unsavory. Lucky for them, their mothers all thought that the poliovirus was somehow linked to it. When she was about six years old, her brother had come down with polio, as did thousands of kids every summer. He was fortunate enough to escape crippling, but most were not that lucky. It was a dreaded disease, for which there was no cure. Hundreds of kids were paralyzed for life every year by it, and no one had the least idea of how to cure or prevent it.

Their parents weren't about to take any chances on their going into the water when it was in that condition, so off they went, by car, to the dam or Dutchers Pond or Francis Pond or Panther Lake, or the Sand Pit. What freedom! What independence! And they never even had to pay for gas. They simply pulled up to the gas pump that was used for the lumber trucks at the mill and pumped their own.

The spring she turned sixteen, however, the back roads were becoming a drag. They wanted to be able to drive to Central Square to see their friends. They wanted to be able to drive home from cheerleading and play practices instead of hitching. They could manage to get to Brewerton by boat in the summer, but school was six miles from there.

There were so many things to do that required a road with a white line. So on her sixteenth birthday, on a cold, blustery, March 1, 1953, morning, George, her best buddy from next door, helped her celebrate her birthday by pounding on the door of the motor vehicle bureau in Syracuse, New York at 8 AM.

She waited the obligatory two weeks after getting the permit to take the test, and by the third week, emancipation arrived in the mail in the form of an honest-to-goodness, legitimate, New York State Junior-Driver's License! Brewerton, Central Square, Syracuse, watch out!

Actually, her mother was reluctant to let them drive in Syracuse. She must have been uncomfortable doing it herself, or she wouldn't have felt that way. Joan didn't remember her ever driving anywhere in the city except to the parking lot of E.W. Edwards Department store, which happened to be on the north side of the business/shopping district and therefore closest in proximity to home. There was one route that she followed to get there, and she would let Joan go that far on her own, but generally she didn't like them to drive in the city at all.

This might have been a disadvantage except for the fact that the new drive-in movie just happened to be in the village of North Syracuse. They didn't have to go anywhere near the city to get to it. It was quite a challenge to direct the conversations with her mother in such a way that they would get permission to take the family car to the drive-in.

The underlying philosophy in the family—that too much fun or enjoyment in life was neither healthy nor desirable—necessitated some rather awkward strategies that could be considered less than upright methods in some quarters. However, Joan knew that if they simply asked to go to the drive-in, which of course was preferable to going to a regular theater downtown, that her mother would just say no. Therefore, they would ask to go to a movie that "happened" to be playing at a theater in the middle of the city.

They would usually begin with something like, "Mom, Singing in the Rain *is playing at the movies downtown. Can we take the car?"*

"No," she would inevitably respond.

Pretending they didn't know why, they would ask, "Why not? It's supposed to be a great movie."

Mom, usually in a disgusted tone, "I don't care how great it is, you're not going! You can just wait until it moves to the drive-in. It always does, if it's decent. If I've told you once, I've told you a dozen times—you're not driving in downtown Syracuse in the middle of the night!"

Innocently disappointed, "Well, then, can we go to the drive-in tonight? It's only a Western, but it's better than nothing."

Mom, still sounding argumentative, "Well, all right, but you listen to me, young lady, I don't want you driving in that city! Do you hear me?"

They were usually out before she was finished so she didn't have time to change her mind.

This strategy served two purposes—it gave Ellen an opportunity to say no, which satisfied her reluctance to let them have too much fun and allowed her the delusion that the drive-in was her idea.

They almost always went to the drive-in with a gang of kids, but once in a while, two couples would manage to go alone. Their parents never seemed curious about what happened in "the passion pit," which had always been a source of mystery. Joan didn't know if the parents of the other kids knew where they were or not, but apparently the adults in Bernhards Bay had lived a rather uninteresting and chaste youth.

Actually, they hadn't really done all that much that was so bad, but they did steam up a few windows now and then, and when they returned home, they always made sure to clean out the overflowing ashtrays.

Chapter 12

If she were to be asked tonight what single thing influenced her senior year in high school more than anything else, she would have to say the Studebaker.

It was her senior year in high school. She had been accepted into music school in December. She was the first and only member of the Webb family to go to college and one of the few in her class to even apply, so she was pretty proud of herself, and she thought her family was, too. That's probably why they gave her such a wonderful birthday present.

They gave Joan her very first car for her seventeenth birthday. She suspected there were two reasons. The most important was the fact that since that particular car, which had been owned by her Aunt Bess, had never been driven any faster than thirty miles an hour, and that was as fast as it would go. The other was that her mother, being the only mother in town with a license at the time, was tired of playing taxi.

That was okay with Joan. It meant freedom. No more school bus. It meant being able to go anywhere she wanted without having to beg for the family car. Instant mobility. What else in the whole world could have provided that kind of independence? She was totally, completely ecstatic! She'd never forget the birthday that turned her into a seventeen-year-old.

It was March 1, 1954. She came down for breakfast, not quite as late as usual, and her dad was still there. He was normally at work by the time she got up. Her mother was there also, and so were an old set of keys on the plate where she usually sat. She thought someone had put them down by mistake, so she simply *moved them aside and sat down with her toast.*

Finally, her father said, "You know, there's something out in the driveway that goes with that set of keys."

She looked up, and he had that little smile that always crept across his face when he was particularly pleased with himself. She looked over at her mother, and even she was smiling. Whammo! *It hit her like a ton of bricks. She grabbed the keys and went flying out the door. She came to a screeching halt and looked around, disappointed. What were they talking about? The only thing there was Aunt Bess's car. She went sheepishly back in the house, feeling like a fool for the display of emotion.*

Her dad said, "What's the matter, don't you like it?"

Suspecting maybe she had missed something out there, after all, she said, "Like what? All I saw was Aunt Bess's car."

Her mother smiled, "Well, I don't think so, Aunt Bess got a new car the other day."

Not wanting to make a fool of herself again, Joan said, "Do you mean that Aunt Bess's car isn't Aunt Bess's car anymore, that it's . . . maybe . . . mine?"

She held her breath.

Her dad said, "I can't think of any other reason it would be parked in our driveway. Your mother and I certainly don't want it!"

She had wanted to scream and yell and holler and jump up and down howling, but she didn't. She behaved myself. She swallowed carefully and said something to the effect that a car was about the most perfect present she had ever had, and thank-you-very-much-can-I-drive-it-to-school-today?

They must have said yes because she could remember pulling up in front of Davis's store, where they waited for the bus each day, and asking Donna, Sammy, Carol, Arena, and George if they wanted a ride to school. They all asked what she was doing with Aunt Bess's car, and when she explained, they all did exactly what she had wanted to do in the kitchen, so she got out of the car and joined them. They screamed and yelled and hollered and jumped up and down and howled. Everyone raced out of the store to see what was wrong. No one in Bernhards Bay was ever that loud just because they were happy!

What a day! When they arrived at the student parking lot, which also served as a quasi-legal place to smoke on school grounds, the rest of the gang greeted them by screaming and yelling and hollering and jumping up and down howling. The next thing they did was skip school.

They skipped school a lot that semester. What the heck? All of them who were going to college had already been accepted, and the ones who weren't going didn't care anyway, so off they went. They drove and smoked and smoked and drove. They were hot stuff, went to matinees, miniature golfing, the greasy roadside stand in Brewerton for greasy hamburgers and fries, and smoked. Smoking was a big thing. It was cool. All the sophisticated movie stars did it, and Joan had an unlimited supply as long as she was careful. She swiped her dad's Camels when she ran out of money.

Every day they went to school, they all crammed into the Studebaker at lunchtime to smoke. When the weather was cold, they sat with the windows up, in a blue haze, through the entire lunch hour. It was a good thing the majority of the faculty also had the nasty habit and couldn't smell them, or the teachers would surely have turned them in to their parents.

They had gotten away with murder that year simply because they all had such good behavior records that no one even suspected about all the forged excuses they brought in. Their whole school career had been without blemish, so they figured that the teachers thought they had gotten awfully sickly. Or perhaps they knew what was happening and simply looked the other way. It was such a small school, with only sixty-five in the graduating class, that they had been the cheerleaders, the sports teams, the chorus, the band, the drama club, and the cast for the musicals. There would have been nothing there had it not been for their dedication and enthusiasm.

It pleased her to reminisce about her senior year. The last semester, one of their favorite teachers, who had also been their senior-class advisor, became very ill. The morning of the last day of school, they thought about what they could do for him that would be special. They decided to get him some flowers. What ensued was now a dreaded phenomenon in almost every school district in America.

She chuckled just thinking about it. She had told her choir about it one day, and they hadn't believed her until she told them all of the details.

Her class of 1954 had single-handedly started Senior Skip Day!

At the prearranged time, Joan asked for a pass from study hall to go to the girl's room. She knew the other three rooms that the seniors were in. She politely knocked on each door and informed the teachers that Mr. Martin, who was in charge of graduation, would like to see all of the seniors in the auditorium, something about graduation rehearsal. It must have sounded plausible enough—none of the teachers objected. The kids made a quiet beeline and slipped straight past the main office and out the door to the parking lot.

Once there, they crammed into about six cars. There must have been at least forty-five kids. Some of them were chicken and wouldn't go, but they promised to keep their mouths shut. It was around ten-thirty when they left.

First, they went to Brewerton for an early lunch of greasy hamburgers and fries. They played the jukebox and danced and had a grand old time. About one o'clock, they decided they'd better start looking for Mr. Andre's flowers which, after all, were the reason they were out.

They drove down Route 11 and finally found a florist. They pooled all of the leftover money and had quite a sizable chunk, so they bought two huge baskets. Discretion being the better part of valor, they decided that a bouquet for their acting-class advisor, Mr. Sullivan, might be a wise thing to do. As it turned out, that second bouquet was very important.

After leaving the first basket with Mr. Andre at his house where he was recuperating, they pulled into the back parking lot next to the cafeteria at school. They were greeted by the "cowards," who promptly informed them that their asses were in a sling. It seemed that the entire board of education, the school superintendent, the county superintendent, and most of the district's clergy were waiting for them. They were overwhelmed. Joan didn't know what they had expected, but certainly not this. There was even talk of canceling the senior trip to New York City!

They knew they had to be strong. They had to act as if they hadn't done anything wrong. Since Joan, Elet, and Barry had more acting experience than the others, they got to hold the flowers and precede the group into the cafeteria.

The powers that be were all there, waiting. The ne'er-do-wells walked into the room in a stunned procession with the flowers leading the way. Joan knew that acting dignified was their only chance. She looked around feverishly and finally spotted Mr. Sullivan. She straightened her back, squared her shoulders, stuck out her chin, made sure her buddies were beside her, and led the parade directly in front of him.

A hush descended on the crowd as if the pope were going to speak. She swallowed hard, trying to stop her knees from knocking, and in her best stage elocution, gave a brief but effective speech.

"Thank you for all you've done for us this year, Mr. Sullivan. We realize how long and hard you've worked, and we want you to know how much we appreciate all you've done since Mr. Andre left. We also took him a bouquet."

Then she had presented him with the basket. By then, he and several other members of the faculty were teary-eyed and clearing their throats.

Maybe they had a chance. Joan summoned up all of the panache she could muster and led the group over to the "head table" where the high school principal was sitting. She explained that they were very sorry to have caused such a ruckus, but they had only wanted to have a chance to properly thank Mr. Andre and Mr. Sullivan for all that they had done. They sincerely apologized and would certainly never do such a thing again.

Mr. Hughes made a halfhearted attempt at a scolding "If anyone should know better, Joan Webb, you should . . ."

She agreed and again apologized. She was truly sorry now. It was easy to act that way because they were in danger of losing the trip they had looked forward to and worked hard for since their freshman year. They also realized how utterly foolhardy their little scheme had been. They must have looked like a bunch of whipped puppy dogs.

The powers that be huddled together. They talked and talked. The kids squirmed and squirmed. They would have kissed their superior's feet at that point if it meant their forgiveness. Every once in awhile, one of those in charge would glance around at them as if to stroke one pointed accusing forefinger over the other, saying, "Naughty, naughty, you don't deserve a senior trip. We had so much faith in you and you let us down."

Just when they all figured they were doomed, the principals broke huddle and Mr. Hughes took the floor. Joan wasn't at all sure what he had said. Her mind was a muddle of self-accusation and fear. She had had as much or more to do with planning this as anyone, so she was truly contrite. Mr. Hughes finally announced their forgiveness with a stern warning concerning their behavior up to and including graduation day. This was Thursday, graduation was Sunday, and the senior trip started Monday.

They had won! They were grateful, ecstatically happy, and they would cherish the joy and camaraderie they experienced with one another that day for the rest of their lives!

The Studebaker was a very unusual color for its age. Most cars that old were either black, dark blue, or maroon. This one was tan. It had a squared-off hood that opened from either side. The hinges ran from under the windshield, down the center of the hood, to the grill. The grill was a slightly inverted V shape that went straight up and down. When both sides of the hood were open, they looked rather like wings.

The fenders looked like donuts mounted to the sides, and the headlights sat on the front bumper on either side of the grill. From the front, with both sides of the hood up, it gave the impression of a scowling bird with a high forehead, in midflight.

There was a running board on the side that was like a stair that you stepped up on before climbing in. The windshield wipers worked on a vacuum so that the slower you drove, the slower they went. This, of course, created a big problem. In a heavy downpour, it was necessary to go fast in order to get the wipers to move fast enough to see by.

The transmission gears and the clutch were so worn out that it was hardly necessary to depress the pedal in order to shift. The motor was so simple it looked like something created from a tinker toy. She could actually fix a lot of the things that regularly went wrong. About every one hundred miles or so, the distributor cap would jar itself loose, and the car would simply quit. She would pull the car over to the side of the road, get out, raise the hood, secure the cap back down, slam the hood, get back in the car, and take off.

The only other problem the car ever gave them that summer, other than the lack of speed, was the taillights. They quit working one night when Donna and Joan had planned to go to Oneida to catch a movie, so they wired an old flashlight to the bumper and secured a piece of red cloth over the end with a rubber band. Worked like a charm.

The movie was great, but as they arrived back at the parking lot, there was a police car sitting there a few feet away from the Studebaker. Their first thought was that he had spotted the homemade taillight and was lying in wait for them to take off so he could nab them. Then they realized that he was probably just sitting there for general purposes while the movie let out.

Well, now, how to turn the light on? They couldn't just mosey up and flick the switch. They quickly formed a rather elaborate plan. Donna was to get in the car while Joan walked around behind where she would drop her purse. While she was rummaging around on the ground, picking up the spilled contents, she was to switch the light on and cough, signaling Donna to turn on the headlights. If they were lucky, the lights would look like they were all going on at the same time.

It seemed to go well. After the lights were on, Joan got in the driver's seat and backed out of the parking space and around the cop. They didn't dare look at him. She put the car in first gear, and making sure she didn't do anything wrong, signaled a left turn with her hand and turned out onto the street. They held their breaths. He pulled out behind them, and just when they were sure they had been caught, he turned a corner and drove out of sight. Whew! They had made it. Stude strikes again!

The summer after graduation had been a wonderful one. She was hardly ever at home. They were either in the Studebaker or in her father's boat. They water-skied, swam, went picnicking on Frenchman's Island, out in the middle of the lake, and visited every state park within a fifty-mile radius. She was gone so much that she seldom had to put up with her mother's moods and pouting. She wasn't home enough to cause any problems, and she realized that as long as she kept her distance from her mother, they got along much better.

Toward the end of summer, one sad thing happened to disrupt the fun. George, her next-door neighbor, who had moved into Mabel's house when they were in sixth grade, went into the marines. He was the kind of friend every girl should have, and they were about as close to being brother and sister as any two people could be without actually sharing the same bloodlines. They confided in one another their deepest secret yearnings.

There was a great big maple tree on the property line between their houses. It was the kind of tree that was made to be climbed, and it hung over the detached garage in the backyard. She spent almost as many hours in that tree thinking as she did sitting beside her lake. After George moved in and they became friends, she invited him to join her. He liked it as well as she did. It became their secret. No one ever knew they were up there because the leaves were so dense that if you didn't deliberately look, you didn't see anything. One of their favorite things to do was sit there and watch as one of their mothers would stand in the backyard and call to them to make them come in and do chores. They never budged.

Even though they weren't lovers, they actually carved their initials in the bark of that tree and surrounded them with a heart. When he left for the service, a huge hole opened up in her world.

The summer wound down to its inevitable close, and when September arrived, she had packed her bags and left with a smile on her face. Ruby and Barry, two of her best friends, were going to Potsdam also. They had spent thousands of hours together during their high-school years singing in a quartet/sextet/octet. The size depended on who was free at the time. Ann always accompanied them, and she planned to follow them to Potsdam the following year.

The other steady member of the group, Elet, was going to Clarkson College, which was also in the village of Potsdam. They were all inseparable, so it wasn't within their realm of thinking that they would ever grow apart. They were all going to the same town, so it would still be just like high school. They would all be together. Little did they realize, at that moment, that the friendships that were so deep in those tender years could succumb so quickly to the responsibilities of budding adulthood.

The day they left was so exciting, however, that they didn't burden themselves with possibilities. The boys were going with their parents because they all had so much to haul, and Ruby was riding with Joan. It would never be the same between them again, but they were so full of anticipation that separation never entered their minds. Within two short years, Ruby would drop out and get married, Elet would be clinging to life in a hospital bed, and although Barry and she both graduated from the Crane School of Music, State University of New York, they really didn't see much of one another.

The Bernhards Bay gang would never be the same, but that day of departure was unmarred by reality. Donna was on her way to Buffalo State, George and Dick were already marines, Sammy was going to work for his father, and Carol was staying home to be with her boyfriend. Joan picked Ruby up at her home in Brewerton, and away they went, happily letting the Studebaker carry them into the future.

By the end of her freshman year in college, however, the car finally began to show serious signs of aging. Her uniqueness, which had always been so charming, was now becoming a detriment. When the mechanics could no longer patch things up, they would go searching in junkyards for replacements, but there were none. The junkyard owners would shake their heads in regret while Joan sadly began to realize that Stude's days were numbered. Her wonderful, loveable, laughable Studebaker, born the same year she was, in 1937, could no longer cut the mustard.

She had made several round trips from home to college, about one hundred and fifty miles each way, and Stude was getting tired. They were also tired, tired of going only thirty miles an hour. They would push her a little harder on each endless trip.

"Come on, girl, you can go at least forty!" But she couldn't.

She tried through, valiantly, but they all knew in their hearts that the trip back to school in the fall would be a sad one.

On the very last trip home that year of 1955, with Stude crammed to the roof with junk, the most extraordinary thing happened! They were going across a bridge in Watertown when what to their wondering eyes should appear but an absolute dead-ringer twin sister! Stude had a family! The kids in the other car must have been as surprised as they were because they were all hanging out the windows, shouting and waving as well! They blasted on the horns and waved and laughed, but for some reason, neither driver attempted to stop.

Even after all the problems they had with her, she was as well-loved as any family pet could possibly be. They laughed that it seemed somehow fitting and comforting that she was not alone, and that when she finally had to leave the earth for good, at least now there was a chance she would be joined by a loved one someday, in that great big buggy-heaven in the sky.

Chapter 13

Just thinking about that car lifted Joan's spirits, but sitting there in the lumberyard that evening, she realized that things had changed drastically after Stude's demise. It was as if childhood had been left behind, and it was time to get serious about life.

When she returned home from school that summer of 1955, the first order of business was, of course, a new car. In her eighteen-year-old wisdom, it seemed to Joan that it would be unfair to ask the family to supply her with another one. After all, she could survive without one, and they had been generous enough the first time around.

The prospect of being without wheels was not one she wished to contemplate, however, so she made the proposal that she would work all summer at any job that was available at the lumber mill if, at the end of vacation, they would chip in whatever was necessary in order for her to get another one. They all felt that was fair, but there weren't any regular jobs available. They already had enough office help and couldn't lay someone off so that she could step in on a temporary basis.

She begged, pleaded, and cajoled. She was desperate. She would do anything, anything at all. It didn't matter what it was as long as she got a car at the end of the summer.

"Anything?" her brother asked.

"Yes, anything!" she answered.

"Are you sure?" he asked.

"Absolutely," she replied confidently.

"Well then," he returned, conspiratorially, "you can work on the pond."

"The pond!" she croaked. "What do you mean, I can work on the pond? Doing what?"

She couldn't believe what she was hearing. The log pond, which adjoined the new modern mill, boasted the worst job in the yard. Everyone hated the log pond. It smelled. No, not just smelled, it reeked! You couldn't even get a good breath without gagging when you were too close. The smell was so intense that many a man had quit and risked being unable to feed his family rather than endure it. It was the place they assigned anyone they wished to get rid of without having to fire them. Guaranteed, they wouldn't last.

She questioned her brother's motives. She smelled something rotten, and it wasn't just the pond. It was like him to want to see what she was "made of." Well, he would find out! If he thought he could get the best of her, he had another think coming, as her mother would have said. Besides, she had asked for it, and now she had it. She couldn't very well say no if she were to hold her head up, to say nothing of the fact that there would be no car at the end of the summer.

She approached the steaming pit that Monday morning as she would have approached one filled with alligators. The closer she got, the stronger the stench. She took off the scarf she had deliberately worn and tied it over her mouth and nose, masklike. It didn't help. Breakfast rose closer and closer to her throat, and she had to fight hard to get it back down. She would not give in. She would beat it if it killed her.

There was a scuzzy-looking man standing on the two-foot-wide catwalk that crossed the pond at the mill end. He had just finished poling a log out of the slime and onto the conveyor belt, which carried it up into the mill to be sawed. He was obviously unaccustomed to seeing a female anywhere in the yard and stopped short to stare. When he realized that the pond was her destination, he spoke defensively.

"What're you doing here, slumming?" he mumbled rudely as if he were challenging her right to breathe.

"I'm here to work," she said curtly.

"No shit!" he replied, unable to process the fact.

Trying to stay calm she said, "If you will show me what to do, I'll get at it."

He looked at her as if she were from somewhere east of outer space and began a stumbling explanation.

"Well . . . you stab those big suckers with one of these here poles and try and work it around them other logs and up onto the pulley here . . . You ain't strong enough to do it, though . . . it takes muscles to move all them logs outta the way."

"Well, at least let me try," she said, reaching impatiently for his pole and stepping up onto the catwalk with him. He ignored the gesture.

The more he contemplated the prospect of working with her, the angrier he seemed to become.

"Then ya gotta spray 'em with that there hose. Why, you ain't even strong enough to press the spray handle to get the stones out, and the first thing you know they'll be breakin' a ban-saw up there and blamin' me for it," he rambled on hurriedly. He held the pole at arms length, out of her reach.

"Give me that pole!" she demanded, lunging for it.

He pulled it back toward his body, and she missed. She threw herself to her knees and down onto the wooden boards of the catwalk just in time to stop from falling into the vaporous steaming sewer.

He thought that was hysterical and began to laugh, and she was getting angry.

"If you don't let me try, we'll never know if I'm capable or not, will we?" she said, trying to be reasonable.

He stopped laughing abruptly and looked at her with growing suspicion.

"What the hell's goin' on here, anyway. Why'd they send some snivelin' girl to do a man's job? You some kinda snoop er somethin?"

Finally realizing the precarious situation she was in, she began to speak softly, trying to calm him down. It wouldn't be hard to drown in the filthy smelling mess below, and she no longer trusted him to have any kind of judgment at all.

"I'm home for summer vacation, and I just wanted . . ."

"Home for summer vacation," he jeered. "Not only do they send some dumb female for me to work with, they send a whiney college brat!"

Now she was really getting mad! Forgetting the circumstances, she hissed, "You look here, you."

"No, you look, girly girl," he huffed. "I ain't workin' with no female! You stay right here if you think you're good enough. They can take this job an shove it up their big Webb asses! They can find somebody else for this shit! I quit!"

He slammed his pole to the ground beside the pond and stomped off.

She waited awhile before going back to the office. She didn't want to see him again and had no desire for another confrontation. When she finally walked in, she could hear laughter from the inner office where her brother's desk was, and her suspicions were confirmed. She had been set up. They were hoping Sir Galahad would quit rather than work with her, and they were right, he did.

When she waltzed into his inner sanctum, the laughter quickly died. She didn't want to let them know she had caught on, so she told them what had transpired. As she did, they had everything they could do to keep their faces straight. What they didn't realize was that she, too, was on the verge of laughter, but for another reason. They thought they had her, but only she knew she could do the damned job! She knew she'd show them. Sometimes her brother displayed a very strange sense of humor, but this time she'd be the one to have the last laugh. They could use her to get rid of a bad worker, but they wouldn't get rid of her that easily!

There was no mention of the problem at the dinner table that night. Jack was at his own house, and she wasn't sure her mother and dad knew what was going on. She certainly wasn't about to complain. She would just be patient and see what tomorrow brought.

It brought sheer delight. Who was waiting for her when she arrived at the pond but Pete Haynes! He had worked for the company from the time he graduated from high school and was one of the most valued employees. He was also a friend and not much older than she. He didn't scoff at her being there but realistically explained that the job was very strenuous. He said that he wasn't sure that she should be trying to do it, but that he would help all he could.

He explained the importance of what they had to do and told her that the reason the smell was so bad was because there were two years of collected sludge at the bottom of the pond, and at the end of the summer they were going to drain it and clean it out.

"Thanks, a lot," she laughed. "Just my luck, they'll clean it after I'm gone."

Depending on how dirty they were, the logs had to soak for several hours before being poled over onto the conveyor belt, sprayed, and sent slowly on up to the mill, fifteen feet above. The trick was to be able to move the other logs out of the way in the crowded water without getting them hung up on one another. You had to be able to push them around and sometimes under each other, which took both brawn and skill.

Pete thought that the easiest way for her to start was to do the spraying while he horsed the heavy logs around. That sounded pretty good to her until she tried to squeeze the handle of the hose. It looked just like the hose of a gas pump, so she expected it to have the same amount of pressure. Boy, was she wrong! When she squeezed, nothing at all happened!

She tried again, harder. Still nothing. She pressed with both hands and got a trickle. Finally, the only way she could make it spray with full pressure was to grip it with both hands, place the tops of her fingers to her bent left thigh and push down as hard as she could with both hands. It also helped to squeeze her eyes shut, hold her breath, and grit her teeth. It was awkward, and she must have looked hilariously funny, but it worked. If Pete thought it was humorous, he never let on.

She mastered the sprayer a little at a time. First she was able to open her eyes, then ungrit her teeth. Then breathe. She was even able to stop pushing her hands down on her thighs after a couple of weeks, but try as she might was never able to do it one-handed. Pete liked to show off once in a while and even tried to spray her occasionally, but that stopped when her strength was built up enough to get him back.

Learning to move the logs around was even harder. Many times she would get the inertia going and almost end up in the drink. She found that as with water-skiing, the most important thing to know was when to let go!

By noon of the first full morning on the job, she was seriously considering going back to school without a car. The house and lunch were across the road, a full quarter of a mile away, and she had to walk. She doubted that she could make it. When she eventually arrived home, she was so thoroughly exhausted that she literally could not eat. She became so nauseated that she got up and stumbled into the living room to collapse on the couch where she stayed for the remainder of the lunch hour.

Her mother wanted her to quit, "I don't know how you expect to keep this up when you can't even eat a decent lunch. You'll be making yourself sick, young lady, and then what good will you be? You'll be flat on your back in bed, if you're not careful. Don't expect me to feel sorry for you when it happens. I don't know why a car is so important, anyway. Everyone else has to walk, why shouldn't you?"

"Thanks, Mom," she thought, "that was exactly what I needed to stop feeling sorry for myself and get back to work. I couldn't have done it without you and the memory of the laughter emanating from the back office yesterday."

From that point on, whenever she felt she could not go on, she thought of those words, that laughter, and that dreadful person who would rather starve than be disgraced by working with a woman. She thanked them all.

By the end of that summer, she had the shoulders of a lady wrestler, huge arm muscles, a completely flat tummy and a 1949 gray Dodge!

Chapter 14

There were so many memories in this place. Their old brown house was still there across the street, but Joan didn't even know who lived there now.

It had been comfortable. The kitchen was large enough to seat them all easily at the table. There was a formal dining room used only for Sunday dinner and when company came. The living room was also large and used more often after they got their first TV set when she was in high school. Also on the first floor was a tiny room they aptly referred to as the "little room." It was just big enough for the radio, a studio couch, her dad's favorite chair, and his smoking stand. Many an hour was spent in that room listening to their favorite programs.

Next to the little room but separated by the stair landing, which emptied into both rooms, was the "sick room." This was a small bedroom with a single bed and a dresser. After Jack moved out to go off to war, it had been used only when someone was ill. It made it easier for her mother to nurse everyone. One fateful night, it became quite a mystery.

Joan had been awakened in the middle of the night by the sound of a baby crying and was intrigued. Sammy's mother, Jean Riccelli, who lived across the street, had just given birth to a baby daughter a few days before. She couldn't figure out why Jean would be there at such a time. She wanted to see the baby, though, and wondered if they would get upset with her if she went downstairs. Her five-year-old curiosity got the best of her and she decided to have a look-see, regardless of the consequences.

She crept quietly out of bed and started down the stairs. The stairway was open, with only the rungs of the banister separating it from the bedroom. From there the room below was in clear view.

She had only descended two or three stairs when she realized there was someone in that room. In fact, there were a whole lot of people in that room. Peering through the rungs down into the gloom below, she could make out her father standing next to the bed. Then she saw the back of the head of a rather stout-looking man but she couldn't make him out. Lying in bed was Jean Riccelli, holding her baby. She just couldn't understand why Jean was there.

Joan sat there for some time, watching, and then a woman she couldn't identify came in and took the baby away.

Finally, as her eyes adjusted more, she was able to make out the identity of the stout man. It was the doctor! What in the world was going on?

Then she really had a shock. The person in the bed moved just enough for her to see the face. It wasn't Jean Riccelli at all. It was her mother! Boy, this was really interesting. Jean Riccelli's baby visiting in the middle of the night, the doctor being there, and her mother in the sickbed, with her dad standing next to her!

Someone she couldn't see very well brought the baby back into the room and gave it back to Joan's mother. Ellen looked at the baby for a while then handed it to her father.

The others had been fussing with an electric light, like a work light, the kind with just a cord and an empty exposed bulb. They put the bulb in the bottom drawer of the dresser and then began folding blankets and towels and putting them in the bottom of the drawer on the other end from the light. Then something really strange happened. Her father bent over and put Jean's baby in there, too!

Eventually, without figuring any of it out, she became bored watching because nothing seemed to be happening. They were all just standing around. Every once in awhile, one of them would stick a hand in the half-opened drawer, but other than that, there was little activity. Besides, the baby was apparently asleep, which meant she couldn't see her anyway, so she went to bed.

The next morning, when she awoke, she was very surprised to find out she had a brand-new baby sister. So that was what all the fuss had been about! The stork had been there! Well, she was not impressed!

"Kids are so much smarter and better informed about those things now," she thought.

Thinking back, it seemed impossible that they could have kept that secret so closely guarded from her. Tummy size apparently didn't mean much, especially to a five-year-old. She *did* remember asking her mother why Jean Riccelli was getting so fat and that her mother's answer had been something to the effect that she also got fat sometimes, didn't she?

Years later, Joan found out that her sister had been several weeks premature, and although it had been increasingly more popular in rural areas to go to a hospital, the majority of babies in their area were born at home. The whole family had been. In fact, they had all been premature, so there wouldn't have been time for the hospital, anyway.

As it turned out, it was lucky for Linda that she was born at home. During that same time, there had been thousands of babies blinded by improper lighting in the hospital incubators.

"I had better think about getting back on the road," she thought suddenly. "How long have I been sitting here? Maybe I should just stretch my legs for a minute before I go."

She opened the door, swung her legs out, and stood up. Suddenly, her head began to swim, and her knees felt as if they were forgetting to hold her up. She grabbed the edge of the door, hoping it would help steady her. She stood there, trying to get her bearings, trying to clear her head, which wouldn't stop spinning long enough to focus. "Focus on the brown house, the memories that are there." Linda's birth . . . her first puppy, Bubbles.

Memories began to overflow and spill out of the past and into her mind, but only the bad seemed to want to be heard. All of a sudden, they wouldn't go away. Something was triggering them, setting them free, giving them a will of their own and threatening to overwhelm her with their power.

"Push them back," she ordered herself with determination.

Then, hoping that if she could get her body under control, her mind would follow, she half-fell, half-sank back into the car seat.

Her mind cleared frighteningly on a scene that she had completely buried until she had seen the Alfred Hitchcock movie, *Psycho*, awhile ago. Here it was again, unbidden, and she was helpless to stop the deluge of memories and terror. The bathroom scene and the violence were the same. Only the outcome was different . . . no one died—not physically, at least.

Four-year-old Donna, Sammy, and Joan were playing with the little wooden boats her daddy had made for her out of scraps from the wood shop. They had an old bucket that took two of them to fill and carry.

They had been cheerfully playing, unattended in the backyard, but for some reason, they decided that it would be more fun to play with the boats in the bathtub, so they gathered them all up and went upstairs.

They drew two or three inches of water in the tub and floated the boats. As time went along, they got more and more rowdy and gradually began getting a little wet. They were laughing and splashing and having a grand old time. Then Sammy deliberately cupped his hands and splashed a wall of water in Joan's direction. It soaked her to the skin, but neither Donna nor she tried to splash him back. She really didn't know why.

After awhile, Joan began to get cold from the wet clothes, and Donna suggested she take her clothes off. Joan complied, and they resumed their roughhousing. Eventually Joan ended up in the tub, with Sammy splashing the others with howls of delight and peals of laughter.

Suddenly, an unadulterated shriek split the air. They froze, paralyzed from the shock of it. Her mother stood in the doorway, looking down at them with a look of unrestrained rage. She screamed for Donna and Sammy to get out of there and get home. They deserted Joan as fast as their little feet could carry them.

They skittered past Ellen in the doorway, leaving Joan alone to face her mother's unbridled fury. She slammed the door shut after them with such force that Joan thought it would splinter and fall apart.

"What do you think you're doing?" Ellen shrieked.

Joan didn't know what she had done, and she didn't know how to answer her.

"Answer me!"

Ellen grabbed her upper arm and in one quick yank whipped her out of the tub and threw her to the floor. Joan lost her balance and fell, hitting her head on the side of the tub. Her terror was so complete she didn't feel any pain from the impact. Ellen reached down and jerked her to her feet.

Joan thought the problem must be the water all over everything, so she grabbed a towel and started frantically dabbing the puddles.

"I said answer me!" Ellen screamed, grabbing the towel and heaving it into the corner. Then she grabbed both of Joan's upper arms and began shaking her violently. Ellen was completely out of control, and Joan was afraid that anything she said would only make it worse, so she didn't dare say anything.

She tried desperately to figure out what was happening, but her young life didn't offer the assistance of experience. Finally, she sputtered, "Please, Mommy, please."

"I'll 'please' you!" Ellen yelled, and letting go of one arm, she wrenched Joan's naked body around and started hitting her as hard as she could in the buttocks with the palm of her hand.

"Ouch, Mommy! I don't know what I did," she begged. "Tell me what I did!"

"You know very well what you did, young lady, and if you ever do it again, I'll blister you within an inch of your life."

She was shouting at the top of her lungs now, and Joan knew she had to get away from her. She twisted hard and got out of Ellen's grasp and flung herself under the sink. It offered no protection though, and Ellen lurched for her, catching her wrist and dragging her back toward the center of the tiny room.

As she raised her hand to strike her again, Joan wrenched herself out of her mother's grip, and Ellen lost her balance on the wet floor. Ellen slipped but grabbed Joan around the waist with both hands. Joan was as slippery as the floor and managed to break free, which caused her mother to land solidly on the floor.

Backing up into the toilet, Joan started crying and screaming, "I won't do it again! I promise, Mommy. Never again!"

Ellen lurched up and grabbed for her. Again, Joan managed to get free because of the water.

Joan tried to wedge herself behind the laundry hamper, but seizing it in one hand, Ellen overturned it, exposing Joan once more to her fury.

Again and again, she snatched Joan in her grip. Again and again, Joan squirmed and wiggled her way free.

It was a steady banter now. "I'm sorry, Mommy! I promise I won't do it again. I'm sorry. Please, Mommy."

She still didn't know what she had done, but it didn't even matter anymore. The only thing that mattered was getting away from her mother.

Ellen started to reach for her again, and she flung her body without regard toward the overturned laundry hamper. She landed on top of it, and as she did, Ellen grabbed a large chunk of her platinum hair and jerked her roughly around. The last thing Joan could remember was her mother's cold, vindictive, accusing eyes as she yanked Joan's face closer to hers.

Joan reached across the car seat and fumbled in the darkness for her purse. Her hands were shaking, and she was crying. In her ears was the echo of, "I'm sorry, Mommy. I promise I won't do it again!"

"I've got to get hold of myself," she thought as she blew her nose and dried her eyes. "This is getting me exactly nowhere, and it's doing me exactly no good, so knock it off!" she demanded.

The correlations between that night and tonight were obvious except that this time she knew what she had done wrong. She was in love with a married man. She had let her love for him color her judgment, and now she was paying for it. As certainly as she had paid in that old bathroom, she was paying now. One part of her wished she could remember the ending of that terrifying scenario, and another part was very glad she couldn't. She had succeeded in forgetting all of it until that night in the theater when it had all come crashing back into her memory.

One thing was for sure—she had to stop this morbid reverie and get her head going in the right direction. She felt as if she had just awakened from a bad dream and couldn't shake off the invisible fibers of gloom.

When that happened to her at home, she usually grabbed a lighthearted book or magazine article. There was no such thing around even if it would have been feasible to read sitting there in the car.

The only reasonable thing to do was to start home again. This time without the stretch, she reasoned. That must have been it—she had just gotten up too fast.

She pulled out onto Route 49 and headed east once more. It felt better just to drive. She went past George's house, which was next to her old brown house. Sammy's was across the street, then there was Donna's street, with Carol's house on the corner. Across the street from Carol's house was the general store, which Carol's father owned. It was the only business in the town other than the lumber company. It also served as the post office. The postmistress, Edna, was Carol's mother.

As far as the kids were concerned, the store's most important function, however, was not for buying groceries or picking up mail. It's most important reason to exist was as a place for the kids to hang out. They spent hours per day sitting on the store steps. They made all their decisions from there, ate ice cream and candy there, planned all their fun from there. It was the center of their social life and was lovingly referred to simply as "the store steps."

They were there so much and interfered with store traffic so much that Mr. Davis finally built a second set of steps beside the old ones, just so they'd have a place to hang out and not be in the way of his customers. They were concrete, no less, and went nowhere.

Directly in front of the store, across Route 49, was the end of the street that Mrs. Tank lived on. Poor old thing, Joan smiled to herself. Well, not really poor. She had gotten everything she deserved. She was the meanest person in five counties.

Anytime they walked passed her house, Mrs. Tank would whip open the door and start screaming for them to get off "her" sidewalk! Well, in Bernhards Bay, them was fightin' words, so they would stash them all away for fall.

She was feeling better already, she realized as she drove along. This was a fun memory. She had told the story many times over the years, and it never ceased to please and liven up a party. The amazing thing was the fact that they didn't all get thrown in jail as kids would be today, she thought.

Halloween was probably the longest-lasting and most highly anticipated holiday in town. For the kids, it was the Fourth of July, summer vacation, and all of their birthdays rolled into one long two-week period. For the adults, it must have seemed like a month, and no one was spared or automatically free from the hassle. The best, or worst, depending on which end of the caper you were on, were saved for the least-liked citizens.

There was a long tradition of prank playing in town, going back for generations, or so they believed. Joan and her friends weren't about to be the first to break that long-established custom.

They planned their strategy for months, saving up all of their mother's discarded thread spools, small pieces of soap, string, and so on. At the end of September, it was time to take action. Hours were spent carving notches around the edges of the little spools. The deeper the V, the louder the racket, but care had to be taken not to get them too deep, or the spool would break after the first few uses, then time would have to be wasted making more.

When the notches were done, they ran a piece of string through the hole in the drum and tied it, working the knot over to the side. Then they would roll the remaining arms-length piece of string around the outside. A sturdy pencil was then inserted through the hole of the spool. It was advisable to tie the pencil to the end of the string so that it wouldn't get lost in the heat of a possible chase.

When the pencil, encased in the spool, was quietly but firmly placed under the bottom portion of a house shingle and the string pulled as fast and firmly as possible, a jackhammer-type blast reverberated throughout the entire house, which acted as its own amplifier. Many a tired gentleman was raised out of a peaceful after-dinner nap with that one!

There was also the inevitable soap for windows, boring and not very original, but effective. They didn't dare buy soap at Davis's store because the adults would know what their intentions were, so if they couldn't find big enough pieces at home, they took the small ones and soaked them in the lake and smushed them together to harden.

They regretted terribly not having grown up, as her brother had, in the era of The Outhouse. *The stories the older kids told them of their younger years invoked envy in the younger generation. The exploits of nailing them shut, stealing the paper, putting snakes and frogs in them, placing waxed paper over the holes, and tipping them over with or without various and sundry occupants were legendary!*

Joan and her friends really had to be creative to top those glorified exploits! Unfortunately for Mrs. Tank, she provided the perfect combination of orneriness and meanness to cause them to rise to the occasion.

For a week they went around after dark, stealing clotheslines. They were very quiet about it. No giggling behind faces, no soaping windows, no rotting vegetables thrown in the road or on porches, no spooling or anything. They worked with a singleness of purpose that they had never been able to muster before.

The town was hushed with anticipation. The adults knew it was the third week in October and wondered why they hadn't started "halloweening" yet. And what was happening to all the clotheslines?

The kids were planning a holiday celebration matchless in the annals of the town's history, and Mrs. Tank was to be the opening ceremony!

They stored the clotheslines down in Charlie Whitney's pasture, under a huge hickory tree. It was the place Joan always went when she really wanted to be all alone. Everyone knew it was there, but because it stood unprotected in the middle of a large pasture, no one but her thought of it as private. They tied the lines in three or four line-lengths so they would be manageable and easily carried. Then, on the appointed night, they crept to Mrs. Tank's house with them.

Working as silently as they could, they tied the clotheslines all together and proceeded to go around and around her house, wrapping every doorknob and window handle along the way. When they finished, they sneaked across the street to watch the fun.

George and Sammy, who had been previously appointed, then came raucously hopping, jumping, and skipping loudly down the street. The kids across the street could see Mrs. Tank through the windows as she started toward the door, getting ready to run the boys off "her" sidewalk. She reached for the knob and turned it, but when she pulled it, it wouldn't open. She tried several times, then ran to the back door. They followed, running around to the back of the house. She tried that door. The same thing happened. They had her! They had succeeded! They had literally tied her in her own house!

She ran back to the front door and started banging on it.

"You little bastards, you let me out of here!" she howled, rattling the door.

Then she ran to the back of the house, hollering all the while, and banged on that one again. Again the kids followed.

Back she went to the front of the house, and then she became silent. They sneaked back to the other side of the house and waited with anticipation. Then the front door slowly opened about an inch, straining against the clotheslines. She stuffed her nose and mouth into the opening and screamed.

"Damn you! Let me out, or I'll call the police!"

And she did.

When the New York State Police arrived from North Syracuse about an hour later, they found the perpetrators in their usual resting place, the store steps. The kids were gloating loudly and could tell the police weren't taking the situation seriously. She called them several times a year, and they were obliged to respond even when they knew it was a farce.

Trying not to laugh, the police made them promise to leave Mrs. Tank alone for the rest of the season. That was fine with them because they had won. She had gotten hers, and they had given it to her. Now they would be the stuff of legends!

Joan chuckled as she drove along. The only other person in town who could compete with her nastiness was Mrs. Noel. According to Joan's nephews and niece, she was so caustic that the day her pet parakeet bit her, it died!

So many memories for so small a town. There had never been a mayor or supervisor, no government whatsoever. The people were responsible to the county, but their little town had no councilmen, no planning board . . . only pillars. Pillars of the community, and Joan's family qualified as one of those.

And when one's family was one of the pillars of the community, one was expected to maintain a proper decorum. *Not* go around getting the first divorce the town had ever had or getting pregnant by a married man! Daughters of town pillars didn't do that. Only town sluts did that.

"Well, my beautiful, peaceful lovely Bernhards Bay," she thought, "I must be the town slut! If I can just manage to get through the next few hours of my life, maybe you will never know."

She drove through Cleveland and tried to keep her mind occupied with more pleasant memories. Unfortunately she was going past that rotten electrician's house. She had been late paying his bill once, and he had "dropped in" to let her know he could suggest an easy way to pay it off. She threw him out, telling him he could rot in hell before she would have anything to do with him. Being divorced was not easy. Men seemed to think you were available for anything at any time. That was another reason David had been easy to fall in love with. He was a gentleman. She wished he were here with her now. She needed his comfort.

Finally . . . home! The reed was beginning to feel like a tampon that was ready to come out.

"Oh, my God! What if it comes out before it's supposed to?" she thought.

What would happen? Would everything stop? Would she have to bring a child to term that was maimed and grotesque? Would she have to say to the twins that the monster was created because Mommy was a slut? She got out of the car and carefully closed the door. She didn't want anyone to wake up.

"Why isn't this over with? I can't do this anymore! I'm exhausted. I have cramps. CRAMPS! What does that mean? Stop, No more thinking. No more feeling. No more guilt. I'm home. Put it away for now. It isn't doing any good."

She opened the back door of the house and closed it quietly. She would sneak in and look at them. That would make her feel better. She would have to be quiet. She didn't want to wake Sally.

"They're so sweet when they're sleeping. One brunette, one blond. So different they hardly look like twins." she thought.

"You've taught me so much since you came to be with me," she said to them silently. "And you've made me wonder about so many things."

When they were babies, she would look at them lying beside one another, sideways in the same crib, and wonder where they had come from. Where had they been before? Did they choose her as she had chosen to have a baby?

A baby, mind you. She hadn't bargained on this double treasure. She used to wonder if they could remember the kicking wars they had in her tummy. Suzanne would sock her in the ribs, and Tracy would kick her in the bladder. Someday she hoped they would both carry babies that kicked them in the bladder! A mother's revenge!

This baby inside her now never had a chance, she thought.

She used to wonder if they knew more about real life than she did. Did they have to forget about where they came from in order to learn what they needed to know to live here? If they could have spoken to her, would they have told her unsuspected wonders about the universe and God and life after death? Did they have all that knowledge stored there in those tiny little brains, waiting to supply them with the stuff of life and things they needed to know to survive it?

"I guess if I were born with it, I sure blew it, didn't I?" she thought, standing there looking down at them.

She continued cooing to them in her mind. "The most important thing you've taught me is about unconditional love. I didn't know such a thing existed. You've taught me that no matter what you do or say, how you act, what you think, you could never make me stop loving you."

She wondered why her mother didn't feel that way about Linda and her. She didn't seem to love people unless they behaved. All her life, she heard phrases like "Get away from me!" "You are a bad girl!" "I don't even want to look at you!" "You make me sick!"

She'd had to build walls around those words so they didn't hurt so much. But that wouldn't happen to her babies. She loved them too much. She would fight any dragons, suffer any brutality, go through any pain life could dish out to keep them with her and keep them safe. No one would ever take them away from her.

"Well, your mommy had better go take that last pill and then get some rest. Good night, my lovies, sleep tight, don't let the bedbugs bite."

Chapter 15

Thursday, October 18, 1965

The lake was extremely calm for an October afternoon. The fresh crisp air smelled so refreshing that it was almost possible to imagine that she was sitting there in peaceful serenity.

What a morning! She hadn't wanted to get out of bed. The reed had kept her awake half the night, along with last night's hotel scenario had created unending circles and cartwheels in her head. Grotesque images of babies emerging from her womb with reeds piercing their skulls and sticking out of their backs, bizarre dreams of malformed and maimed babies marching in rank and file, coming ever closer to her. She had awakened several times in a cold sweat, panting from imaginary flights away from the ghastly sights.

She hoped that she had done the right thing, taking the reed out earlier. It was frightening, but she didn't know what else to do. It couldn't have been helping anything, anyway. She could tell it had disconnected because she could hardly keep it in when she went to the bathroom. It was a terrifying thing to do, but there certainly wasn't anyone she could call for advice.

"Hello, I have an eight-inch reed stuck in my unmarried pregnant uterus. Could you tell me, pretty please, what to do with it?"

The call to school to tell them she wouldn't be in had been as frightening as the nightmares. She hated to call Herb and tell him she was sick even under normal circumstances. The teachers all felt guilty waking him up at the crack of dawn to make him start calling the substitute list. It was worse this time because she was actually lying. She had to tell him that she wouldn't be in tomorrow, either. She wondered if he had believed her claims of the flu.

Well, maybe she'd be able to get some respite now that the girls were down for their nap and Sally was busy in her room. She had been right—what she needed was a little "lake time" as she used to call it.

Climbing down the long flight of stairs in front of the house hadn't been easy, but it felt good to just sit there and contemplate. It was peaceful enough to disregard the cold.

There had been a long period of time in her life when she hadn't been able to seek the solace of her lake, and she had sorely missed it. All her college summers, except the one she spent earning her new car, had been spent in school. She had accelerated her program in order to finish and get married sooner. Now she seriously questioned the wisdom of having done it, but hindsight was always easy. At the time, she had been madly in love with her intended, and it seemed the reasonable thing to do.

Looking back on it now, that first year of marriage was like a dream in some respects. Atlanta, Georgia, was about as far away from Bernhards Bay, New York, as any place in the world could be. The amount of trouble she found herself in most of the time attested to that fact.

The trouble was caused by an ignorance of the society she found herself forced into as the wife of a Fort MacPhearson, Third Army Band member, but it was fueled by her own stubbornness and a streak of innate rebelliousness. It was 1957, and there had already been some rumblings in Little Rock.

The first incident occurred a few days after their arrival by car, having spent their honeymoon on the drive down the Eastern Seaboard. John's band was giving an outdoor concert in the amphitheater in northern Atlanta. She hadn't had time to meet any of the other wives yet, so she rode to the concert with John. She stayed with him until he had to go tune up with the band, and then she took her seat in the audience.

The band, in full dress uniform, took its place on stage, tuned, and then stood as the band director took to the podium. The band seated itself, the director raised his baton, gave the downbeat, and they began to play. The audience stood immediately and respectfully placed their right hands over their collective hearts in reverent silence.

"Wait a minute," she thought in amazed confusion, "they aren't playing 'The Star-Spangled Banner,' they're playing 'Dixie'!

She didn't know what to do. People all around her were already staring at her as she continued to sit there. She didn't understand why the band would put that old song in front of the national anthem, and she certainly didn't understand why everyone would stand up and cover their hearts over it!

Looking around, she was beginning to realize that she should stand up too because through the process of mental osmosis, she was getting the distinct impression that if she didn't, she might regret it.

Just as she stood up, the song stopped, and everyone else sat down. There she was, standing alone in an amphitheater of several hundred people, hand over heart, just as the band began playing, "Oh, say, can you see." She didn't know whether to sit or faint!

She could smile about it now, here in the safety of this "Northern" dock, in all of this peace and quiet, but at the time, she had been terrified. She was also too stubborn to sit down. Ah, the sweet innocence of youth! She got out of it unscathed, however, because the audience probably felt she was more trouble than she was worth. Just another Damned Yankee!

She was standing in line at the motor vehicle office, waiting to get her Georgia driver's license. It was insufferably hot. Even native Atlantans were having trouble that day. She spotted a water fountain, and since her tongue felt like a piece of tanned leather, she looked around for John. He could save her place in line while she dashed for a drink. She finally spotted him sitting on a marble bench, leaning against the coolness of the marble wall.

She waved him over and explained, then made her way for the much-needed drink of water. Just as she was beginning to slurp thirstily, she felt someone grab the collar of her blouse and literally yank her roughly back and away from the fountain. She thought that she was being attacked and felt momentarily threatened. Then, as she whirled around trying to get her balance, she saw that it was John.

"Get away from that fountain," he hissed.

She had never seen him express any anger before and was as astonished by that as she was by his actions.

"What's wrong?" she gulped as she choked on the water she had half swallowed.

"What's wrong?" he said incredulously. "It's a 'colored' fountain, that's what! Can't you read?"

He pointed to a sign above the fountain that said 'colored.'

"You can get into trouble drinking out of a colored fountain!"

He was so close to panic that she was hesitant to argue with him, but she was thoroughly confused.

"But it isn't colored. It's white. It's as white as the one we have in the kitchen!"

At that, the most startled expression came over his face, then it changed to amusement, and he began to laugh. She had never heard him laugh that hard.

"The 'colored' refers to the skin color of the drinker, not to the shade of porcelain the fountain's made out of!" he said, doubling over, trying to suppress his laughter.

"I'll never get it right," she thought, remembering that she had read about segregated water fountains. She wasn't at all sure she wanted to get it right but sighed her defeat and searched around until she found a proper 'white' one.

It seemed at times that there were so many rules and regulations that it wasn't worth going out of the house, but school was about to start, and she had her first teaching job. She figured the children would be a little more forgiving. The school she was going to teach in had never had a choir, and she was really looking forward to it.

She had flown to Atlanta the March before they were married, for a job interview that John had set up for her. Between seeing him for the first time in months, her first job interview, and her very first plane ride, she had been very excited.

She had never been that far south and was enthralled by the beautiful gardens and parks. It was only March, but there were flowering trees, bushes, and roses everywhere. She had never seen dogwood and magnolias. It was almost ethereal to the senses, and she drank in every last bit of the sights and aromas. It was like being in a foreign country.

The whole trip went off as if she could do nothing wrong. The Fulton County administrators that she met were gracious beyond belief. They didn't seem to care that she had no training or experience. They said they needed a breath of fresh air to stimulate their public schools, and she would be able to assist in doing that.

They also didn't care that her major was in music and not in classroom even though she was interviewing for a fifth-grade classroom position. As a matter of fact, they seemed delighted because they would be among the first in the state with elementary music being taught formally.

The idea was that some of the other teachers would take her students for academic work, and she would take theirs for music. It sounded great to her. She would be a welcome part of a faculty and would be able to contribute something no one else was able to do. She was completely delighted. She flew home feeling she had the world on a string.

After all the social boo-boos she had made after returning, however, she wasn't so sure about everything. School started at last, though, and the first week went without a hitch. They had settled on a good schedule for swapping students and the fifth- and sixth-grade choir, which was being touted by the teachers and principal as the best thing that ever happened to the school, was all auditioned and ready for its first rehearsal the following week.

On Friday, there was a countywide teacher's conference and luncheon. Joan was actually disappointed at not being able to teach, but she was also excited about the conference. Everything in the state was run on a county basis. Teachers were hired by the county, as there were no such things as individual districts, and her principal had invited her to join her at the table of the county superintendent! Joan knew it was a great honor.

She had a wonderful time explaining their program to the superintendent, and he seemed very impressed. Her principal bragged happily over the fact that it had all been her idea in the first place, and a great time was had by all. That came to a quick halt after the superintendent asked her THE question.

"Tell me," he said, "how are the school districts up North dealing with the 'Negrah problem'?" he asked, seeming genuinely interested.

She found out later that "Negrah" was the term used when an educated Southerner was trying to falsely show respect for the race. They couldn't quite get their mouths around the accepted term, "Negro."

"Oh, there isn't much of a problem up there," she had offered innocently. "I guess it might be the fact that there are less Negroes in the North, but we don't really have a problem. We just all go to the same schools, and no one makes a fuss about it."

She smiled, realizing now that she should have been more aware of attitudes and what she now knew must have been transpiring around that table, but she just generally assumed that intelligent people were of the same mind about such things, no matter where they came from. The question in and of itself should have warned her, but apparently she didn't want to be warned. She just went chattering along.

"There were quite a few Negroes in my class at college. Most of them were from the New York and Long Island area and were much better prepared musically than I was. One student, as a matter of fact, was so good at conducting that most of the faculty was secretly jealous of him. His name was Pete Bagley, and I wouldn't be surprised if someday he had a world-famous choral group. There just didn't seem to be any problems, not where I went to school, anyway. I had a Negro roommate my sophomore year. She was an excellent piano player and accompanied our girl's trio when we performed."

She felt, later, that the last was apparently the straw that broke the camel's back. The superintendent excused himself from the table, as did most of the others, but since it was time for the afternoon meetings to start, Joan really didn't think much of it. Everyone was getting up and making their way to their assigned places. John was picking her up after the meeting, so when it was over with, she just said good-bye to everyone and left happily for the weekend.

She must have been one of the few on the staff that had a relaxed weekend because when she arrived at school on Monday morning the entire fifth- and sixth-grade schedules had been reworked, the students had been reassigned, and somehow she was no longer needed.

Most regrettably, the county had hired too many teachers, and since she was the last one hired, she had to be the first to go. They hoped she would forgive them, but there just wasn't one thing that could be done about this deplorable situation. No, there were no other schools in Fulton County that need teachers, either. They were so very sorry and upset, but as she could see, there just wasn't one thing that could be done. All said with a beautifully polite and proper Southern regret.

Then there was the bus incident. Their car was being worked on, so she was forced to ride the bus to do some Christmas shopping in downtown Atlanta. She had never ridden a city bus in her life, much less in the South. She had no idea how much they cost or where they went. When the bus stopped, she got on the nearest door, which was in the middle of the bus, and walked up front to ask the driver how much it was and pay him.

This accomplished, she turned around, and not seeing any empty seats in the immediate front section, she walked back toward the rear and took the seat that was one row behind the middle door. Immediately in front of her was a young woman with several bags of groceries and a crying baby.

As usual, it was a stifling day, and there was no air-conditioning. She could hardly breathe in there. The baby was crying because it was hot, too. She wished the driver would hurry up and get going so they could at least have some breeze from the windows. When she looked up at him, she noticed that he seemed to be staring right at her in his mirror. She couldn't understand why he would do that and looked away. A few moments later, they were still just sitting there, so she looked again, and again he seemed to be staring at her.

Finally, he disgustedly threw whatever it was he had been holding in his hand to the floor and came stomping toward the back of the bus. She thought she must have done something wrong again and cowered a little in her seat, waiting to be reprimanded.

He stopped at the seat in front of her, leaned threateningly toward the woman with the baby, and said, "you know very well you ain't supposed to be sittin in front of a white woman. Move!"

"Wait a minute," Joan stammered, "I sat down after she did. She's got a baby and groceries and—"

He interrupted, smiling sweetly at Joan, and said, "I'll take care of this, if you don't mind, Ma'm."

She was appalled, "Look, I never would have sat down here if I'd known it was going to cause a problem. I'll move."

"No you won't, Ma'm, she will," he said, never taking his eyes off the young mother.

The woman began to try to gather the child and groceries up in her arms, but Joan couldn't take any more.

"You stay where you are," Joan said to the young woman, "I'm sorry I caused this to happen. I'm getting off this bus."

She grabbed her purse, pushed her way past the objecting bus driver, and left through the middle door. As she started walking back toward her street, Joan heard him yelling something that had to do with her being a God-Dammed-Yankee-Troublemaker. She hoped she hadn't made it worse for the woman by protesting, but she was glad she had gotten off the bus.

When the protests really started in Little Rock, some time after they left Atlanta, she knew in her heart that they were long overdue.

Looking back at that fall of 1957 from her 1965 dock, she knew she had also had problems with repression. She trickled her fingers through the cold October water, thinking that she felt she understood what it was like to experience repression, but in her case it wasn't because of skin color, it was because she was a woman. It couldn't compete with the racial prejudice she had witnessed, but it was very real.

In some respects, racial prejudice today was a lot further along than women were, she realized suddenly. Things had improved tremendously in Atlanta since she was there. The city was now becoming a leader in desegregation, or so she'd heard. Women were no better off anywhere, though.

Twenty hours. Nothing had happened yet. She wondered how much longer she would have to wait. He said twelve to forty-eight hours. When would it start?

Chapter 16

Her lake. Her solace since a child. She had had to really take the bull by the horns to get this place, but it had been worth it. It wasn't ideal, just a remodeled old camp, but she loved it. Yes, the cliff was too high, but that was part of why it was so beautiful. She could lie in bed at night and watch the moon through the huge picture window as it bounced its beams off the water below.

The stairs that went down to the water were too rickety. Maybe one of these summers, she would be able to afford to get some work done, but work or not, she loved it. It was on her lake, and it was all hers. Well, it was hers and the bank's, but basically it was hers, she thought proudly.

Everyone had thrown up their hands in despair when she decided to buy it after the divorce. It was as if she had no idea of how to care for her own kids. Then there was the fact that most women weren't supposed to own houses by themselves. She was doing it, wasn't she? She might be the only woman she knew who had a mortgage in her own name, but she was making the payments. Why shouldn't she be able to own it by herself?

Her mother and father had been against it because they were convinced that the kids would fall off the cliff. In the first place, there was a ledge three feet below the top that was so dense that a mouse couldn't have fallen through and been injured. It was so dense that the place for the stairs had to be hollowed out of the brush and an upper landing built. The stairs descended through the landing, and there was a gate there that would make it impossible to fall.

Their doubts had made it difficult for her to keep her confidence up. Her mother had always done that to her. Just when she would begin to think that she was competent and able to do something or other, her mother would find some way to chip away at the confidence until she began to doubt herself again. It had been unlike her father, though. She had decided it had something to do with his being overprotective of his grandchildren, but it had still been at her expense.

Even if it had been possible to fall off the cliff, the twins were bright enough to understand the danger and stay away from it. Yes, they were very young, but they did as she asked because she had faith in them.

Sitting there, below the dreaded cliff, in all this peacefulness, it was hard to believe what was happening inside of her. Maybe it had just been a four-month-long nightmare and wasn't really true. Maybe she would wake up and find out it had never happened, it had all been a bad dream. She hadn't really gone to the Hotel Syracuse last night. She was not really sitting on this dock with a dying, rotting baby in her womb, waiting for him or her to abort him or herself.

Maybe she wouldn't have to worry about the sand pail she had found in the toy chest and then stashed in her bedroom closet. As she had feared, a three-pound coffee can had been impossible to find, so the large red pail would have to do. It seemed rather ironic to her that it was to be put to such a use. She didn't know if it would work because she didn't know what to expect. If this were just a nightmare, maybe she wouldn't have to worry about that or about wearing a housecoat all day and having a towel handy in case something started.

She wondered if Sally would tell on her if she knew. Regardless of the situation she was facing, she knew that she had been lucky to find Sally. Joan certainly felt lucky to have her, but would she keep quiet if she found out? It would make this day so much easier if she could trust her. She didn't think Sally was mature enough to keep it from her foster family, though. It was so explosive that it would be all over Camden within hours of their learning about it.

The people at school would feel secretly sorry for her, but they would have no choice but to fire her. She had earned tenure, but this would come under the "decency clause." Even if she weren't caught or arrested, they would still have grounds to let her go. What kind of example would she set if they kept her? They just plain wouldn't be able to.

She wondered if this baby would ever come out.

"Will I have labor pains?"

"Will it hurt?"

"Will it be like having a baby, or will it be so broken up there won't be any pain?"

"Will there be little arms and legs? Fingers?"

"Was this hurting the baby?"

"Was it still alive in there?"

"What does it look like?"

She was angered at the thought that if it hadn't been illegal, this could have been done months ago, when the possibility of pain was nonexistent. Then it would have been so simple!

"Who do they think they are, putting us through this? This is our pain, not theirs. It is none of their business! Because it's illegal, it has taken much longer, and the one who has to suffer the most is the only one who is completely blameless!"

"I'm so sorry, little one," she thought. "I pray you don't hurt. It's been so long. At least that awful reed is gone. Maybe that made it better for you. I'm so, so sorry. Please forgive me. I have to think of your sisters. If I didn't do this, the authorities would take them away from me, and I know you wouldn't want that. Please, please forgive me."

Oh, God, she had to stop doing this. Get back up to the house. Get some rest before Ann got there with the other prescription. She wanted to be rested when Ann arrived. Unlike Sally, there was no need to worry about Ann. What would she have done without her? Who could she have turned to except Ann?

She decided it was time to go back up to the house, up all sixty-seven steps. It had always been part of the game to count them. Hand in hand, one twin on the step ahead of her and one on the step behind, always making sure whoever brought up the rear would lead the next time. They had mastered the counting easily.

She began the steep ascent but found it was more difficult than usual.

"Twenty steps. Guess I'll sit and rest for a minute," she thought, gasping for breath and trying to find a comfortable step to sit on.

The lake looked dark, like an October lake usually did. If the sun had been shining, it would have glanced diamonds off the surface, but the day had turned dreary, making it look like crinkled aluminum foil.

"Oh, lake, my lake," she thought, laboring for breath. "Will I ever be free enough of this anguish to truly enjoy you again?"

It was time to get going. She was really tired. It must be all the emotional turmoil. Supposedly that kind of turmoil took more toll than just plain physical effort. She got up unsteadily and resumed the climb.

"Dear Lake God," she pleaded, "please forgive me for what I'm doing. I know you understand. I know you don't look down on us with vengeance. You wouldn't create us with bodies that were designed to seek the love of another and then punish us for doing just that very thing."

"The God that lives in church punishes us and says we should hate our bodies."

She couldn't understand why. If he created them in his image, why should they hate their bodies? Should they hate something God himself created? It didn't make any sense.

Supposedly, he was a loving God, but she couldn't believe that. If he were as loving as they were supposed to believe, he wouldn't play tricks on people, would he?

"Resist temptation," saith the Lord! "I am the one who created your body in a manner in which it can be tempted, but if you can't resist that temptation, you will be a failure, and I will not love you anymore. Hah, hah, hah! GOTCHA! Go straight to hell. Do not pass GO. Do not collect two hundred dollars!"

She had wondered about those church teachings since she had been a child. So many of them hadn't made sense and still didn't. If he created little babies in his image, then why was it necessary for them to be baptized before they could go to heaven? The answer was always the same. They had to be forgiven for their original sin. What original sin? Had their parents committed the sin they were being forgiven for in the act of their conception? If that were the case, then why did the church condone sex at all? If it were so sinful it had to be driven out of the baby it created, then why was it all right to do it, married or not? It seemed to her that he was the one who needed the forgiveness for torturing people like that.

What kind of a god would do those things, she wondered. A loving one? She didn't think so. Maybe it was the church's doing. Maybe the church had to create sins in order to have something to hold over their heads. Without sins to be forgiven, why would they need the church at all? If they had the power to go directly to God, why did they need an organization with ministers and priests?

Fifty-two steps. She was getting dizzy again, like last night. She thought she'd better sit down before she fell. She sat with her head in her hands, trying to make sense of it all.

She knew her lake god would encourage them to love themselves. Be happy. He wouldn't be testing them all the time to make sure they were worthy of his love. He wouldn't care if they were worthy, He would love them, no matter what, and would accept them into his heaven. He would be kind and gentle, not mean and spiteful.

She should get started up again. She stood up slowly.

"Good-bye for now, Lake God. Please stay with me and guard me from harm. Protect my babies. Watch over them, just in case."

She felt woozy as she slowly climbed. Maybe she was coming down with the flu after all.

Chapter 17

The twins were waiting patiently for her from the top step of the front porch, staying obediently away from the cliff. Just the sight of them lifted her spirits. They looked adorable in pigtails with their light blue one-piece corduroy jumpsuits.

"Thank you, Lake God," she whispered. "Thank you for my precious daughters."

"Mommy, Sally wants to know if you want her to start supper," Tracy said.

"Yes," Joan answered, completely winded, "but I'd like to talk to her first." "Suzanne, come help Mommy, will you? I'm very tired today."

"Tracy, would you tell Sally I want to see her in the living room?"

Suzanne helped as much as her little body could, and they gradually stumbled up the front stairs, across the small porch, and into the living room.

"There," Joan said, sinking gratefully into an easy chair.

Sally came into the room half-dragged by Tracy. She eyed Joan with obvious concern.

"Are you feeling all right?" she asked.

"Yes," Joan responded, trying not to raise Sally's suspicions.

"I'm just very tired, and I'm afraid I may have picked up that stomach bug that's been going around school, but I'm sure it's nothing serious. Would you mind getting supper by yourself?'

She looked placated and said, "Sure, I'll get it. What were you going to have?"

"The pork chops I bought Thursday should be eaten soon, so why don't you cook those and some boiled potatoes. That would be easy. Cook one for Suzanne, too, just in case. I keep hoping that one of these days, she'll want something besides a hot dog. Maybe tonight will be the night."

"Were you planning on a vegetable?" Sally inquired.

"Just make whatever you want," Joan said, trying to keep the exhaustion out of her voice.

"I think I'll lie down for a little while. Call me if you need anything."

"Mommy, I don't want you to lay down," Tracy whined. "I want you to play. We didn't play today."

She tried to tug Joan out of the chair. Joan let her succeed at the tugging because she really needed the assistance, but as she stood up, she put her arm around Tracy's little shoulders and hugged her close.

"Mommy needs to take a nap first. You already had yours, and now it's Mommy's turn. We'll play later. You go help Sally get supper."

She knew Sally wouldn't be overjoyed at the prospect of "help," but she had to divert Tracy's attention away from her for the time being.

"Besides, the cartoons are probably on. You can watch them for a while."

"Okay!" they squealed delightedly as they rushed out to the family room, which was right next to the kitchen.

Her bedroom door was right across from the chair she had been sitting in, so she willed herself through it and on over to the bed where she flopped with relief to be alone and to lie down at last.

She must have drifted off because the next thing she knew both girls were shaking her, and Suzanne was trying to get her to get out of bed.

"Come on, Mommy, supper's all ready, and Sally says it's going to get cold. Come on."

They climbed up onto the bed.

"She's got applesauce to go with the pork chops, and she said we can have some of the cake she made yesterday for dessert," Tracy said breathlessly as they bounced up and down on the mattress making windmills with their arms.

"Stop!" Joan shouted angrily. "You're making me dizzy!"

They stopped abruptly, not accustomed to having her raise her voice to them. "I'm sorry," she said guiltily. It wasn't their fault that she didn't feel well.

"Mommy didn't mean to yell. It's just that her tummy doesn't feel good. It feels like she's coming down with the flu or something. Do you remember how you felt last spring when you both had the flu?"

"Yes," they both answered.

They had been very ill, and she knew they would remember and understand how she was feeling.

"Well, that's the way Mommy feels right now. I'll eat later. Tell Sally to leave mine on the cupboard. Okay?"

"Okay," they intoned sympathetically.

"Anne and Ray are bringing Amy out to see us later, so you go eat, and after you're done, you can bring all of your clothes that you've outgrown, and we'll sort them out for Amy, all right?"

They had been looking forward to seeing the baby for some time and were excited about giving her some of their hand-me-downs. Both jabbering at once, they headed back to the kitchen. She could hear snippets of their conversation as they told Sally what was happening.

"Amy is coming to visit, and we're going to give her some clothes. Mommy doesn't feel good . . ."

She thought to herself that this was not the time to be coming down with the flu, but she knew that it hadn't lasted long with the people who had recovered, so she told herself that she'd feel better in the morning. That seemed to be the way it affected people.

She didn't remember falling asleep, but she realized that she had, when she heard all of the commotion coming from the kitchen. The dog was barking at the top of her lungs, and the twins were talking excitedly.

"Here's the baby! Here's the baby."

It was obviously Ann and Ray. She hoped Ann hadn't had any trouble getting the prescription filled. She willed herself out of bed, not wanting Ann to worry needlessly. She just wished she could shake the weariness and nausea.

There was quite a racket from the kitchen as she made her way unsteadily into the living room. She would just sit down there and let them come to her. No need in trying to get out there—her knees were a little weak. She might stumble, and everyone would get all upset. The house was very small, so the short distance between the kitchen door and her chair in the living room made it easy to hear the greetings and conversation.

"Hi, kids!" Ann said.

Joan could tell Ann was puffing under the weight of either Amy or the inevitable paraphernalia that always accompanied babies.

Ann continued depositing things on the kitchen table as she asked, "Where is your Mommy?"

"In the bedroom," Suzanne replied, "Where's Amy?"

"In the bedroom?" Ann demanded, as if alarmed.

"No, I'm in the living room," Joan interrupted.

Ann looked up and spotted her and said to the girls, "Ray has Amy. She fell asleep in the backseat, and he's getting her out of the car. You wait for him while I go talk to your mommy for a minute."

Ann headed through the kitchen as Joan once again thought how lucky she was to have such a friend.

"What's the matter?" Ann said immediately after she was out of earshot of the kitchen.

"I just feel like I'm coming down with the flu or something. I'm a little nauseated, that's all," Joan replied

"You don't look very good to me," Ann said, being careful to keep her voice down.

Sally was doing dishes, but Ann didn't want to take any chances on being overheard.

Joan looked at her. "No, really, it's just a bug that's been going through school. Everybody has had it, and my symptoms are exactly the same as theirs—lightheadedness and nausea."

Ray came into the kitchen with the baby, and there was more ruckus as the dog deemed it necessary to reassert her responsibilities as family protector.

"Oh, Duffy, be quiet," they heard him say, speaking as if the dog should know better than to bark at him. He came into the living room carrying the baby. The two kids and the dog followed close at his heels.

Forgetting caution, Ann said to him, "Ray, look at her. She looks awful, don't you think?"

Ray scrutinized her carefully and was about to express his opinion when Sally came into the room.

"Well, I feel just fine," Joan said., "Thanks for getting supper, Sally. If you're all done with the dishes, you can take the car if you want. I won't be going anywhere with company here."

"No thanks," Sally said, sounding tired. "I think I'll just go up to my room and watch TV and go to bed early. If you want any supper, I left it out on the cupboard to be reheated. Good night."

"Good night," they all mumbled back as she made her way up the stairs.

As soon as Sally was gone, Ann said, "Well, good, I'm glad she's out of the way for the evening. Now, Ray, why don't you take the baby into the family room and let the kids play with her for a while?"

He realized she wanted a chance to talk with Joan alone and said, "Okay, come on, kids. Let's find some of her toys, shall we?"

Ann, following along behind, said, "Yes, I'll help."

She was only gone a second and then returned with a glass of water and her purse. She handed Joan the water and rummaged through the purse.

"Here's your prescription," she said quietly, opening the bottle and handing Joan a pill.

"Thanks," Joan said as she swallowed it, hoping but not at all sure it would stay down.

"Did you take the rest of the other pills?" Ann asked, concerned.

"Yes, I finished the last one last night, I'm just fine, really. Just tired. It's all the tension and waiting. I really mean it when I say that I think I have a touch of that bug."

Her words rushed together, spilling out like water. It was so good to have someone to talk with she almost cried, "But this morning that damned reed came out!"

"Came out!" Ann said in horror. "How did that happen?"

"Do you know that awful feeling when a tampon is ready to come out, and it pushes down as if it will come out of its own volition if you don't take it out?"

"Yes," Ann answered unbelievingly.

"Well, that's exactly the way it felt. I could tell it wasn't up in my uterus anymore the way he said it should be, so I didn't see any point in leaving it in. I pulled it out."

"What did you do with it?" Ann asked, frightened.

"It was soft, not brittle the way I had seen it before he put it in, so I bent it in several places and then wrapped it with toilet paper and threw it in the trash in the bathroom. Then I took the kitchen and bathroom trash out in the back and burned it like we always do. It's gone."

"That's good!" she said, relieved.

"You know, I feel terrible about this, but Ray has a lot of work to do to get ready for a very important meeting tomorrow, and we can't stay very long. I wish you'd call the doctor and tell him how you feel before I leave."

"Oh no," Joan said, "it's late, and I would probably have to call the medical service, and then we'd have to wait for him to return the call. It would probably take a long time at this hour of night. Besides, I've felt exactly this same way many times. I'm sure it's nothing to worry about. I'll call him first thing in the morning if I don't feel better, I promise."

"Well, all right, if you're sure, but I'd still feel better if you'd call him, even if it takes a little while," Ann said stubbornly.

"I'll make a bargain with you," Joan said, not wanting to disturb the doctor. "I'll call him later tonight if I still feel the same. Is that better?"

"Promise?"

"Yes, I promise," Joan said, convinced that she'd feel better. "Now you get going. It's a long drive, and, Anne, thanks again for everything."

"You're welcome. Just don't forget your promise. Maybe I'll call you when I get home."

"Okay, fine," Joan would agree to anything just so Ann would leave and she could lie back down. It was tiring to have to act cheerful when she felt so rotten.

"Call me later," Joan said.

"All right," Ann replied, getting up and calling into the other room, "Ray, get the baby wrapped up. We're going."

Ann disappeared into the family room, and Joan could hear all the preparations being made for leaving. As they moved back into the kitchen and started out the door, Ann called to Joan, "You take care. I'll talk to you in a little over an hour. Throw a kiss to Amy, girls. You watch out for your mommy, she doesn't feel very well tonight. Bye-bye."

And they were gone.

Joan was struggling to get on her feet when the twins came into the living room. "Do as Ann said and help me, will you? Help Mommy go lie down on the bed."

Suddenly she was hit with what felt like a cold blast of icy wind, and she began to shake uncontrollably.

"Get Mommy an extra blanket, will you? It's cold in this room tonight."

Suzanne headed for the closet to get her blanket as Tracy exclaimed loudly, "Oh, oh! We forgot Amy's clothes! Mommy! We wanted to give her the clothes!"

Tracy was almost crying, so Joan said weakly, "Well, go try to stop them."

She found the bed, and for the second time that evening flopped gratefully into its comfort. She shivered violently as Suzanne tried to get the extra blanket over her.

From the bedroom, she heard Tracy as she shouted for Ann to come back. Then she didn't hear anything. All she did was feel the incredible cold. It seemed to be permeating every pore in her body with its arctic iciness. She thought that she had never been this cold. She couldn't stop shaking. The bed was freezing. How did it get that cold?

"Somebody get me more blankets," she pleaded quietly. "Please, I'm so cold."

"JOAN! What's the matter?"

Ann was shaking her and talking at the same time. "I think you're having convulsions!" she said loudly, fear in her voice.

"No, I'm okay," Joan chattered. "Just so cold. Please get me more blankets, Ann, please! This is such a terrible time to come down with the flu. Please, there are more blankets in the twins' room. Get them for me, will you?"

Then, resolutely, as if nothing in the world could change her mind, Ann took charge.

Chapter 18

"Joan, listen to me. This is not the flu! This is what the doctor warned you about. You are having chills. People get chills when their temperature gets really high."

Ann felt her forehead.

"My God!" she exclaimed. "You're burning up! There's no question now, we have to call the doctor. He said that if you began to run the slightest fever to call him, remember?"

Trying not to agree, Joan whined, "Yes, but it's so late. It's too late to call him now."

Joan knew by Ann's tone of voice that there was not much point in arguing with her, but she tried.

"I'm going to tell Ray what's going on, and then get the girls ready for bed. I'll be right back."

Ann rushed out of the room.

What seemed like a second later, she was back. "Now, tell me his name," she demanded.

Joan knew any disagreement was useless. "Okay, it's Dr. George," she said, almost unable to get the words out through the tremors. "His office is in the Medical Arts building, downtown."

"Don't you have the number written down?" Ann said incredulously.

"No, I didn't dare have it around. Get the phone book. I'm so cold I can't stand it, Ann. I can't stop shaking. It's Dr. William George. In the phone book. Syracuse, Medical Arts building."

"Okay, here it is," she said, dialing. "I can't believe it. He has his home phone listed."

"Ann, be careful, it's a party line. People listen. Ann, I'm scared."

"So am I," Ann answered quietly.

"Hello? Dr. George? Thank God, you're there! I can't give you my name on the phone, but I'm the friend of a patient of yours. I'm on the verge of panic, and I need you to listen carefully. You only saw her one time, but she told me you were very understanding and had said that if she ever had unexplained symptoms and began running a fever, she was to call you immediately. Do you understand what I am trying to tell you? This is a party line—there are neighbors who could be listening."

Ann listened to his response.

"Okay," she said, handing the phone to Joan. "He wants to talk to you."

Joan panicked. "No! I can't. Someone might recognize my voice."

"You have to!" Ann interrupted, thrusting the phone toward her forcefully.

Joan acquiesced and said meekly, "Hello?"

A strong deep voice answered, "This is Dr. George. I know what your problem is. I have other patients who have been in the same condition. Do you understand?"

"Yes, but . . ."

"I have to know your name," he cut in.

"But this is a party line and . . ."

"It doesn't matter! Tell me!" he demanded.

"It's Joan, Joan Winter," she could barely speak, she was so traumatized with fear.

"All right, Joan. Good girl. Now put your friend back on."

She handed the receiver back to Ann. There followed a series of hesitant answers.

"Yes . . . Okay . . . I understand . . . I'll try . . . It's Orleans 5-8246 . . . I don't know how high. She's shaking almost uncontrollably. Yes . . . I understand . . ."

Then she hung up. She looked at Joan, her face white with fear. Joan realized at that moment that they had a real problem. This wasn't the flu. It was what Ann feared. For the first time since leaving the hotel, she was afraid for her life. Not afraid of being caught this time, but afraid of dying.

Ann spoke, measuring her words as if she were forcing herself to keep control.

"He's going to call right back. He's setting up a hospital admission. I'm going back out to talk with Ray. Will you be all right alone for a minute?"

"Yes, go do what you have to do."

Joan tried not to think of the consequences and the chain of events that had set them in motion. She could hear Ann talking to the kids and to Ray. Her tone of voice was a giveaway as to which of them she was addressing.

"All mothers talked like that," she thought.

She couldn't make out what Ann was saying, but she thought that if she could stop shaking, she might be able to understand. But she couldn't, so she stopped trying.

Ann returned in a few minutes with the air of someone who had efficiently accomplished a mission.

"Ray is all set with the baby. The twins are getting their pj's on. They know you are sick and might have to stay in the hospital all night to get better. They're fine. I'll call Sally down just before we leave so we can avoid a lot of questions. Okay?"

The "okay" was more of a question about Joan's understanding rather than one seeking approval. Joan sensed that she was no longer in control of decisions about her welfare and was again glad that Ann was there and was such a good friend.

"Why hasn't he called back?" Ann asked the air impatiently. "I can't believe how long it's taking."

It dawned on Joan what the problem might be, and she offered through chattering teeth, "the party line. Someone might be on the line, preventing him from getting through. If someone's on, they're supposed to hang up if there's an emergency. Check it."

Ann lifted the receiver quietly and replaced it. "Yes, they're on."

"Maybe . . . they'll hang up in a mi-minute," Joan stammered. "If they g-get curious, they might listen. I don't know who they are. Just wait a minute and see what happens."

"Joan, you're getting worse, fast. I can't wait. I'm going to do it." She picked up the receiver and began speaking so quickly that Joan didn't have time to object.

"Ah, pardon me, excuse me," she said sweetly. "We have a slight emergency, and I'm expecting a call-back from a doctor. Would you mind terribly hanging up and talking later? Oh, thank you very much!"

There was a pause, and then Ann said, "There, they hung up. Maybe I should call him back, it's been busy so long."

She thought a minute. "I will."

She dialed. "Hello? Dr. George? This is the friend again . . . I'm sorry. This is a party line, and I didn't realize there was someone on the line. I had to ask them to hang up and . . . Memorial Hospital? Okay, right away. No, there aren't any ambulances way out here. It takes about an hour . . . all right, we'll hurry as fast as we can."

She hung up with that same white-fear expression she had the last time, but this time, Joan thought she saw her hand tremble as she replaced the receiver. She quickly left the room and called up to Sally, barking directions.

"Sally, can you come down here? Ray, come help me with these blankets, she's freezing!"

Ann continued, "Sally, she's very ill. Thank goodness the twins called to us as we were pulling out of the driveway. I've spoken with my doctor, and he wants us to take her in to the emergency room at Memorial Hospital. He will call her family doctor in the morning. What's his name?"

"Dr. Brown," Sally answered, surprised at all the preparations.

"Oh, that's right," Ann lied as if she hadn't remembered. "He's from Cleveland. I won't bother him at this hour. The arrangements are already made. No use changing them now. Our doctor is already on duty," she said officiously.

"No need to bother Dr. Brown. Ray, would you go start the car so it will be warm when we start out? Kids, your mommy is going to be fine. Say good night and give her a kiss. Sally will put you to bed."

"But she doesn't let us kiss her when she doesn't feel good," Tracy said.

Suzanne agreed, "She's afraid she'll give it to us."

Ann smiled reassuringly, "Well, I think this one special time will be all right."

They looked rather bewildered, so Joan rustled up all the energy and confidence she had and reached out to them. "Night-night, Lovies. You be good for Sally. I love you."

She hugged them to her, ready to burst into tears. "Give me a kiss. Sally will read you your night-night book," she said, her voice breaking with emotion.

Anne realized what was happening and quickly took charge again.

"Okay, let's get you in the car," she directed.

Suddenly Joan felt sick to her stomach.

"Ann, I'm afraid I'm going to throw up in the car. There's a sand pail in my closet. Will you get it for me?"

"In your closet?" she asked as if Joan were crazy.

"Yes, on the shelf," Joan managed. "Please get it. Hurry."

Ann returned with the sand pail as Ray was ushering Joan out to the car.

"There you are. Climb in—can you?" he said protectively.

Somehow she managed to get into the backseat, and they tucked blankets around her.

"I'm so cold," she said, grateful for the extra warmth. "I'm so tired."

She sank gladly onto the seat with relief. She could hear the twins shouting their good-byes from what seemed like a very far-off place as the car began to back out of the driveway, then she closed her eyes and drifted dreamily, not cold anymore.

"We've got to hurry!" Ann said urgently.

"The doctor said this is really iffy. We may be too late already. He says it sounds like a massive infection. Her internal organs may already be shutting down. Ray, what are we going to do if something happens while we have her in the car?"

"I hear them talking up there," Joan thought cagily, chuckling to herself.

"They think they're so smart and that I can't hear them. Must be their mothers didn't teach them any manners, whispering and keeping secrets from friends. Well, I can hear them," she giggled craftily as she wafted in and out of reality.

"Oh look, here's Bernhards Bay again. Seems like I just went through here a little while ago."

Memories took over as the sounds of the car and its rhythmic movement mesmerized her mind.

There's the school again and the church next door and the cemetery. That cemetery was lots of fun to play in. The gravestones made great places to hide behind for cops and robbers. The side of the hill that led up to it from the backyard of the school was filled with lilies of the valley every spring. They always smelled so good.

There were grave markers in there from the early eighteen hundreds! They probably weren't in the right places anymore, though. Frank Crandall used to pull them up and make piles so he could mow the grass faster. Everyone said he was so smart that he knew exactly were each one went back to, but the kids saw how helter-skelter they were when he was working, and they didn't believe it.

Did they ever have fun in that school, too! The first warm spring day always brought some shenanigan or other. They just couldn't help themselves.

One time, when Mrs. Clarence went out to the bathroom, the boys boosted each other up to the clock that was right over the only door in the room. They set the hands ahead. Not much, just a few minutes. Then they all scrambled back to their seats, and when Mrs. Clarence came back in, they were all hard at work.

They held their collective breath and were absolute angels until the clock said three o'clock. When she announced that it was the end of the day, like she did at three o'clock every day, and it was really eight minutes of, they knew they were on to something! They left as all-innocent as they could, but as soon as they were far enough away, they let out a yelp of victory and ran down to the lake as fast as they could run.

Not wanting to take any chances by overusing their newfound early dismissal routine, they decided that they wouldn't use it just any old time. They'd save it for especially nice days or special occasions. It was quite a few days before the boys climbed up there again, and this time they set it twelve minutes ahead. That worked too!

They kept adding a little time until they gradually got up to fifteen minutes, and it was still working. They waited and waited for the most absolutely perfect day to try the next one. Finally, one day, they all agreed that it had arrived. Then they had to wait for Mrs. Clarence to go to the bathroom so they could change the clock.

The minutes crawled by. Lunchtime came. She hadn't left the room all day, so they didn't want to go out. They had to make up reasons for someone to be in the room all the time to keep track of her movements. They didn't want to miss their opportunity. They took turns going in the room, using all kinds of excuses, like looking for an apple or chalk for hopscotch or anything they could think of. They couldn't leave her alone and take a chance on her going to the bathroom without their knowing about it.

Finally, after lunch, the time came. She had just finished sixth-grade social studies when she looked around to make sure they all had something to do and then left the room.

It was a silent scramble. They looked like the players in an old-time movie, pantomiming directions at each other, trying to work fast and be quiet at the same time so she wouldn't hear them. Suddenly, just as Ronnie got balanced up on Carl's shoulders and had succeeded in advancing the clock by twenty minutes, they heard the girl's room door squeak open and then bang shut. The two boys were standing right in front of the door. The whole room gasped, quietly. They all held their breath, expecting the door to fly open and Mrs. Clarence to slam right into the boys.

Everyone froze stone quiet, waiting. Nothing happened. Then they heard footsteps crossing the small foyer to the "little room" door and then some quiet tapping on it. They were saved! She was going to talk with the other teacher. Ronnie and Carl disengaged, and they all beat it back to their seats.

By the time "three o'clock" came, they were so hot and excited that all they could think of was swimming. They decided to run home, throw their suits on, and meet back at the dock as fast as they could. That was a big mistake! The only ones who made it to the dock were the ones who didn't have any parents at home, and that wasn't very many.

They should have known better than to go home twenty minutes early. There were a million places they could have gone, but no, they had to wait for the perfect day, and they had to go swimming! Their early dismissals came to a very fast end! They had been caught!

Chapter 19

"I wish she'd quiet down! What time is it?" Ann asked impatiently as the car moved steadily down Route 49.

"Seven forty-five," Ray answered distractedly.

"You might as well relax. I can't go any faster. We sure don't want to get stopped with her blabbering away like that in the backseat. They'd surely think she was drunk. Either that, or they could see she's sick and want to know what was wrong with her."

"Well," Ann offered, "I wouldn't mind them giving us an escort so we could get there quicker. With Amy in the car, I wouldn't want you to go any faster without some help. They wouldn't have to know what the problem was. Listen to her! We could say we stopped for a visit and found her this way. I think you should flag one down if you see one. She sounds worse already."

"They're whispering in the front seat again," Joan said to herself. "Their mommies didn't teach them any manners! But that's all right. I like them anyway."

They had a great time at recess at Bernhards Bay School. Sometimes Mrs. Clarence would ring the bell to come in after the regular half hour was over with, but other times she'd forget. They realized that she forgot a lot easier and for longer if they went to get her a string of fish to take home for supper.

Every spring, a kind of fish they called suckers would come up the creek next to the school to spawn. They got real good at stoning them. If she saw them out there, she'd let them stay out longer.

They'd usually play softball until it was almost time for her to ring the bell. Then someone would "discover" some suckers, and they'd all run over to the creek and start the slaughter. They were usually very good but not very fast. The only thing that mattered, though, was how many they got for her supper, so they took their time.

Sometimes she'd teach them things that she had no idea she was teaching. Her size told them things about the adult human form that were startling.

She had to wear all kinds of corsets, slips, brassieres, and who knew what all. Everybody knew that no part of the female body should be allowed to bulge, stick out, or in any way make itself known, and neither was any garment that was supposed to conceal it.

Well, Mrs. Clarence's size required that she wear so many of these garments that sometime her body couldn't tell what the rest of them saw was happening as she performed certain tasks, such as writing on the blackboard.

There were no copy machines then, so almost everything had to be done on the blackboard. Those were the days when talking about sex was illegal except when they were by themselves, looking at the pictures in the Sears and Roebuck catalog. So Mrs. Clarence made board work real interesting. She'd start by reaching up so high that her dress would be pulled up when she raised her arm and her slip would show. Wahoo!

Then as she wrote further and further down the board, her slip gradually disappeared under her skirt. Then, when she started bending over to write on the bottom part, the top of the back of her knees would begin to show, then the bands of her stockings, and then lordy, lordy, last, but not least, her garters! They loved board work!

They didn't know much about sex or anything like that. The only time they even saw any underwear was when it was hanging on the clothesline. Never when it had a living person in it! Except for Mrs. Clarence, of course.

They also loved it when the music teacher came once a week. Well, Joan guessed she was the only one who really liked it because nine times out of ten when Miss Tyler got ready to leave, the air would be mysteriously missing from her tires, or a spark plug would have disappeared. Never anything threatening but always annoying.

Actually, Mrs. Tyler was the reason Joan had wanted to be a music teacher. She loved music so much that in fourth grade she made up her mind that someone had to go out in the world and prove to people that music was something that should be fun, not dreaded.

She loved it because she was always a star in all the plays and programs they performed for the town and the church. She especially liked the annual Christmas program when she got to be the angel and wear a white crepe paper dress with a halo and carry a star-shaped sparkling wand that looked like magic.

"Hah, Hah, the Christmas Angel got knocked up by a married man."

Ann laughed. "I sure wouldn't want an escort around right now," she said thankfully.

"Don't worry," Ray assured her, "we'll be there in a little while. I'm just happy Amy is too tired to wake up every time she erupts like that."

"Yummy, charred marshmallow! The crispier, the better!"

"Oh, brother!" said Anne. "I hope she isn't getting worse."

When you don't care if they get charred and crispy, it doesn't take long to cook them. The kids had a special place for hotdog and marshmallow roasts, down on Winn's Point. It was a little point about a hundred yards long and fifty feet wide that stuck out into the water. On one side there was a small sandy beach, and on the other, some docks where Mr. Winn kept his rental boats. The tip end of the point was about big enough for ten kids and a bonfire between the huge boulders.

The hotdogs were thirty-two cents a pound, which included about eight dogs. They pooled their money for the chips, rolls, and dogs and took turns bringing the ketchup and stuff like that from home.

From August on, they tried to have corn. They swiped it. It couldn't be store-bought or be grown by anybody's family who was with them. They never discussed this out loud, but it had to be stolen—just like the apples and grapes in the fall. Well, they didn't steal very much, just enough to have a little fun.

They couldn't figure out why, but they never, ever stole a decent ear of corn. Of all the gardens and fields they raided, they either got cattle corn that was tasteless or corn that was too young or so old you couldn't chew it.

There weren't many gardens to choose from since World War II ended, though. Everyone used to have a garden. They were called victory gardens, and if you didn't have one, you were called unpatriotic, which was a very serious thing to be.

Everything was dedicated to the war. It wasn't just gardens. For some reason, cream was in short supply because the troops needed it, so ice cream disappeared, and so did butter. It had to be sherbet and margarine. Oleomargarine, it was called at the time. Talk about awful!

It came in clear plastic bags and was pure white, like lard or shortening. There was a capsule of yellow food coloring in each bag that was supposed be kneaded into the margarine and make you think it was real butter. Fat chance! No way in the world anyone who had taste buds could mistake that stuff for butter. And to make things worse, it was always up to the kids to do the kneading. You could stand there for hours working it, and the best you ever got was this ugly looking stuff with yellow streaks through it.

Joan didn't like sherbet, either. She remembered driving along, seeing signs that advertised ice cream for sale in little roadside stands. Every time she saw a sign that said Ice Cream for Sale, she would beg her daddy to stop because she always hoped beyond hope that it would be true, but it always turned out to be that awful sherbet!

Gum was real scarce, too, so it became a very important thing to the kids. This was great for Joan because she had a big brother who was in the war, and the soldiers could buy it. Every once in awhile, he would send some home. One of the happiest days of her life was the day she got a package from him all the way from overseas. Inside was a pair of real wooden shoes from Holland, a satin pillow that had a poem, "My Sister," written on it, and whole box of Teabury gum! She was the most popular kid in the school for days until it finally ran out. The most fun was saying no to one of the almost-sixteen-year-olds who wouldn't give her a piece of gum the week before.

Another very important item to all the kids was sugar. It was rationed just like gas. In order to buy either of them, you had to use coupons along with your money. The number of coupons you got depended on how many people you had in your family. A whole black market sprung up for the purpose of illegally buying those things. No one in Bernhards Bay did this much, though, because the town was so small. Joan's mother said everybody would know if someone was doing too much baking or traveling. You couldn't get away with much when there were only two hundred and fifty people in town.

The problem with sugar was getting every last speck out of every bag you had. They'd stand for hours, shaking and shaking 'til finally they couldn't hear any more granules rattling around.

The amount of gas coupons you got was decided by the kind of job the owner of the car had. There were different kinds for people who had to drive for a living. You didn't go anywhere just to go. You needed an excuse. It was easy to understand that the troops needed gas more than they did at home. Tanks, ships, and planes were more important than joyriding around. The ice cream was another thing, though . . .

Lots of things were different about that war. For one thing, they didn't figure the United States was free from invasion. Japan killed several thousand men in a surprise attack on Pearl Harbor, so what was to stop them from doing it again?

War bonds were a biggie. If you had any money, it went to buy war bonds, which were supposed save American lives. Even the kids all saved to buy them and went door-to-door selling them. Everything they did was for the war. It was all anyone thought about or worked for.

They saved and collected aluminum in every way, shape, or form. Cans were washed, and both ends taken off so they could be crushed by stepping on them. They also got aluminum from peeling it off the inside of cigarette and gum wrappers and making aluminum balls. They collected newspapers too, but she couldn't remember why.

They also collected milkweed pods. They grew alongside of the railroad tracks and roads. They grew on stalks and were these sausage-shaped things with pointy ends that were so sticky you had to use kerosene to get the stuff off your hands. They made parachutes with the white stringy stuff inside the pods.

In the whole country, all anybody thought about was winning the war. The newsreels that they played before the movies started always showed our boys doing some good deed or other. The enemy never did anything nice, though. They even tortured women and children. They were really bad. Our boys would never do stuff like that. They only shot at people in self-defense.

People had little flags they hung in their windows. They were made out of satin and shaped like a shield. The background was white and had a red border, and they were trimmed with gold fringe. In the middle was the same number of stars as the family had boys in the service. A blue star meant they were alive, and a gold one meant they had been killed for their country.

Telegrams were very important. They were the only way the government told families about their loved ones. Usually it was always bad news. When you saw the postman coming toward your house with one, you wanted to run in the other direction.

Joan found one on their kitchen table once. It said, "The United States Department of the Army regrets to inform you that your son has been seriously wounded in action." Joan grabbed it and ran to the mill office, crying, but her mother said that he was really all right. He had called before it came so they wouldn't get scared.

Until the war came, they'd only read about airplanes in their Weekly Reader Magazine *but they'd only seen a few real ones. After the war started, though, they flew over all the time. Poor Mrs. Clarence, every time one flew overhead, the entire school would empty out. They'd all run out in the yard, waving and hollering to beat the band. No matter what Mrs. Clarence was doing, they'd take off.*

Because of planes, all the houses had to have special curtains called blackout curtains. When the sirens rang at night, you had to run home and help your parents get them over the windows so the enemy planes couldn't see the lights and tell where their targets were. If you didn't do it right, the air raid warden gave you a fine.

She remembered the day the war ended in Europe. Her daddy piled all the kids onto the back of one of the Webb Lumber trucks, and they went all over Bernhards Bay and Cleveland, waving and shouting and blowing the horn. Pretty soon, everybody was following them, some in cars and some on foot. What a parade! It was one of the most fun things she had ever done because the war was over and the "Boys" were coming home!

"Thank goodness, she's finally quieted down," Ann said as they turned the last corner before reaching the hospital. "I didn't want her laughing and carrying on when we arrived."

Cautiously, Ray said, "I'll pull the car up to the emergency-room door. Whatever you do, don't give them your name. As soon as you see they safely have her, get back in the car. I want to get out of here before they start asking questions."

"I don't think we have to be concerned about them," Ann said. "They don't care. They just want to fix the problem. It's the police we have to worry about, and I don't think they're here."

"Nevertheless, I'd feel better if we left right away," Ray said. "We can't tell them anything Dr. George doesn't already know, and there's no need in having to stick around with Amy here, anyway."

"You're right," she said. "You know, she's awfully quiet back there. I'm getting concerned. Look, there's a guy in hospital garb. Pull up near him. Hurry, Ray."

Pulling up to the curb, Ann rolled down her window and asked if he worked for emergency. "We have a patient to see Dr. George. Can you help us?"

"That's what I'm here for," he said congenially, opening the back door and sticking his head in. "Not in too good shape, is she?"

He disappeared through the hospital door and returned quickly with a younger version of himself and a stretcher.

"Don't offer any information beyond what we already told him," Ray said under his breath. "We can't afford to get involved in this any deeper than we already are."

The two men did their job quickly and easily, then stopped at Ann's window. "She's unconscious and hot as an oven. Is there anything you want us to tell the Doc?"

"Not really," Ann said quickly. "Dr. George is supposed to be waiting for her. Just tell him she's here. Her name is Joan Winter. We spoke to him before we left her house. Nothing has changed as far as we know. He'll know what to do."

"We have to go now," Ray interrupted. "We have the baby here with us, and have to get going. Thanks for the help," he said as he began pulling away.

"They sure are in a hurry!" said the first orderly to the other.

"I wonder what's wrong with her that they left so fast. I hope it isn't something illegal, or we'll be here half the night answering questions."

They made their way into Emergency as the younger man called loudly, "Hey, Margaret, tell Dr. George his date is here."

Chapter 20

"My God, she's a mess!" Dr. George exclaimed. "Get her vitals, temperature first. It sure took them long enough to get here! Where's the woman that brought her in?"

"Harry said they left as soon as they got her on the stretcher," Nancy replied. "They were in a big hurry, according to him." She quickly busied herself with her preparations.

"Well, you can't really blame them," Dr. George replied as he continued to look her over. "No one can afford being implicated in something like this. If she survives, she can thank that friend!"

Thoughtfully, he stood looking down into the inert face below him. He continued aloud as if trying to put his finger on something, "There's no hemorrhaging. I don't understand that."

"There wasn't any blood when I removed her underwear, either," said the nurse. "I thought it was strange, too."

"Well, I've handled lots of these cases, and I've never seen anything quite like this before!" he said as if searching his experience for an explanation.

"Her temperature is very high, 103 degrees, Doctor." Nancy's voice reflected the concern she felt.

"Get an I.V. started before you continue. We may be too late already," he said regretfully, still staring down at her.

"She's so young, and if I remember correctly, she has twin daughters at home."

"Yes, Doctor," Nancy said as she efficiently went about setting up the intravenous. *"Doctor Patterson . . . Prof Pat . . . Prof Patterson,"* Joan muttered in a weak singsong voice.

"I wonder who this Patterson character is? Do you suppose he could be the guy who did this to her?" As if to himself, he continued, "I doubt it. If a real doctor did this, I'd like to think he would have done a cleaner job than this obviously was!"

"Alex, Alex, Alex Bay! Wowee!"

"The delirium could be an indication that her vital organs are beginning to shut down," he said emphatically. "The body just can't take this kind of infection without help. If we can get on top of it, we have a chance of saving her. If we can't, she's a goner!"

His anger reached the surface for the first time.

"What's her blood pressure?" he demanded.

The nurse answered evenly. She had worked with him many times and knew the anger was not directed at her but at circumstances beyond his control. "Seventy over fifty," she replied.

"Jesus! I can't understand it! According to her friend, it's only been twenty-four hours! How could this infection be so far advanced, so fast?" he almost shouted in frustration.

"Her pulse is very weak, too," Nancy added. "A hundred beats per minute."

"Is the I.V. running smoothly?" he asked.

"Yes, it's good."

"Then start 1.2 million units of penicillin. We have to shock her with it. It's her only chance. When you finish that and the catheter, get blood and urine samples down to the lab. We need to know exactly what we're dealing with here. In the meantime, I'll order a room and find someone to stay with her. She needs constant monitoring."

It was too bad Prof. Patterson's wife couldn't have come along like she usually did. Joan was always a little uncomfortable around her. She thought it was probably because Mrs. Patterson was the secretary for the Crane Department of Music and for Helen Hosmer. Miss Hosmer was the department's chairman, and she was the conductor of the world-famous Crane Chorus. Joan strived to emanate her in her own conducting and rather worshiped the ground Miss Hosmer walked on, so she found her secretary to be intimidating as well.

Joan couldn't wait for the day she could actually test the skills she had learned from Miss Hosmer in her own classroom. She didn't want Prof Pat's wife to find any fault with her that she could report back to her idol, so it was actually a little refreshing not to have her along for a change.

Good old Prof Pat, she thought to herself as they drove along. She was lucky to have had him as her voice-major teacher. He was such a sweetie. She was able to escape once a week with them! Sometimes she just went to their house for dinner, but tonight was special.

He had managed to get a set of keys to the graduate dorm, which was right on the other side of the fire door in the middle of her hallway. Grad students were on one side, undergrads on the other. The grad students could come and go as they pleased, but that wasn't the case for the undergrads. Apparently they hadn't had enough women graduate students to take up an entire wing of the dorm, so they just used half of her undergraduate dorm. She would be able to return after curfew, and all she would have to do was open the exterior door and the fire door with the keys he'd given her, and she'd be home!

Too bad this dorm arrangement hadn't existed during the regular session, she thought. She could have gotten accustomed to this freedom. She was starting the last six hours of her academic work, getting married in a few months, and was still being treated like a juvenile with a curfew at eleven o'clock. It was even illegal for her to go beyond a fifteen-mile radius of campus without permission.

Well, tonight she was going eighty miles without permission, planning to get back after curfew and even sneak through the graduate dorm to get to her own room! So there, powers that be! She almost wished she could tell them. Maybe she would, after she graduated.

Last week's outing had been fun.

"The St. Lawrence Seaway connects the Great Lakes and the rest of the middle of the country with the Atlantic Ocean," said the tour director. "It runs from the east end of Lake Ontario, north and east along the Canadian border and out to the sea. The Seaway System is a system of locks that opened the midsection of the U.S. to international trade."

The tour had been every bit as impressive as she had expected, and afterwards they all went to a nice restaurant about halfway between Potsdam and Massena. It was great to eat something besides dorm food.

Tonight it was back to the St. Lawrence again, but this time it was to Alexandria Bay, in the Thousand Islands, which was a hundred miles south and west of the Seaway Project. It was a gorgeous area that she had always felt comparable to Niagara Falls in beauty. It was one of New York State's best-kept secrets. The restaurant they were going to tonight was on one of the islands and had a boat that picked people up at the town dock! Cool!

She was excited about the boat ride. It would be the first one since returning to school last fall. The break between the regular session and summer school had been very busy with wedding plans so there hadn't been any time for boating. No matter, the wedding was in just a few weeks, and then they would be on their way to Atlanta, Georgia, for a year. After that, it would be back home for student teaching to complete her degree.

Prof Pat had been a great deal of help to her in meeting her academic and voice requirements. He had pulled a lot of strings in her behalf. She couldn't have accelerated her program without that help and not being able to accelerate would have prohibited her from getting married that summer.

"You know, Prof Pat," she said, looking across the car seat at his middle-aged, rather generous profile. "I owe you so much. It was great of you to help me with my voice requirements the way you did. It certainly wasn't anything you had to do. I couldn't have accelerated my program without your help."

"Don't think a thing of it," he said paternally. "It was my pleasure. You've been a very rewarding student to work with. I enjoyed being able to do it for you."

"Well, I just want you to know how much I appreciate it," she said gratefully.

"It was good for me, too," he said. "I was getting lazy until you came along and inspired me to start the girls trio and male quartet tours again."

"Oh," she said, surprised. "I thought you did that every year as part of the public relations program for the music department."

"It's true that I did the tours for years, but I was getting tired of making all those hotel arrangements and dealing with public school administrators over the scheduling. Then there were the professors on campus who didn't like the time it took away from their classes. I had to answer to them, also."

"No," he said decisively. "I wouldn't have bothered the last two years if you hadn't wanted to be in the girl's trio."

"Well, gee, thanks!" she said enthusiastically. "We all had a great time touring. I guess I owe you another one!"

"Let's not talk about that now," he said as if the accolades were embarrassing him.

"You know, you look lovely with your hair like that. You should wear it that way more often."

"Thanks," she replied happily.

She had never fixed it pulled back that way. She was experimenting for the wedding so she was happy for the compliment even if it had come from a father figure.

"I'm real sorry Mrs. Patterson couldn't come tonight. What a shame to miss out on an island dinner, complete with a boat ride!"

She was so excited that she was feeling benevolent and really sorry that Mrs. Patterson hadn't been able to join them. She also had been very good to Joan.

"Well, she isn't crazy about boats," he said easily, "so don't feel too sorry for her. Besides, she has a tendency to get seasick, so that, combined with the cold she has, wouldn't have been good for her."

"That's strange," Joan said curiously. "When we were at the Seaway, she told me she loved boats."

"Not boats," he said hesitantly, "ships . . . she likes big ships, not the kind we'll be going on tonight. She would be frightened."

"Oh, good," she replied, then realizing it sounded like she was glad Mrs. Patterson had stayed home, she added, "I mean . . . I'm glad she isn't missing something she would really enjoy."

They traveled a few more minutes, and then she spotted a familiar landmark. She had been to the Thousand Islands many times with her parents, so the Alexandria Bay welcome sign was familiar. It formed a giant arch over the street and was made of neon.

"I always make a bet with myself over which letter on the sign will be out," she said, laughing easily. She couldn't remember ever seeing it all in working order at the same time. That was almost part of its charm.

"So you've been here before then?" he asked, seeming rather disappointed.

"Oh, yes, many times. My dad would make a spur-of-the-moment decision to go somewhere, and my mom would usually get angry and complain about not having time to get everything ready for a trip. Then they would compromise on the Thousand Islands because it wasn't very far and didn't take as much preparation."

"But," she said enthusiastically, trying to assuage his disappointment, "I have never had dinner on an island before!"

They drove under the sign and past the beautiful old Victorian homes that had been summer places to the rich at the turn of the century. They had become permanent residences for local people as the rich made their way to other, more exotic reaches of the globe after the invention of the passenger jet. Hints of their former elegance could be seen on some, others were in sad need of repair, but most had simply limped along into the twentieth century, their beautiful old handmade gingerbread trim being replaced as it rotted with newer, "better" trim. They were well cared for, if not groomed the way they had been originally intended.

Most of the old gracious resorts had long since disappeared, a majority of them in flames. The newer resorts were busy this time of year, and the town seemed to teem with activity. There were restaurants, gift shops, boat tours, art galleries, and almost everything else that would make up the usual description of a summer vacation spot. They found a parking space on a side street and began to walk.

As they neared the town dock, activity seemed to take on a more frantic pace, with tour boats, privately owned yachts, and kids in little runabouts, all seeming to compete for the same dock space. Finally they saw the shuttle for the restaurant and made their way along the dock.

She had never been on the St. Lawrence River in anything but a large tour boat, so the ride was almost a brand-new experience for her. The difference in perspective the smaller craft provided enhanced the beauty of the area, and it was breathtaking.

She hadn't remembered so many islands so close together and thoroughly enjoyed the ride. She was quite disappointed when their driver informed them that the next island up ahead was their destination. He promised that the ride back would be a different route, which made her more willing to climb ashore when they arrived.

The restaurant was in an old mansion, which had been beautifully remodeled. They were led directly to their table by a pleasant hostess and settled down in anticipation of an enjoyable meal.

"That was a beautiful ride," she said breathlessly.

"I've been on tour boats in the islands but not a gorgeous launch like that. Did you like it, too? You seemed rather preoccupied," she said, concerned that he wasn't having as much fun as she.

"I was just thinking how much I was going to miss your exuberance, your love of life," he said regretfully.

"But you don't have to worry, you have plenty of students around you all the time," she reasoned.

"Not like you, my dear," he offered. "What would you like to drink? A martini?"

She wasn't much of a drinker and didn't really know one drink from another. "I don't think so," she said. "I don't even know what it is. I usually have a grasshopper or a sloe gin fizz."

He seemed surprised. "But, my dear, they're so sweet! Have a martini with me, they're much better."

She held her ground. She just didn't like the taste of hard liquor. "No thanks, I don't like most drinks. Grasshoppers and sloe gin fizzes are the only ones I've ever tasted that I like, but either one will be fine."

He finally realized that she wouldn't change her mind, so he ordered a martini for himself and a grasshopper for her. When the waitress returned with the drinks, she asked if they would like to order dinner. Joan said yes and he said no, so they compromised and told her to return in a few minutes.

"I really don't know why you are in such a hurry, can't you relax and enjoy yourself?" he asked, with just a hint of accusation.

"Of course I can," she answered, surprised at the question. "I'm having a marvelous time. Just getting away from campus is good enough, let alone having dinner on an island!"

"Well, I'm glad. I'm having a wonderful time, too," he said, pleased.

"I really am hungry, though. I didn't have much of a lunch today. I spent most of the time in the library, working," she hinted.

"All right, if you insist," he said, beckoning the waitress.

"Have you decided to order after all?" she said pleasantly.

"Yes," Prof Pat answered, "but we need menus. We haven't seen one yet."

"Oh, this must be your first time here. We don't have menus. We have one entrée per night, and tonight it's fried chicken. I hope that meets with your approval. It's really delicious," she said apologetically.

"Then fried chicken it is, but I must confess I was looking forward to a nice big steak," said Prof Pat.

"Fried chicken is fine with me," Joan volunteered. "Could I have French fries to go with it?"

"Of course. And you, sir?"

"I'll have a baked potato, please, and Italian dressing on my salad."

"Mine too," Joan said.

"Very good," she smiled. "The vegetables are served family style. I'll be right along with your salads."

She hurried off toward the kitchen.

"That was easy," Joan said, pleased that the one item was something she liked. "Yes, I wasn't aware there was no menu," he said, annoyed. "I apologize, my dear."

"No, I really meant it. I love fried chicken. My family didn't eat in restaurants much, so I don't like a lot of the things they usually have on the menus. I don't like rare meat, so prime rib and steak are out. Chefs are always insulted when you order it well done, and they usually won't cook it that way."

"Well, most people think it becomes too tough when it's cooked through," he said. "Personally, I like mine very pink in the center."

"That's your prerogative," she replied, "but people don't allow us well-doners that privilege, so I'm happy to have fried chicken. I don't like to experiment."

The waitress arrived back with the salads, and they dug in, continuing the conversation about restaurants and food in general, which led inevitably to dorm food and the rest of the meal was spent pleasantly discussing campus life from both the student and professor points of view.

"Are we going to have dessert?" the waitress asked, wheeling a cart of luscious-looking desserts to the table.

Joan had never seen a dessert cart before and was totally impressed, not only with the idea but the selection as well. She chose a gooey, sinful-looking chocolate thing, and he settled on a piece of pie. Just as they were finishing dessert, the band began to play.

"This dessert is delicious. I've never had anything like it before. It's sort of a combination of pudding, brownies, and an ice cream sundae. How's the pie?" she asked.

"Just marvelous. The band sounds good, doesn't it? Would you care to dance?"

"Oh, I don't think so," she said, trying to hide her surprise. She really had no desire to dance with him.

"I should be getting back. My classes are early tomorrow."

She didn't know when it had happened, but she suddenly realized that the mood had changed subtly.

"Just one, then. I'd like a dance that I can remember after you've gone. It will be the thing I remember when I think of you. I won't take no for an answer," he said, standing up, "so you might as well come willingly."

"If you put it like that, then okay."

She reluctantly took his extended hand, and he ushered them out onto the dance floor. As his arm went around her, she stiffened, trying to keep at least some distance between them. She was becoming uncomfortable but wasn't really sure what was happening. Was she overreacting to an innocent request to dance?

As they moved across the floor, she happened to look around at the other diners and noticed that several of them were watching them curiously. One couple was leaning across the table, heads close together, obviously talking about them.

She began to back away from him just as he was starting to put pressure on the middle of her back to draw her nearer. Neither of them succeeded in their attempts, so they remained pretty much the way they had been. They were close, but not unreasonably so.

Then he bent his head down close to her ear and whispered, "Joan, did you mean it when you said you didn't like to experiment?"

"Oh, yes," she said, taking the opportunity to back away from him a little. "There are lots of restaurant foods I don't care for or even want to try."

"I wasn't thinking about food," he said, drawing her closer again, "I was thinking of something more physical."

"More physical than eating?" she said, surprised. "What are you talking about, Professor Pat?" She wasn't at all sure she wanted to know.

"I was thinking of you and me experimenting—for instance, in a shower."

"WHAT?" she almost shouted. "What are you saying to me?"

Without waiting for an answer, she went on, appalled, "I don't understand! I think I'd like to go now."

She backed away from him and started for the door. She was completely horrified. It was all she could do to keep herself from running. Out of the corner of her eye, she could see him going toward the table to pay the check. By the time he paid the bill and came outside, she was already sitting in the boat along with several other people. Unfortunately there was no one else in her double seat, so he was able to sit down next to her.

He put his arm over the back of the seat, and as the boat moved away from the dock, he slipped it down around her shoulder. She couldn't move. There were no other empty seats, and she didn't want to cause a scene, so she just sat there stiffly, pretending to watch the scenery. Several times he tried to rub her shoulder, and each time she turned her body or shifted her position in the seat in order to move away from his attempted caresses. He didn't seem to take the hint and kept right on trying.

When they reached the town dock, she quickly headed for the car, warding off any attempt on his part to stop somewhere else. Her only hope was to get back on campus, and the only way to do that was to go with him. She would have to think of a way to get out of this unbelievable situation. It had taken almost an hour and a half to get there, and before she could do anything, she had to get back to familiar territory.

"Oh, my God," she thought to herself as they drove along. "I can't believe this! He's an old geezer! He isn't even good-looking. What did I do over the past three years to make him believe I would want this? I must have led him on or something without realizing it."

The girls in her dorm were always kidding her about being naïve. They called it "Bernhards-Baying."

"Watch out, she's 'Bernhards-Baying' again," they would tease.

It had always seemed funny, but this was far from funny.

She must have done something, she thought, searching her mind for some incident that would justify this behavior. She must have done something really stupid to make him think she would be interested in him. He knew she was getting married soon. She just couldn't understand this.

She'd had professors put their hand on hers, and one wanted to give her a back rub to "help her relax" before taking a conducting exam, but this was different. This was planned. Every bit of it had been carefully set up. It struck her that his wife might not even know they were out together! She probably thought he was in rehearsal somewhere on campus!

Somehow she had to play along just enough to get her hands on those keys. They'd throw the book at her if they discovered she was out this late at night. Actually, it was grounds for dismissal. She had to find a way to say no, but not quite. First she had to get back to town. They were really in the boondocks. She didn't have the faintest idea of where they were or how far it was to the next town. She didn't even dare look at her watch.

"Don't move," she said to herself. "Pretend nothing is wrong. You'll figure out something when the time comes."

Then he tried to put his arm around her again and pull her toward him. She didn't move. She sat there and deliberately pretended nothing was wrong. She knew she would be all right as long as the car kept moving. The drive seemed interminable, but just as she was getting very discouraged, she saw a familiar-looking gas station up ahead.

"Thank goodness," she thought, relieved. "Here's Canton—only ten more miles to go. Thank you, Canton."

At least she knew where she was now. She just had to stay calm and not move.

She wished she could figure out what she had done. She couldn't even remember ever hugging the man. All of a sudden, he seemed like such a creep! He was old and ugly! It made her sick to think of him that way. It was true that she had heard rumors about professors and students, but she really hadn't believed them. She figured that the girls who led professors on probably had it coming to them. Everyone knew there were girls on campus who were like that, but she wasn't. She wasn't like them, and she didn't want any part of this!

She was grateful when they arrived at the first bridge in town. Once they got over it, most of the motels in town would be behind them. She didn't think he would ever dare take her to a motel. They might be caught. The state teacher's college wouldn't put up with that kind of thing, would it? Then they reached the second bridge!

His husky voice broke the silence. "Where would you like to go, Joan?" he asked intimately.

"Well," she thought quickly, "how . . . ah, how about behind my dorm?" She knew if she could get that close, she'd at least feel better. "Think! Think what to do next," she demanded to herself.

"Yes, that's a good idea," he smiled. "There is a large parking lot back there, and no one will be prowling around this late at night."

"Oh God," she thought to herself, "he really thinks I want to do it!"

Then out loud, trying to keep her voice steady, she said, "Professor Pat, before I forget, could I please put the keys in my purse? I wouldn't want to get to that door later and realize that I had forgotten them."

As they pulled to a stop in the parking lot, he turned the car off and said, "Of course, my dear."

He reached into his pocket and said with mock surprise, "What's this? But first, the keys. Here you are, my dear."

He extended his right hand toward her, and she took the keys. She put them in her purse, which she held tightly in her lap.

His left hand held something that looked like a jewelry box, but she wasn't sure and didn't really care. She had the keys! With her right hand, she started to reach carefully for the door handle.

Then he said, "I was hoping you would be cooperative and see things my way, so I bought this gift for you today with that in mind. Here, take a look."

He handed her an expensive-looking gift box and sat back, looking very pleased with himself.

She opened it and tried to act excited. "Oh, Prof Pat, how wonderful of you. You shouldn't have done that." Her right hand reached the door handle as she continued to thank him, "I can't tell you how much I appreciate this."

She had the handle in her hand, and as she yanked it and pushed, she said, "you'll never know how happy you've made me. You've been just wonderful."

She threw herself out of the car and slammed the door as hard as she could, "Be sure to tell Mrs. Patterson how sorry I was that she couldn't have joined us."

Then she turned on her heels and ran as fast as her legs would take her toward the dorm.

She heard him start to protest, but the words faded quickly as she made her way toward the back door. "Don't run away . . ."

"I made it!" she shouted silently to herself. "That bastard! That son of a bitch!"

Then she realized she still had the jewelry! She couldn't think about that now. She had to get the key ring out of her purse. She was glad there were only two keys on it.

She fumbled with her purse and the jewelry box. She had to hurry. She wanted to look and see if he was coming toward her, but she didn't dare take the time. The first key she tried worked. She considered heaving the jewelry into the parking lot but knew she couldn't just leave it there for people to wonder about. She gratefully entered the graduate dorm and quickly closed the door.

She couldn't take time to congratulate herself on her Academy Award-winning performance because she still had a ways to go before she was really safe. Would he try to come in? She had to get to the undergrad door fast. He'd never dare try to go in there. She had to be quiet. She didn't want anyone to hear her and make her stop to explain what she was doing there.

The door opened easily, and as she closed it behind her, a wash of relief enveloped her. She was safe. She was home. She still couldn't be seen with street clothes on, though. As she made her way toward her door, she began to feel sick to her stomach. She quickly opened the door, grabbed her pajamas, and ran for the bathroom where she vomited for almost half an hour.

"That bastard! That son of a bitch! I'll kill him if he comes near me again! Who does he think he is? I'll show that dirty rotten . . ."

Chapter 21

"Where are the ice cubes?" the nurse demanded, "I sent for them ten minutes ago. Her fever's getting out of control!"

"They'll be here in just a minute," said her companion as they emptied bottles of rubbing alcohol into a large vatlike stainless steel bowl. "They had to go down to the cafeteria to get them."

"Well, I hope they hurry! This is critical. We've got to get her fever down fast!"

A third nurse hurriedly pushed a cart, topped with bags of ice, through the door. Working quickly, they filled the alcohol bowl with ice and then followed the ice with a single-bed-sized terrycloth blanket. They swished the blanket around in the icy alcohol, and without wringing any of the alcohol out of the blanket, they lifted it and slapped it onto the bare body of their patient, covering her from ankles to neck.

A bloodcurdling shriek escaped Joan's throat as she began flailing her arms about, trying to pull the freezing torture off her searing flesh.

"What are you doing to me, Professor Pat? Stop! Stop it! You're killing me. Please, I can't stand it! Somebody make him stop!"

She was trying to regain rational thought, but at the same time she was crying, begging, and fighting uncontrollably, trying to pull the blanket off.

"Somebody make them stop! Please! I can't take any more. Why are you doing this to me?"

Her breath was sucked out of her by the cold each time they rewet the blanket and slapped it back on. Somehow she had to make them stop. She had to make them understand what they were putting her through!

Dr. George came into the room, an anxious expression on his face, "Hold up, Nurse, maybe she's beginning to cool down."

They left the blanket in place as they backed away to make room for him at the bedside.

"Joan, do you hear me? Can you understand me?" he asked.

She looked at him, hatred pouring forth, "You're the one making them do this to me aren't you, Professor Pat?" she raged, pulling at the blanket.

Dr. George leaned over her, one arm on either side of her body, his hands on the blanket, successfully pinning her down.

"Yes, I'm making them do it, Joan, but I'm Dr. George. You came to me with a problem several weeks ago. Do you remember? A friend of yours brought you to the hospital a little while ago. You are extremely ill, and we need your cooperation."

"Cooperation!" she cried accusingly. "How can I cooperate when they're trying to freeze me to death?"

"Joan, you have a very high fever. We must get it down immediately. We can't wait for aspirin or some other medication to lower it. This is the only way."

Still breathing heavily from the shock of the cold and the exertion, she began to make sense out the whole thing. Ann had come to the house. They had called the doctor. Yes, they called Dr. George.

"Dr. George, I'm s-s-sorry," she chattered, "I wasn't thinking straight, but can't you make them stop?" she begged weakly.

"I'm sorry, I can't. We must get your temperature under control before we can operate, and if we don't operate, you will be dead very soon. Do you understand? If you fight us, I'll be forced to restrain you, and I don't want to do that."

He was speaking quietly, in a soothing manner, trying to calm her down, and even though she knew from her own classroom skills that he was doing it deliberately, she responded.

"How long will they have to k-k-keep it up?"

"Until your fever comes down. Only a few more minutes," he said reassuringly.

"W-W-Well all right," she said reluctantly and braced herself for the next onslaught of cold.

They resoaked the blanket and laid it more carefully on her body this time. It was almost easier when she was fighting them—at least she had been moving around. Now she was forced to lie there and knowingly accept their healing torture.

Both of her hands began to smart at once, and she realized for the first time that there were needles taped in the back of them both, connected to hanging bottles of liquid. She must have disturbed them when she was trying to fight the nurses off, and now they were very painful. She decided she had better keep still so they would stop throbbing.

One of the nurses took her temperature, and they were all pleased when they announced they had succeeded in getting the fever down somewhat. They put a dry sheet over her freezing nakedness, but she was becoming disinterested and foggy. Vague thoughts of hall lights moving and people looking down at her faded in and out. People whispering. Glaring lights. Masked faces. Dr. George.

"Joan, listen to me, we're in surgery. The alcohol bath brought your fever down a little, and we don't feel we can wait any longer. Do you understand what I'm saying?"

"I think I do." Her mind seemed to be wandering around, but she could catch it once in awhile if she concentrated real hard.

"I'll do everything in my power to make sure you come out of this, but you must understand that you probably won't be able to have any more children. We'll try to do just a D and C, but I can't guarantee anything. We might be forced to remove your uterus. The important thing right now is your life."

"That's okay, Doctor. It's all my fault. Do what you have to do."

"We're going to put you out now. Is there anything you want to tell me?"

"Just take care of my babies," she pleaded desperately.

"Yes, I promise," he answered gently. "Dr. Brown will know what to do, won't he?"

"No! He'll call my mother! I don't want my mother to know about this!"

Then, realizing for the first time the full implication of the dire circumstances she was in, she knew there was no choice. Accepting defeat, she agreed.

"Oh, I don't know. All right. I guess it will have to be all right. I don't know what else to do. I can't think," she conceded.

Her mind was straying again, but as she struggled to capture it and bring it back, Dr. George said, "I don't want you to worry about it. I'll take care of everything. Now I want you to count backwards from one hundred. Can you do that?"

She thought that of course she could count backwards from one hundred. What a silly question.

"Out loud, please," he said firmly.

"Okay, One hundred, ninety nine, ninety eight, ninety . . . what comes . . ."

Mommy says I have to be brave and show the boys up. Sammy and Jimmy were supposed to get their tonsils out last week, but they chickened out. Daddy says afterwards I can have all the ice cream I want to eat, but he says at first it will hurt so bad I might not want anything to eat even if it's ice cream. But he said it wouldn't last very long, and it was better than having tonsillitis all the time, which made you get sore throats, too. So I might as well get one bad sore throat and make the rest of them go away. So I said we should do it. I sat right up on that wagon while the nurses took me for a ride and the doctor showed me his round mirror with a hole in the middle to see through. Then he bet me I couldn't count backwards with a mask on my face, but I did. Boy! Daddy was right. It was one big sore throat, but it was better the next day. Sammy came over to see me, but I didn't give him any ice cream. If he'd been as brave as me, he wouldn't have any more sore throats.

"What are her vitals?" he demanded.

"They're hard to get. I'd say sixty over forty. Heart is still a hundred per."

"Well, let's see what we're dealing with. That bastard must have been a real butcher. He obviously didn't sterilize anything, or the infection couldn't be this widespread so soon. Give me vitals if there is any change at all, even the slightest. I still don't understand why there is no hemorrhaging."

They worked efficiently. The silence was broken only by an occasional comment regarding the carelessness and apparent callousness of the perpetrator of the offense that had caused the massive infection.

As he was finishing the work, Dr. George exclaimed, "I've seen a lot of botched abortions in my life, but never anything like that, so much infection! Well, I hate to do it, but get the usual samples down to the lab. It can't be avoided."

One of the nurses that had worked with him for years said pleadingly, "Doctor, isn't there some way . . . ? Hasn't she been through enough?"

"We've obeyed the law for years, whether we agreed with it or not. We can't stop now." he remarked as he took off his gloves. "The important thing is that she's alive; although for how long, I can't say."

He slammed his gloves into the nearby sink and walked back toward the operating table. "I want her in a private room. This bug is too virulent to risk putting her in recovery, and I want twenty-four-hour nurses. Greene is to be one of them. She's the best in the business."

He leaned down and softly said, "Joan, Joan, can you hear me? Wake up now. Come on, little lady. It's time to open your eyes. I want to talk to you."

He began to shake her shoulder gently.

She came back to semiconsciousness but felt something was very wrong. They hadn't done anything! Nothing had happened. She opened her eyes for a second, and now everyone seemed to be getting ready to leave. They had moved her back onto a stretcher and were about to wheel her out of the operating room.

"Wait!" she said as loudly as she could. "Aren't you going to do anything? You told me you were going to do a D and C. You didn't do it. Am I still going to have this baby?'

"It's all right," Dr. George assured her.

"You don't remember anything because of the type of drug we used to put you under. Everything is fine. We did the D and C. It's all done," he said, patting her shoulder reassuringly. "We didn't even have to take the uterus. Barring complications, you could even have another child someday."

"Really?" she said weakly. "The baby is . . . gone? It's all over? I don't have to worry anymore? It's really over this time?"

"Yes, it's over, the baby is gone. You have nothing more to worry about."

She had the feeling he was still talking, but the sound seemed to get farther and farther away, and her eyes wouldn't focus, so she closed them and gave in to sleep.

"Okay," he said gently, "let's get her to her room. She has a lot of work to do to survive the next twelve hours."

One of the nurses' aides, who had helped with the alcohol bath, interrupted the usual routine. "But I don't understand—you took the fetus and all of that infected mess out of her. Why is she going to have such a hard time surviving?"

Dr. George looked around the room at the young women who had been assisting him. "Well, let me try to explain. It wouldn't hurt you seasoned veterans to listen to this, either. Sometimes I think you get pretty careless because you think it could never happen to you."

He looked down at Joan to make sure she was unable to hear him and began, "This condition is called 'Sepsis.' It's a very complex situation, which is caused by a total body infection. It's accompanied by high fever and dehydration. The lymphatic system becomes so overwhelmed by the immense amount of bacteria that it is prevented from functioning properly. When that happens, a hormonelike substance, which is produced by the bacteria, causes an abnormal vascular response called dilation and constriction. This cuts off blood supply to the vital organs such as the brain, heart, liver, and kidneys, causing them all to shut down simultaneously."

"Oh, my God, I had no idea," the young aide said. "I thought once you removed the fetus, she'd automatically recover."

"The fact that we removed a vast amount of offending bacteria will help immensely, but it is far from a guarantee that she'll improve. It may have been too far advanced for the procedure to help. Only time will tell us that."

"Thank you, Doctor," one of the older women offered.

"Your thanks to me would be best expressed if each of you would make an appointment with my office, even those of you who are unmarried, so that we can get you all started on the new birth control pill. Tell my receptionist that you work with me here at the hospital, and there will be no charge for your first visit."

The nurses all looked at one another and then at him. They were surprised and slightly embarrassed.

He placed his hand gently on Joan's shoulder and said, "I don't enjoy this procedure. Anything I can do to prevent it, I'll do gladly."

Now," he said quietly, "let's get her to her room. If we're lucky, she'll be a real fighter and beat this."

Chapter 22

Friday, October 19, 1965
Early Morning

Joan sensed there had been someone in the room with her. Every time she started to wake up she could feel her presence. She was quite sure the woman had been taking her blood pressure. She had started to come to when she felt a great pressure on her arm. She had wondered why someone was in her bedroom, taking her blood pressure, but she was so tired she decided that it really didn't matter much. She'd figure it out later.

She almost woke up once when the woman was leaning over her, whispering into her ear. She wished she could remember what she had said, but Joan could only remember that she liked the woman and felt comfortable with her there. Maybe she would remember in a little while. She'd get some more rest first, then she'd feel better . . .

"Good morning, Nurse Greene," Dr. George chimed cheerfully as he bustled into the room. "I didn't hear from you all night, so I presume we didn't lose her. How is she doing?"

Nurse Greene straightened her crumpled uniform and tried to look as if she hadn't lived in it for the past ten hours. "She's doing quite well, I think. There was a point at which I almost called you, but then she seemed to rally a little."

Dr George stood looking down at his patient. "It's hard to believe the shape she was in yesterday."

He reached down to take her pulse. "Amazing. We were right—she's a real fighter!"

"Yes, she definitely is. She kept talking in her sleep about her twins. I even know their names. They're Tracy and Suzanne. I think they're probably responsible for her surviving."

"I wouldn't be surprised. How are her vitals?" he asked.

"Improving, Especially in the last couple of hours."

"Well, I hate to wake her, but I have rounds and a woman down in delivery, so I don't know what the rest of the day will bring. There is something I have to discuss with her."

Greene leaned down and gently massaged Joan's shoulder. "Joan, Dr. George is here to see you," she said softly.

Joan tried to wake up, but the cobwebs wouldn't completely part. She couldn't brush them out of the way. She knew someone had been talking, but it was from a long ways off. She couldn't quite seem to get to that place where she heard the voices coming from.

"Joan."

It was a man. She knew there were two of them, a woman and a man. They wanted her to wake up.

"I'm trying," she thought.

Her eyes were like lead. They felt as if they were glued shut.

"Come on, Joan," the woman's voice encouraged. "Dr. George is here to see you, and he wants you to wake up."

"Oh, Dr. George," she thought. "I like Dr. George. He was so good to me that day."

Then, as if a light bulb had been turned on, her mind cleared, "Dr. George," she said weakly.

"Hello there, young lady," he said, obviously pleased with his work. "How are you feeling?"

"Okay, I guess," she said weakly. "You could probably tell me better how I'm doing," she said.

"You're physically much better than last night, but you still have a ways to go before you're out of the woods. We're still administering massive doses of penicillin."

"But I'm okay as long as the infection doesn't start getting worse?"

"Physically, yes," he said.

There was that word again.

"Why do you keep saying 'physically'?" she asked.

She felt so weak she wasn't sure she could concentrate enough to understand.

"Well, that's why I'm here so early. There is one more thing you have to be concerned about. Now don't panic, but there is a slight chance you will be visited by the police."

"The police!" she said, adrenaline making up for the weakness.

"But it's all over now. How could the police—"

"Because whenever something like this happens in a hospital, the lab is required by law to test and report the findings to the police."

"Oh, my God!" she groaned.

"In your case it was obvious there was foreign matter involved, and it had to be reported. There was no choice," he said sympathetically.

"Great," she said with as much sarcasm as she could muster. "What am I supposed to do now? I can't just get up and run away! I'm trapped!" She started to cry.

"Joan, calm down, please," he begged.

"Calm down! Calm down! That's easy for you to say. I'll still lose my kids and my job. What good did it all do anyway? Why didn't you tell me this before?"

"Because it would have done you no good to know, that's why," he said reasonably. "You didn't need to be worried about this part. At the time, you had all you could possibly handle and then some."

"Then tell me what to do," she pleaded.

"First of all, I need you to calm down. You won't do yourself or anyone else any good if you keep this up. Now, listen to me carefully."

He pulled a chair up next to the bed and took her hand, "There is a very fine line here, and one that is very difficult to prove. In order to take action on this, they have to prove that the foreign material was introduced with the sole intent of causing the abortion and for *no other reason* Do you understand what I'm saying?"

"Yes!" she said horrified. "You want me to tell them I put something inside myself for pleasure. I think I'd rather die," she groaned.

The nightmare wasn't over. It might be just beginning. Her head was reeling with anger and shock. She was having difficulty absorbing it all. Would it never end?

"No, you wouldn't rather die," Dr. George said emphatically.

"The police deal with this sort of thing all the time, just like I do. They think nothing of it, it's an everyday occurrence," he reassured her.

"Well, it might be for you, but it isn't for me," she said.

She was feeling hopeless and helpless. "I'm not used to it! I'm not used to any of this! I just want to go home! I want to see my babies! I thought it would be over with time and time again, but it just keeps going on and on and getting worse!"

"No, it isn't," Dr. George said firmly. He grasped her shoulders with both hands and tried to make her focus.

"Listen to me—you survived! Most of the people who arrive in the shape you were in, don't. You fought it. We heard you fighting it in you—rantings during the fever. You have fought too hard and have too much to lose to give up now!"

"But you don't understand—all they would have to do is take me to the police station, and everyone would find out!"

He looked at her with calm understanding.

"I've had a lot of experience with this sort of thing, and I don't think they would take you to the police station. I've never heard of them doing that. If they do come around to question you, just deny everything. You don't need to explain or make anything up. Just deny everything they say. Don't offer anything. Answer their questions with a simple *yes, no,* or *I don't know.* No matter what they say, stay calm and deny it. If you do this, there will be nothing they can do. I'm sure they'll give up if you remain calm and firm."

"Okay," she sniffed, trying to act as if his valiant effort to calm her down had worked. "I'll try."

"That's what I like to hear! I'll do everything I can to convince them that their questions won't yield anything substantial. They probably won't even bother with you, but I had to make sure you were prepared."

"I sure hope you're right," she said, relieved that he was so sure of the situation. "You won't get into any trouble for helping me, will you/"

"No, all I did was step in and try to solve a problem that was started by someone else. I have absolutely nothing to worry about."

"That's good. I'd hate to cause you trouble after all you've done for me," she said gratefully.

"Don't you worry about me, I'll be fine. There is one more thing I have to tell you, though," he said with regret showing in his face.

"Now what?" she said defensively.

"It isn't much, but I feel I have to put you in isolation for a while. This infection is of such a nature that it could infect other people. Also, you aren't in any shape to be exposed to any more germs. For the time being, everyone coming in or out of the room will have to wear a mask, gown, hat, and gloves. This is just a precaution. You're on the mend, as I said, but not totally out of the woods yet. I just don't want to take any chances. Look at it this way—maybe all of the paraphernalia will discourage the cops!"

He grinned mischievously as if that would give him great pleasure. Then he got up and smiled at the nurse. It was obvious that they had a great deal of respect for each other.

"Greene here is the best nurse I know. I've put her on private duty with you. She's been here since you came out of the OR last night, and she'll stay as long as I feel you need her. We even moved in a cot for her."

"Thank you for the compliment, Doctor," Greene responded.

As she spoke, Joan realized she had heard that voice on and off all during the night, giving her encouragement and urging her to fight.

"You talked to me last night, didn't you?" Joan asked her appreciatively.

"Yes, and you were quite the conversationalist!" she chuckled.

"I'll bet," Joan answered weakly. She was beginning to feel better, but all of a sudden, she felt an oppressive tiredness begin to descend on her, and her eyelids began to get heavy.

Dr. George started toward the doorway and then turned. "You've become a pretty important person around here. You were quite a challenge. Everyone has taken a personal interest because they hate the butchery that goes on out there. They finally had a chance to save someone, and they're grateful to you for letting them do it!"

"I had no idea—" she said emotionally.

"Well, it's true," he replied, moving back toward the bed.

"Now they need you to be brave and try as hard as you can to stand up to this one last problem with the police if it becomes necessary. Believe me, they're all behind you, and so am I."

"Thank you, Dr. George," she managed. "I don't know what I would have done without you. You've been so understanding."

"I'll keep in touch with the nurses' station. They'll keep me posted and let me know immediately if the police show up. Now I want you to get some sleep. You have a lot to do to get over this infection. Be brave. Keep your chin up."

He patted her affectionately on the head as he turned to go, "take good care of her for us, Greene."

As he reached the door she reached the limit of her wakefulness. Worried or not, she couldn't ward off the sleep any longer and began to succumb gratefully.

Chapter 23

Friday
Late Morning

She heard a strange noise and woke up, startled by her surroundings. Then everything came back to her quickly. She realized that she had slept very deeply. It was the kind of sleep that offered no clues to any dreams that might have occurred. She could tell by the light outside that it was late morning. She must have been asleep for quite awhile.

Looking around, she realized that Greene was nowhere in sight. That was a good sign, she reasoned. If Greene had been concerned, she wouldn't have been left alone. She had a cot in the room, but Joan couldn't imagine that she had gotten much sleep last night. She certainly deserved a break.

Joan heard an elevator start up and begin an ascent from another floor. Her heart stopped. Dr. George's warning rushed at her. She listened intently as she heard the door open and close and then heard footsteps walking away from her room down toward where she supposed the nurses' station was.

She couldn't believe that the elevator was right outside her door! That's probably what had awakened her, she thought. Then another thought crossed her mind. Every time the elevator was used, she would have to wonder who it was, and if they had come to arrest her. Why couldn't she be down the hall somewhere? This was going to be awful being so close!

As if that weren't enough, she was in isolation! She hadn't heard of anyone being in isolation since she was a kid. Carol had rheumatic fever when they were in grade school and had to be inside for what seemed like months. Donna and Joan would go to see her, but they had to talk through the window. They took her comic books, but before Mrs. Davis could give them back, she sterilized them by baking them in the oven.

"Maybe that's what I need," she thought. "I need to be baked."

Her heart leapt to her throat as she heard the elevator start up again.

"Damn! I've got to stop this. Enough is enough. I'll deal with it when and if it happens. No more worrying. If they *do* come, I'll pretend I'm talking to Clem Northrup!"

That would make it easy, if she could keep a straight face.

Clem Northrup was the only excuse they had ever had in Bernhards Bay for the law, and he hadn't "taken office" until Joan was in high school. Actually, he worked for the township, not for Bernhards Bay. He just happened to live in Bernhards Bay, and since he had no physical office, the Bay became his central area. His responsibility reached to Cleveland and Constantia. Those who knew him knew better than to feel any more secure because of his new status. As a matter of fact, there was nothing to be feared to begin with, so there was no reason to rejoice at this appointment.

One night, when Joan's parents were away, with their approval she hosted a pajama party. The girls got bored a little after dark, so they decided that they needed a little more diversion than just learning how to smoke, so they called Clem.

They were afraid that he might recognize the voices of anyone who grew up in the Bay, so they selected a good friend and annual summer resident, Anne McKnight, to do the dirty deed.

They called him, and Anne told him that she was Mrs. Young, who lived in the lakeside area the natives referred to as "the grove." There were five streets in Bernhards Bay, two of which were regular straight streets. The other three started and ended with State Route 49. Joan lived on the corner of State Route 49 and one of the loops that went down to the grove. If you went down her street and went left, you would be taken behind several lakefront cottages, and then it turned back up toward Route 49, past several local houses, including Donna's, ending at another corner of Route 49. If you went to the right when you got to the end of the grove road, you would travel past the back of a few more summer places, then across and around a large apple orchard. It, too, made it's way back to Route 49. The three streets actually formed the letter W, with Joan's corner being the middle road.

Pretending to be Mrs. Young, Anne told him she had a prowler and asked him to check it out. Then they turned out all the lights in the house and waited for the fun to start. They knew he would have to go past Joan's house to get to the grove.

They had just started to get bored and go back to smoking when Clem came roaring off Route 49 on two wheels and headed down toward the lake. A monstrous whoop went up as they cheered him on, hoping that Mrs. Young's son, Wally, would be home. They had known the kids from the grove for years, and although they considered themselves a little above the natives, they generally all got along well.

Joan and the others could hear the gravel and dirt battering back and forth under Clem's car as he made his maniacal romp down the road. He looked every bit the picture of a Keystone Cop making that turn.

The girls raced as fast as they could up the stairs to the bathroom where they all crammed into the window to watch him barrel down the road. About halfway down, his headlights disappeared from view. They wondered why, because the road there was straight until it made the two turns. They waited there in silence—or at least as much silence as six teenagers could muster. They waited and waited and then, Bam! *He came roaring back again and wheeled a right turn onto Route 49, heading for the middle of town and the other leg of the grove road.*

The girls ran to Joan's mother's bedroom where they could see bits and pieces of the other road. This was the road where Donna's house was, and all of a sudden, they could see his headlights heading right for her house. Then, as mysteriously as before, the lights disappeared. There were a few minutes of nothing, and then there he was again, but this time he was traveling slowly. He didn't come back their way again, and after a few minutes, they went back to practicing looking "cool" and coughing and choking.

It wasn't until the next day that they got the whole story, and that was every bit as funny as anything they had imagined. After going home in the morning, Donna called to say her that her father had seen Clem the night before. He had tried to arrest two old-timers who were innocently coming back from night fishing. They just laughed at him and left!

Then, later in the day, they learned the other half of the story, which was even funnier. Joan was in the backyard, hanging clothes on the line, when Wally and Ronnie Nass, Joan's boyfriend, came ambling up the road. She had a hard time listening to the story and not giving away what she knew would be disastrous information.

It seemed that the entire grove had been in an uproar the night before. Clem Northrup had called and asked Wally if the prowler was still around. Wally, who had never heard of a prowler in the first place, had consulted with one of the neighbors, who in turn asked the other neighbors if they knew anything about a prowler. The upshot of it all was that the entire grove sat up most of the night with a various assortment of guns, clubs, and knives, guarding their boats! Joan almost howled. Clem had stopped his car and flashed his light around halfway down Joan's loop. Then he stopped the fishermen halfway down Donna's loop, but our hero evidently never got anywhere near the "danger!"

"Please God," she prayed, "if the cops have to come, let them send Clem!"

Chapter 24

Friday Afternoon

She was startled when Nurse Greene bustled radiantly into the room in full isolation regalia. She looked exhausted but happy.

"They tell me you don't need me anymore, so I'll be saying goodbye." She busied herself picking up and organizing her things.

Joan watched her with affection. "I'll miss you, but I'm glad I'm well enough not to need you," she said.

Nurse Greene continued her packing. "Your vitals are picking up nicely. You should be back to normal in no time at all."

Two men came in, grumbling about having to don the mask and other clothes and began folding up the cot that had been brought in for Greene to rest on. They acted like they were in a permanent state of low-grade anger and disenchantment. They slam-banged the lone chair out of the way and finally but noisily dragged the cot out into the hall, pulling off the garb as they went. She could hear them complaining until they were out of earshot.

Greene ignored them completely as if their attitudes were totally insignificant, and she continued gathering her things. "It's hard to believe you were in such immediate danger only last night, but that's what Dr. George told me to expect. Actually, he said I'd be done today, one way or the other. He said that you would either be better or dead, and he was right!" Greene quipped.

"Well, I'm sure I don't have to tell you that I'm glad the operative word is 'better,'" Joan laughed weakly. It had been a long time since she had laughed.

Greene smiled sheepishly. "He didn't say it exactly that way. He wasn't *that* callous about it."

"Don't worry," Joan said, enjoying Greene's embarrassment.

Joan would miss her. She had given her tremendous encouragement, and although Joan couldn't remember anything specific that Greene had said, she could remember her whispered urgings.

"You know, I don't think it would have turned out this way if it hadn't been for you. You helped me a lot last night, and I want to thank you," Joan confided.

"Believe me, it's been my pleasure. Most women don't come out of it, so when someone does survive, it makes us very happy."

She took Joan's hand and squeezed it conspiratorially. "It's like we won one for a change!" she triumphed.

Greene gave Joan a quick hug and, with tears just beginning to moisten the corners of her eyes, was gone, but her enthusiasm and the forcefulness of her being remained.

Joan had always thought that even as girls, they should strive for the masculine traits of responsibility and independence. Just by her general attitude, Greene made her realize that these weren't necessarily male qualities. They were human qualities and should be embraced. Greene was responsible, independent, feminine, and very proud of it. She seemed to be the personification of some of the female characters Joan had read in Ayn Rand novels. Greene was the first real-life female Joan had known who possessed those strong traits.

She had thought that her desire to be strong and independent was something to apologize for, as if it somehow pitted her against things or people male, and that because she wasn't actually male, no matter how well she succeeded, she would still come out a close second and less feminine or less of a person for having tried.

Greene was a woman of deep conviction who took pride in her profession. Somehow Joan knew she would never forget her. She had touched some place in Joan that she hadn't known was there. It was a feminine place.

Her musings were rudely interrupted by the sound of the elevator starting up from the floor below.

"Damn!" she thought with outrage. Just when she thought she could relax a little, that lousy machine started up again.

"What am I going to do? I can't live with this fear for the rest of my life!" she thought despairingly.

Just as she hoped it wouldn't, the elevator stopped on her floor. She listened, wondering which way they would walk. The footsteps headed in her direction. She panicked.

"They're coming! This isn't funny anymore! Don't admit anything! Deny everything! Just say nothing happened!" she rehearsed, swallowing hard.

A woman stood in the doorway. Thank goodness! It wasn't likely that a woman would be a cop.

"Are you Mrs. Winter?" the woman asked sweetly.

"Yes, I am," Joan replied, relieved.

"Good evening," she said pleasantly, coming into the room and adjusting the isolation gear over the required uniform.

"I'm from admitting. You've slipped through the cracks, my dear. You were never officially admitted," she chimed.

She made it sound like it was one the greatest mysteries of the twentieth century.

Joan was so relieved that she didn't care who she was as long as she wasn't from the police.

"I hope that didn't cause too much trouble," Joan offered.

The sudden supply of adrenalin that her body had supplied for the possible onslaught withdrew and left her weak.

"No trouble at all," the uniform chirped. "We'll take care of everything.

"May I sit down?"

"Be my guest," Joan answered weakly. She might be much better, but she was rapidly losing whatever strength she had gained from her nap.

The woman sat down and officiously placed her clipboard on her lap. "Your full name, please?"

"Joan Webb Winter."

"Address?"

"Box 238, North Bay, New York."

"Is there a street address?"

"Yes, but I don't get mail at home. I have to go to the post office," she replied, losing energy fast.

"Just where is this North Bay?" she asked as if it were probably a place she would not want to come from.

"On the north shore of Oneida Lake," Joan said defensively.

"Do you have insurance?"

"No," Joan lied, taking a sudden dislike to her.

"What is your husband's occupation?"

"I don't have a husband," Joan answered coldly.

"But our records say you are a Mrs.," she said in surprise as if her records could not possibly be wrong.

"I had one once, but I got rid of him," Joan answered flippantly, deliberately trying to aggravate the woman's sense of propriety.

"Well!" she huffed. "Are you covered under any insurance of his?"

"No." The woman was getting visibly upset, and in spite of her weariness, Joan was enjoying every minute of it.

"How do you support yourself if you don't have a husband or insurance?" she asked incredulously.

Suddenly, Joan realized that however much she was loving the volley, she was getting much too tired to continue it, so she decided to be nice and get it over with.

"I'm a teacher," she confessed.

The woman's attitude did a sudden about-face.

"Oh," she cooed, "if you are a teacher, you must have insurance."

"Well, yes I do, but I don't want to use it. I'm not going to put a claim in."

"Oh, my goodness, my dear, why ever not?"

"I just won't, that's all," came the caustic reply.

Joan didn't really consider this any of the woman's business. If she opted to pay the bill out of her own pocket, who did this person think she was to question it?

"This is highly irregular!" the woman said indignantly.

"I'm sure it is," Joan replied nonchalantly.

"Where is your place of employment?"

"I can't say."

"Well, my dear," she sputtered, annoyed. "If you don't want to use your insurance, you must tell me the place of your employment so that the hospital can garnishee your wages should it become necessary!"

Joan knew her state of exhaustion was probably responsible, but she was getting very tired of the chirping, meddlesome person and wanted nothing more than to be left alone to get some rest.

"I will guarantee the hospital that I will pay the bill. I will sign anything you want, but I will still not tell you where I work or who the insurance carrier is."

The woman leaped off her chair in total disbelief.

"Well, I'll have to speak to my superior about this! We will see what happens!"

"Your superior won't get the information either," Joan said wearily, "but I will sign a note for whatever I owe the hospital."

"My supervisor or I will see you in the morning!" she said threateningly and stomped out of the room.

"That's fine," Joan muttered quietly and rolled over on her side. Her annoyance was not strong enough to hold back the deluge of sleep as it overtook her.

Chapter 25

Friday evening

This time she felt as if quite a lot of time had elapsed as hospital sounds began to wrap themselves around the uncomfortable feelings she was having about making mistakes. What was it? She tried to reason, to focus on what she had been thinking. No, not thinking, dreaming. She had been dreaming, but about what?

Without moving her head, she opened her eyes and surveyed the immediate area. Then she remembered. The hospital. The pregnancy. The abortion. The operating room. It all flooded back like a nest full of rattlesnakes, squirming, writhing, and worming their way into her consciousness.

Mistakes were like that. They happened without expecting them, and then there they were to haunt and heckle and deny happiness. She felt like her whole life had been a mistake. She couldn't get away from the idea. Every time she turned around when she had been a child, she made one. Half of the time, she didn't even know that she had made one until she was punished for it.

Suddenly she knew that she had been dreaming of one that she had so successfully buried, that she remembered it now for the first time in years. How strange. She knew that at the time of committing it that she had had no idea of the ramifications of what she had done. It didn't take long to discover that the consequences of disobeying her mother would be the suffering of the most excruciating embarrassment she had ever experienced as a young child. Now she could chuckle about it, but at the time she had wanted to drop off the face of the earth.

She loved family reunions. It was the only time she got to see her cousins when they weren't working on the farm. She wished there had been some girls her age, but she liked the boys anyway. Marvin, Garner, and Dale were her favorites, and they were about her age.

Living on a farm was hard. They had to work all summer. They always called her "city slicker" when she'd go to visit overnight. They had to get up at the crack of dawn to do chores, and when she'd go downstairs for breakfast, they were usually finishing theirs and had already been up for hours. "City-girl time" they called it—as if Bernhards Bay were a city! They kidded each other a lot, but because there were more of them, they usually won.

She didn't go down to the barn anymore if it was milking time. They tried to teach her to milk the cows, but she could never get any milk out. Then they'd tease her for that. Often she became the target to see who could squirt the milk the farthest. If Uncle Harry had known about it, they would have been sorry for wasting all that milk. She could never figure out how they could aim it so good. They could hit a bull's-eye from ten feet away.

One year they had the reunion at a small lake that had picnic tables and a little beach. There was also a great big building with a jukebox, some pinball machines, and the biggest mounted moose head she had ever seen. The eyes seemed to follow wherever she went. It was creepy.

It was a very hot day, and her mother had forgotten to pack her bathing suit. The boys were all in the water having a grand old time and she asked her mother why she couldn't go in with her dress on. The answer was emphatic. No, she would get cold and get sick from it.

She stood on the shore and watched the boys until she couldn't stand it anymore and went back and begged her mother some more. This time, Aunt Elizabeth was there and suggested that maybe it would be all right if she just went wading, so they reached a compromise.

She raced out and kicked her shoes off, wading delighted into the cool spring water. It felt soooo good! She started running along the shoreline, holding her skirt tight so it wouldn't get wet. She stopped and watched the boys splashing each other and having such a great time that she decided to go back and give her mother another try. She turned around and started for the shoreline when WHAM, *her cousin Dale hit her from behind with a full-blown tackle, and she went under.*

At first it was great. She pushed him back, and he shoved her under the water again. They were laughing and carrying on when it hit her. She was in real trouble! She got scared and started running for the shore.

"What's the matter, chicken?" they teased.

"Joanie's a sissy. Can't take the water!"

She really didn't want to leave because the water was the only place where she could beat them. She could outswim and outdive them, but because of all the farmwork, they were stronger and could beat her at anything else. She was tempted to stay and give them a run for their money, but she didn't.

She knew that her only hope was to go fess up and try to get forgiven. It didn't work, though. Her mother was so mad that she just wouldn't listen. She grabbed Joan by the arm and dragged her across the dusty parking lot to where their car was parked and made her take off all her clothes. Then she went to the trunk and got a blanket, which she threw at Joan

"Next time maybe you'll do as you're told, young lady," she spat.

"You get under that blanket and stay there until your clothes are dry!"

She slammed the door and proceeded to spread Joan's dress out on the hood of the car. Then she actually hung Joan's underpants on the car aerial. Joan wanted to die right there in that car.

She slithered down on the floor. It was so hot the sweat was already pouring down her forehead and upper lip and almost everywhere else. It was hard to get a good breath between the heat in the car and the heavy blanket. She huddled on the floor and plastered herself against the door, trying to make herself as invisible as possible. She snaked her arm between the seat and the door to make sure it was locked. Then she crawled across the floor and checked the other side. They were both locked, so she scrunched down and listened. Nothing. Maybe the boys didn't know.

Then she heard a really loud whisper. They must have spotted her panties on the aerial! She knew if she could hear a whisper they weren't very far away. Maybe they wouldn't realize she was inside the car, and they'd go away. She wondered why they were being so quiet. Maybe they had gone back swimming. Then she heard some feet shuffling and some pushing and shoving. There was another loud whisper and a quiet snicker. She squeezed her eyes shut to protect herself from what she knew was coming. Then it happened. They were real quiet at first. Starting with a long, drawn-out, singsong chanting of her name.

"Jooooanieeeeeeee, where arrrrrrre you?"

They kept at it for a while and then changed the dialogue.

"We know where you're hidiiiiiiing."

They went on unmercifully, repeating the same derisive words over and over again. Then she heard a tapping on the window. They kept up their teasing and then changed it again.

"We see your underpants. We see your underpants."

Every time they sang it they got louder.

She started to cry. She didn't know what else to do. She couldn't look at them, but she knew that they knew where she was, and for some reason that made everything worse.

Then she heard a shout from the softball field on the other side of the car, "What do you boys think you're doing?" It was Uncle Harry. "You boys get away from that car and leave her alone."

There were some indistinct mumblings and grumblings as they shuffled off as fast as they could.

She could breath easier. Well, not really—it was too hot. Then she heard Uncle Harry's voice again. "Harlan, did you know that Joan is in your car with the windows rolled up?"

"Maybe Daddy will rescue me," she prayed.

Her mother showed up a few minutes later and said that maybe her clothes were dry enough. She handed them to Joan and told her to get dressed. They left soon after that, and Joan had been very relieved that she wouldn't have to see her cousins again for a very long time.

The old familiar feelings of mistake-born guilt started to engulf her, and she got "that feeling" in the pit of her stomach for the millionth time. It was a feeling of regret, stupidity, unworthiness, and self-reproach, all rolled into one neat, efficient little emotion. It overtook her whenever she made a mistake and lasted as long as the severity of the incident warranted.

If it were a simple mistake such as voicing a wrong opinion at the supper table, it would only last overnight. If it were something major, such as flubbing a high note at the end of a solo, she didn't sleep well for days. The note would just keep going around and around in her head while she lay in bed, feeling like a slave to her own mistakes and praying for the blessed relief of sleep.

Lying there in the hospital bed, she realized that she was falling back into those old habits. She hadn't done this to herself for a long time over insignificant matters. The pressure she had been under had obviously taken its toll. She would get over it as soon as she separated those old feelings from the new ones brought on by the pregnancy. The work she had done with Dr. Reed had helped her tremendously with guilt. She knew she would be able to process it all successfully. It would just take some time.

She could look back on that childhood incident with a degree of amusement now, and she knew that eventually the guilt that had been brought on by the abortion would also become tolerable. Dr. Reed had given her the tools. She just needed time to use them.

Making mistakes had been unforgivable when she was a child. She knew that was true because no one in the family had ever admitted to having made one. They were never wrong. They were always and forever perfect. She seemed to be the only one who made mistakes.

Her own rambunctious nature made it worse. She was such a tomboy when she was little that she was constantly hurting herself. This caused a real dilemma for her because she knew that if she went crying for solace and a bandage, she would be punished for being dumb enough to get hurt in the first place. She would be spanked for falling down and skinning a knee or hitting her thumb with a hammer, anything. It always seemed to her that her mother was deliberately rough when she cleaned up a boo-boo.

"You sit still and stop your sniveling, young lady, or I'll give you something to really cry about," she would snarl.

This could be followed by a crack on the leg or some other thing that was equally as uncalled-for.

Joan recalled being dismayed one day when Donna went home crying with a bloody elbow. She didn't really want to go home with her, but she wanted to keep playing, so she did. Joan thought that maybe Donna's mother wouldn't get quite so mad at Donna if she had company with her. That's the way it always happened at Joan's house.

Instead of losing her temper, picking her up, and slamming her harshly in a chair, Donna's mother knelt down and tenderly gathered her in her arms and hugged her and whispered to her comfortingly. When Joan went home with a bloody anything, all she got was a slap. Yes, mistakes were costly in her house.

Joan could only imagine the gruesome outcome if her mother found out about her latest error. It certainly wouldn't be pleasant. She knew she would be disowned, disinherited, and disfamilied. She didn't care about the money, she just cared about her family, and they would all side with her mother, she had no doubt. One didn't make mistakes as despicable as this and stay on speaking terms, family or not!

She heard a familiar voice clear its throat and turned to find Dr. George standing there in the doorway. She was happy to see him and grateful he had interrupted the unhappy musings. "Hi!" she smiled.

"Well! Don't you look better?" he grinned, coming into the room. "Yesterday, I really didn't know if you would still be with us by now."

"I know," she said lightly. "Nurse Greene clued me in on what you told her. 'Better or dead,' I believe it was."

He blanched at the idea that she knew what he had said, but he could tell by the smile on her face that there was no malice in her heart.

"I don't believe I used that terminology, but in essence, that's the way it was. Tonight is a different story, however. 'Patient recovering nicely' would be today's story."

He looked genuinely pleased, which pleased Joan in turn. She noticed that he didn't have his uniform on under the required isolation duds. He was in civilian clothes for the first time since she had known him.

"Are you going home now?" she asked.

"Yes, but I forgot to tell you something this morning," he said.

By now, she was pretty much shell-shocked and expected the worst. "Oh, no, not something else to worry about!" she groaned suspiciously.

"Now don't worry. I just forgot to tell you that I spoke with Dr. Brown this morning. He understood perfectly and was very concerned about you. I spoke with him again a little while ago to inform him of your progress, and he said that as long as you were doing so well, he would call your mother and let her know where you are."

"Oh, my God!" Joan said disbelievingly.

"Wait a minute, don't get upset. He wasn't going to tell her any details at all. He was merely going to tell her that there had been some sort of emergency and that your friend thought you should have it checked out and brought you along with her when she returned to the city."

"Oh, okay," Joan said.

There was no use trying to make him understand her fears, so she felt that she might as well let it pass for the time being and pretend there was nothing else to dread.

"I haven't heard a word from the police," he said. "I feel good about that. Every hour we don't hear anything brings us closer to their forgetting it completely."

"I sure hope so, Dr. George," was all she cared to say about the subject.

"I'd best be going now," he said, giving her that now-familiar pat on the shoulder.

"Get a good night's sleep, and I'll see you in the morning."

Just then, Ann came in the door, adjusting the mask as she walked. The hat was in her hand.

"Hi!" she said before looking up.

"Hello there," said Dr. George.

"Oh, I'm sorry, I didn't know . . ." she said squashing the hat on her head and frantically trying to adjust it.

"That's all right," Joan said, "I'm glad you're here."

"Dr. George, I want you to meet my friend Ann. She's the one who called you and brought me in."

They simultaneously extended their gloved hands to shake. Dr. George was the first to speak.

"Joan knows how lucky she is to have a friend like you," he said.

"She also knows how lucky she was to have a doctor as understanding as you," Ann replied.

"Well, isn't this sweet?" Joan said. "Both my rescuers in the same place at the same time. Thank you and thank you," she said, nodding from one to the other. She was deeply moved all of a sudden and began to tear up. "From the bottom of my heart," she blubbered.

They all chuckled together, and after a few moments, it was possible for Dr. George to make a polite exit. Claiming family responsibilities, he made his excuses and left.

Once they were alone, Joan couldn't wait to hear news from home.

"How are the twins? Are they worried about me?" she said, concerned.

"No not really. Sally calls me whenever they want news. I just keep telling them that you are fine and that you send your love. Sally says that every time there is a reference to a hospital on the TV, they rush over to it and tell her that's where you are."

"Boy, I miss them!" Joan said. She was almost disappointed they didn't seem to miss her, but at the same time she was glad.

"How are you feeling?" Ann asked, concerned.

"A little tired right at the moment, but I'll tell you, a lot better than last night!"

"I called the nurses' station this morning, but they wouldn't say anything specific. You know how they are, but they did say that you were doing as well as could be expected. I didn't know if they really meant it or if that was a standard answer for everything."

"Last night was pretty iffy, from what Dr. George said. It was pretty much touch and go. There was a special duty nurse who watched me all night. She helped me a lot. I wasn't so scared when I knew she was around. He let her go this afternoon."

"Then he must know you're going to be all right," Ann said happily.

"Yes, that's what he told me," Joan said, without matching her mood.

"What's wrong? I would think you'd be elated."

She knew Joan too well for Joan to be able to disguise her feelings. "Well, there are several things I'm concerned about. Have you spoken to David?" she asked apprehensively.

He had stood by her until now, but she wasn't sure he was prepared for everything that had transpired, and she was afraid he might decide the whole thing wasn't worth the aggravation.

"You needn't worry about him!" Ann smiled knowingly. "He called me right after he called your house last night, and Sally told him you weren't home. I guess he didn't even ask her where you were. He just hung up and called me."

Joan breathed a sigh of relief at the news that he wasn't going to desert her.

"I can't get over how he has stood by me, Ann. He could have told me to get lost and denied everything. It would have been so simple for him."

"I think you're wrong there," she said with conviction.

"It wouldn't have been easy for him at all. I think he truly loves you. It isn't just a fling with him—that much is obvious. The minute I made it clear that as far as I knew you were all right, he asked to come out to see me. He's been there twice today. Actually, he's becoming rather a nuisance!" she smiled.

"Well, I'm sorry he's pestering you, but I'm relieved to know for sure how he feels." Her eyed brimmed with grateful tears.

Ann went on, "When he got there this morning and I told him what the nurses had said, he actually broke down and cried. He sat down at the kitchen table, put his head in his hands, and sobbed like a baby."

"I guess I'm lucky in more ways than one," Joan said, overwhelmed at his reaction. She had never had a man cry over her before. It was a heartwarming experience and filled her with more love than she had thought possible.

"Oh, Ann," she said intensely. "I owe you so much."

The tears finally had their way.

"Dr. George said that if you hadn't brought me in when you did, I would have died. No questions about it. Now you're taking care of David and making sure he's all right. How on earth am I ever going to repay you?" she cried.

There had never been much outward expression of emotion between them, and Joan felt that her outburst might be embarrassing her friend, so she didn't go on. She sniffled loudly, and Ann handed her a handful of tissues.

"I'm sorry. Everything has been so bottled up, it had to come out sometime. Lucky you to be here at the right moment."

Joan dabbed at her eyes in an attempt to get herself under control.

"That's all right. What are friends for?" Ann said lightly.

"Well, not for having to save your life from a botched abortion! I sure am glad we forgot to give you those clothes for Amy, or we wouldn't be having this conversation!"

"There is something I have to tell you that you won't want to hear," Ann said simply.

Joan had a pretty good idea of what it might be. "What's that?" she queried.

"Your mother," Ann said dejectedly. "She's been harassing me all day. She's been calling Sally, too. Sally doesn't really know anything, so it isn't bad for her, but I hate to keep lying to your mother and telling her I don't know anything."

"You've got to!" Joan pleaded. "Just for a little while longer. She can't find out the truth!"

"I know. I won't do anything that foolish, but I'll be glad when that part of it is over. She's coming in here tomorrow, whether you want her or not. She's obviously livid with Dr. Brown for not telling her anything except that you are going to be all right, and she obviously doesn't like being kept in the dark. She's loaded for bear."

"I figured," Joan said simply. "Some things never change," she thought.

"You know, I should be going. Ray is watching Amy, and he's very tired. I should get back." She began to gather her things and then reached in her purse and handed Joan a letter.

"This is from David," she said, happily handing Joan a letter. "I thought I would save it for last so you could enjoy it in private."

Nothing short of the news that she would survive would have made Joan happier.

"Thanks," she said gratefully. "Thanks, Ann."

"You take care and get better," Ann said, squeezing the hand that held the letter. "I'll see you tomorrow." She left quietly.

Chapter 26

Saturday, October 20, 1965 Morning

Joan thought that she must have rested well because unlike the previous times, she had no recollection of any unpleasant dreams. As she came fully awake, she heard the rustle of paper and remembered the letter. Her hands trembled as she opened it to read his words for the first time since last night.

> My Dearest, Dearest Darling,
>
> My heart aches that you must endure the things you are going through and that I can't be there by your side to comfort and support you. I beg your forgiveness for having put you in this danger and beg you to continue to love the love that we share. I live for the moment that I will be able to hold you in my arms again and express the true depth of my love for you.
>
> Until then I remain,
Your Adoring,
David

How sweet that he sought her forgiveness, she thought warmly. She felt that it was his forgiveness that needed to be bestowed upon her.

Her early morning reveries were rudely interrupted by the promised visit from the admitting office. This woman didn't look quite as contentious as the last one had been, so Joan thought perhaps this one would be more reasonable.

"I'm sorry to bother you this early, but we need to get this cleared up as soon as possible," she said.

"That's fine with me," Joan replied noncommittally.

"My name is Mrs. Horn, from admitting. My assistant tells me that you refused to give her some pertinent information yesterday," she said as she took a seat.

Joan decided that it might be in her best interest to stay on the good side of this woman, and since she seemed reasonable, she decided to cooperate.

"I'm sorry to have caused trouble," Joan started, "but I just can't afford to have my employer find out about this situation."

"What situation?" Mrs. Horn asked curiously.

"There is no doubt in my mind that I would lose my job if this gets out. If that should happen, I wouldn't be able to support my family, let alone pay this hospital bill. This situation wouldn't be covered by my hospitalization anyway, so I don't understand what all the fuss is about."

Mrs. Horn considered her carefully and replied, "I don't understand. What situation? Why wouldn't it be covered?"

It didn't seem possible to Joan that after what she had gone through, the offices didn't know what had happened. Mrs. Horn looked at Joan and then at the chart hanging on the foot of her bed. She removed it and scanned the contents. "Oh, I see!" she said, dismayed. "So that's the problem!"

"Now perhaps you can understand why I can't put a claim in for my insurance to cover the cost," Joan said, a little indignantly.

"Well, yes," she apologized, "I can. I'm sorry, I didn't realize that you were the one who . . ." She trailed off, not certain how to finish the sentence.

"The one who had the abortion," Joan finished for her.

Sheepishly, Mrs. Horn said, "If you don't mind my asking, how do you intend to pay the hospital?"

"If you will bill me, I'll pay it off in three months' time, Mrs. Horn. I'm sorry—that is your name, isn't it? In the tenseness of the moment, I forgot."

She nodded, and Joan continued, "I'll sign a note to that effect, which I told your assistant yesterday, but she wasn't interested in listening."

Joan had the upper hand for a change and decided to take advantage of it.

"I understand now." Mrs. Horn said quietly.

Joan wanted to continue making her point and went on, "You can certainly trust me to make the payments because I couldn't afford the publicity if you decided to come after me."

Standing abruptly, as if she suddenly realized her mistake and wanted to run away, Mrs. Horn said, "I'll have the note drawn up and sent up for your signature this afternoon. Our apologies, we didn't understand."

"Thank you, Mrs. Horn," Joan said gratefully.

Mrs. Horn started for the door and then turned and said quickly, "I'm very happy you made it. We were all rooting for you." Then, as if she shouldn't have said anything, she disappeared through the door.

"Well, my goodness!" Joan thought, "Greene was right—they do care!"

As swiftly as Mrs. Horn had left, the dread hit Joan. This was the day her mother would be there, demanding answers to her questions. She thought that maybe she would rather be questioned by the police. She could anticipate their attitude more accurately. All she really knew was that just like the police—she couldn't admit anything to her mother, either.

Thinking back over her life, she wondered just how many times she'd had to face her mother over something the woman perceived to be terribly wrong. Most of the time, her mother's own silent rage fueled the flame and made the simple mistake of a child into something that was blown out of all proportion to the "crime."

Her mother was unmerciful if she thought Joan had done something that would bring embarrassment to the family. One time in particular, she remembered her mother had started hitting her with her hand for some infraction. Then she got angrier with Joan because it was Joan's fault that her hand hurt, so she rolled up a magazine and began hitting her with that.

As was the case in many incidents such as this, Joan really didn't know what she had done. When she asked what she had done, her mother's reply to her question was always the same, "Well, if you don't know by now, young lady, I'm certainly not going to tell you!"

Her favorite method of punishment was what she called a "switching." This consisted of deliberately hunting around for a green twig that would make the perfect switch. If it were too dry, it would break, so the fresher off the tree it was, the better. The "switch" would then be applied to the back of her upper legs in direct proportion to the seriousness of the nasty deed. It stung and smarted very badly, but it was concealed under her skirt and healed fast and didn't leave much evidence.

As Joan became older and bigger, the switching became verbal and eternal. Sometimes her mother would go on for what seemed like hours, haranguing about the same thing over and over again. Always interspersed with the accusations of Joan's wrongdoing were statements of the lack of respect shown her by "everyone" and how no one knew what she had to go through, how overworked she was, or how no one cared whether she lived or died.

Joan couldn't remember ever having quiet, peaceful times at home. They didn't exist if her mother were in the house. It was a constant diatribe of what to do, how to do it, or why it shouldn't have been done.

"If you don't do such and such, I'll. etc., etc., etc."

Therefore, Joan spent as little time at home as she could manage.

Now the old dread-knot in the pit of her stomach was tightening up again at the prospect of her mother coming in. She wished she knew when to expect her so she could relax a little until it was time to get emotionally ready.

Then the morning brightened considerably as Dr. George came bustling into the room with such energy and bounce that she thought it must be his day off and he was just stopping in for a second. He laughed at her suggestion of it and said that he had been up for quite some time but had just finished a difficult delivery and that the mother and daughter were doing just great!

The unabashed love he displayed for his profession made Joan feel even more strongly about him.

"You really enjoy your work, don't you?" she asked, sure of the answer.

"I most certainly do!" he answered enthusiastically.

"I have a feeling you enjoy yours, too," he said as he looked at her challengingly.

"Guilty as charged," she quipped.

"I hope you feel as well as you look today."

"I feel fine," she answered happily. "I haven't heard a word from the police, so I'm hoping they aren't going to do anything."

"I doubt they'll pursue it at this point. They usually would have appeared by now if they had any intentions in that direction," he said confidently.

"I just realized that you're the second person to come in without a mask and all the other paraphernalia. Does that mean that I'm not in isolation anymore?" she asked.

"Yes," he returned. "Your blood work shows great improvement, so I removed your name from the list."

"That's good," she replied, relieved.

"Do you have to rush off to rounds or anything right now, Dr. George?"

"Not right this minute," he responded. "Why?"

"Because if you have a minute, I'd like you to explain to me exactly what happened and why I was so close to dying."

He drew a chair up close to the bed and made himself comfortable. "First of all, this so-called doctor, do you know his name?" he asked.

"No, I don't," she replied. "The only name I know is the friend of the baby's father who helped us. He only knew one name also. Apparently, each person knew only one other name. That way they would have a harder time determining who was responsible. Everything was pretty tight," she explained.

"Tell me what he actually did to you," Dr George said kindly.

"He put a reed in my uterus. It was awful!" she shuddered, thinking about it.

"A reed—what do you mean by a reed?"

"Well, it looked like a piece of bamboo that had been woven and whittled into a point on one end and a ball on the other, supposedly to keep it from falling out."

"Oh, yes," he said reflectively. "It's called a lamineria. It's made out of dried seaweed, a natural growing material. Difficult to identify."

"But if it's seaweed, how did it get so hard and brittle?" she asked, not at all sure he was correct.

"Through the drying process, I'd guess. You see, after inserting it through the cervix, the natural body fluids cause it to swell up and expand the opening in the uterus. I just don't know how he thought that in and of itself would start the process."

Something occurred to Joan. "Would some kind of pill have helped?"

"A pill? What kind of pill?" he asked, encouraged.

"I think they're in my purse, in the side stand. Can you reach it?"

He handed her the purse, saying mischievously, "Here, you find them. I would never search a lady's purse, even with her permission."

She found the bottle and gave it to him. He looked it over, examining it carefully.

"How many did you take?" he asked.

"Only one, the night Ann brought me in, the night after the procedure. It was right after I took it that I began shaking so badly."

"What happened to the lamineria?" he asked, looking as if it were beginning to make sense.

"It came out about noon or one o'clock the day after he put it there. Well, actually, I took it out because I could tell that it had dropped so far it wasn't in my uterus anymore."

"Now I understand!" he said, pleased that the mystery was solved. "These pills are designed to contract the uterus. The two things together would have definitely worked, but the fact that you lost the lamineria and only took one of the pills explains why the contractions never started."

"In layman's terms," he said thoughtfully, "the infection was so advanced when you arrived, and your blood was so thoroughly poisoned by it, that the natural filtering process that's usually carried out by the lymphatic system had begun to break down."

"When a bacterial infection is that intense, the blood system reacts in such a way that the vital organs such as the brain, liver, kidneys, and the heart become so starved that they actually begin to fail all at the same time. In your case, we were minutes away from that failure."

"Oh, my God!" she said. "You just made the hair on the back of my neck stand right straight up! Now I understand why the timing was so important," she said.

She was grateful to finally understand it all but feeling rather weak-kneed at the same time.

"Well," he said, getting up suddenly, "let me quickly check you out."

He took her wrist in his hand and checked his watch.

Jokingly, he began, "I do have other respon . . . say, what's this? Your pulse is racing. Are you all right?"

"I don't know," she answered. Then, as if making a confession, she blurted out, "My mother is coming in, and I'm scared to death. Would that do it?"

"Certainly it would!" he said, surprised. "What kind of monster is this woman, anyway? You spent a good deal of time talking about her when you were delirious."

Joan answered thoughtfully, "I've tried to figure her out for most of my adult life. She's stubborn, suspicious, distrustful, always right, and thinks that whatever goes wrong does so for the specific purpose of doing her harm."

"If she's that bad, why do you even bother with her?" he asked incredulously.

"She's the only mother I've got. And besides, if she throws me out of the family, I'll never see the rest of them. I have a brother and sister who have kids, and I don't want to deprive my kids of their family," she answered simply.

"Well, I was going to pull the I.V., but let's leave it there. Maybe it will make her a little more sympathetic."

"It's a good try, but I doubt it'll work," she said dejectedly. "I have to figure out something to tell her that will make sense, so she won't keep questioning everyone about what's wrong with me. She's been driving both my babysitter and my friend Ann crazy with her questions."

"Are you serious? Do you mean to tell me that if I explain to her that you were within a few minutes of dying, she wouldn't forgive you?" he queried.

"I doubt it," Joan answered. "She's the most unforgiving person I know. She holds grudges for a lifetime. She wouldn't have forgiven me if I had died. Why would she do it when I'm alive?"

"If she's that bad, I'll mislead her to keep her off your back, but I'll have to inform Dr. Brown. Is that all right?" he asked

"Yes!" she said happily. "I know he'll understand."

"All right," he said. "Do you have any suggestions as to what to tell her?"

"Me?" she asked, surprised.

"Well, I really don't know much about you. Perhaps there is something in your way of living we could use . . ."

She thought for a moment. "How about a water-skiing accident about two months ago?" she asked hopefully. "I fell and I was really lame for a couple of weeks."

"Hmmm, possible . . . highly unlikely, actually, but to a layperson . . . we could manufacture an abdominal wall puncture that could result in a latent infection . . ." he thought out loud.

"Dr. George, you're wonderful. It sounds good to me!"

Conspiring further, he said, "Tell you what—are you expecting her this morning?"

"Yes," she replied, enjoying the fun he seemed to be having.

"Then I'll tell the head nurse to detain her and send for me when she arrives. I have quite a few patients to see, but it would be worth it to intercede for you."

With that, all of the rest of the pent-up emotions she had been holding in for so long became impossible to dam up any longer, and she started to sputter, "Dr. George, I . . . I don't know h-h-how to thank you." She sniffed, "how can I ever repay you . . . first you save my life and th-then . . ."

"Now there, don't get all red-eyed, you don't want to give her any more ammunition, do you? I'll see you later. If there are no problems tonight, you can probably go home tomorrow. Chin up . . . and remember, I'll take care of your mother!" he said confidently. "Before I'm through with her, she'll be a pussycat. See you later . . ."

And he was gone.

Chapter 27

Saturday Early Afternoon

After he left, she realized that he was the only person, except Dr. Reed, that she had ever told about her relationship with her mother. She had never told her husband—it would have had no impact on him, so why bother? She guessed that Ann knew some of it, but it always made Ann uncomfortable when she brought it up, so she didn't, very often.

Certainly no one in their little community would believe it. Ellen was always so nice when other people were around. That's why Joan stayed away from home as much as possible unless she had a friend with her.

Ellen was known as a hard-working Christian woman who served the church and God. She wouldn't hurt a flea. Of course she disciplined her children—didn't everyone? She would never be cruel or hateful or take out her frustration on her children, would she? No, the community would never believe it.

Now that she thought about it, her sister might know. She wondered if she had ever treated Linda that way. She wondered if Linda could trust and confide in their mother when she couldn't. Joan was quite certain that she wouldn't have been able to either.

She remembered one time when she went to visit her grandmother and tried to elicit support and sympathy from her mother but got an emotional slap in the face instead.

It was always fun at first to visit her grandmother, but her home was in a place that was even more rural than Bernhards Bay. It was a little place called Amboy Center and had about ten houses in it and a church and a gas station. There were no kids her age to play with, so she would become bored easily. To make matters worse, it was almost impossible to carry on a conversation with her grandmother because she was very deaf. Her eyesight was also going fast. The family knew that it wouldn't be long before she would have to sell her house and move in with her children.

On one occasion in particular, it was even more difficult to make her understand. Joan had been trying to ask her to make a favorite dish, which no one else in the family could do as well. It was her special baked vanilla pudding. The only way she could make her grandmother understand what she was asking her to do was to drag out as many of the ingredients that she knew went in it and put them on the sideboard. When her grandmother saw the cornstarch box, she realized what Joan was asking her to do and went happily about the chore.

Joan was looking forward to having the pudding for supper that night when "it" happened. She had gone to the bathroom and there "it" was—blood in her panties! She panicked!

Why was she bleeding? Was it cancer? It must be cancer Mom had had cancer, and there had been blood in her panties because of it. She had to go to the hospital and have an operation because of it. She almost died. She had to go all the way to Boston to get it fixed. She was gone for weeks. What should she do? First of all, tell Grandma.

"Grandma, there's blood in my panties."

"What?"

"THERE'S BLOOD IN MY PANTS!"

"What? Speak up!"

She was already shouting so loudly that she was afraid all the neighbors could hear her.

"Never mind," she said, dejectedly. Joan knew she would never make her grandmother understand.

"I don't know what you're saying," her grandmother shouted. "Come and eat your supper."

Joan did as she was told but could hardly choke down the vanilla pudding.

After supper she had to do something. She was really scared. She remembered Mable and some of the older girls talking about something that happened every month that had to do with blood. It was all very hush-hush and mysterious. She had tried to ask her mother about it because the girls had seemed so embarrassed, but when her mother didn't understand her right away, Joan changed the subject.

She knew she should call home, but she was reluctant. First of all, it was a long-distance call, which no one ever made, and secondly, the whole thing reminded her of another time she had tried to ask a question of her mother. They had been sitting in the kitchen facing each other with a bushel of string beans between them, which they were preparing for canning. On her mother's lap was a large pan into which they were putting the beans after snapping off the ends.

"Mommy," she had begun as she snapped away, "there's something I wanted to ask you."

"Well, I hope it isn't one of the foolish questions you usually ask," her mother responded.

She wasn't sure whether it was foolish or not because she didn't understand it, which was why she was asking it in the first place. She wasn't quite sure what to do, but she pushed on because she wanted to know. Maybe she should ask in a different way.

"It's a word I don't understand," she said carefully.

"Well," her mother said with a strange look on her face, "what's the word?"

"Fuck," Joan said.

"WHAT?" her mother shrieked.

Then, without warning, her mother slapped her, hard across the face. Then she jumped to her feet, spilling the beans all over the floor. She kicked the bushel basket out of the way and grabbed Joan by the shoulders and started shaking her as hard as she could.

"Where did you pick up such language, young lady?" she demanded.

"Mable," Joan stammered. "M-M-Mable said it!"

Her mother slammed her down and tore out of the house, leaving her bewildered in a pile of beans. She assumed her mother was on her way to Mable's house.

Well, she knew that wrong or not, she had to call home. This could be serious, and even though it was a long-distance call that was too expensive to make, she had to do it even if her mother got mad at her.

The phone itself was a problem. In this rural outpost, it was necessary to go through an operator. There weren't any dials on the phones. This one was a long rectangular wooden box that hung on the wall. It had a shelf about three quarters from the bottom. Sticking out from the box above the shelf was a small horn that was used to speak into. The receiver hung on the side of the box and was also shaped like a horn but was slightly different. It was attached to the phone by a cord.

On the opposite side from the receiver was a handle. When the handle was cranked, everyone on the line, which could be several people, heard the ring. A different pattern of rings was assigned to each household on the party line. If it was your ring, you answered it. Sometimes you answered it when it wasn't your ring if you wanted to snoop.

She lifted the receiver and cranked one long crank, which called the operator. She hoped to goodness no one was listening in. She knew this call might be something that would end up with the old familiar, "What would the neighbors think?" routine.

The operator finally answered, and she asked her to please connect her with Cleveland 2402. She heard the two familiar short rings on their more modern desk-type phone and then her mother's familiar greeting, "Kneello."

She always answered the phone that way when she was at the office and trying to impress someone. Usually Joan thought it was silly, but now it seemed menacing.

"Hi, it's me," she said apologetically.

"Oh," Ellen answered, sounding like she was sorry she wasted her cordial greeting.

"Could you come back to Grandma's and get me?"

Joan squeezed her eyelids together, anticipating what the response would be like.

"Why?" her mother demanded.

"There's something wrong."

"What's wrong?"

"I don't know what it is," Joan pleaded.

She knew her mother would get angry if she said the words "underpants" on the phone, in case someone was listening, so she didn't know how to answer.

"What do you mean, young lady, that you don't know what's wrong?" she insisted. "You are calling me long distance on the telephone, and you don't know what's wrong?"

"I know what it is, but I don't know what it means," she tried to explain without saying a wrong word.

"Well, you'd better know what it means pretty soon if you expect me to stay on this phone long distance!" Ellen spewed.

Finally, Joan couldn't take it any longer, she just wanted someone to be kind to her for a change. She wanted someone to try to understand her. She began to cry but fought it back, knowing that crying would just make her mother angrier.

"I don't want to say it on the telephone."

Joan managed to talk normally by pushing her head down as hard as she could on her neck, which kept her voice from trembling. It was a trick she had learned out of self-defense. It always helped her to stop crying.

"Now, you listen to me, young lady, you had better get talking and telling me what's going on if you expect me to come chasing up there this time of night! Do you hear me?"

"Yes, I hear you," she answered. "But I don't want to say it."

Finally, she couldn't stand it any longer, "It's something in my underpants!"

She closed her eyes and waited for the verbal onslaught.

There was silence for a few seconds as if Ellen were about to make up her mind about something. "Well, why didn't you say so in the first place?" she asked sharply. "I suppose I'll have to come and get you."

"Okay," Joan breathed, relieved.

"Good-bye," she said and hung up the phone.

Joan was glad she was coming, but when she arrived and Joan showed her the panties, she was livid.

"Do you mean you dragged me all the way up here this time of night just because you started to menstruate?" Ellen demanded accusingly. "I thought it was something serious, like pinworms. As if I don't have enough to do, I have to go chasing all over the countryside for you. You get yourself in that car, young lady, and I don't want to hear another word out of you until we get home. Do you hear?"

Ellen stomped in to talk to Joan's grandmother, and by the time she got in the car, she was in a little better frame of mind. She actually talked a little on the way home but not about what was wrong with Joan, and Joan didn't dare ask.

When they arrived home, Ellen ordered her upstairs where she grabbed a bunch of rags from the ragbag and threw them at her daughter telling her to pin them inside her pants.

"Tomorrow you get yourself over to Davis's store and get some sanitary napkins. If you think I'm going to get them for you, you've got another think coming!" she pronounced.

"I'm not sure what to do with these," Joan said, indicating the rags.

"If you think hard enough, you'll figure it out," was her mother's reply.

Well, at least she knew it wasn't cancer, and if they had sanitary napkins for it, someone else had to have it, too. It must be what the older girls talked about, after all.

Suddenly reality was standing in the doorway in the form of her mother. She gulped. Her heart and mind got all tangled up in the familiar flip-flop they always did when she felt she had done something wrong.

"Um, come on in," Joan said, embarrassed by her nervousness.

She hoped her mother couldn't hear her heart pounding. When she was a little girl, her mother seemed to know so well what she was up to that Joan believed that her thoughts were broadcast across her forehead like a one-line ticker tape, and all her mother had to do to read her mind was to read the built-in news clips.

"I see you still have an I.V. running—are you all right?" her mother asked rather sympathetically.

Joan wondered what was wrong. Why was she being so concerned?

"Oh, ah yeah, I'm fine. Just a little tired. Ah, how are you?"

"Well, of course *I'm* all right," she said sweetly, seemingly surprised at the question. "I'm not the one in the hospital!"

"Oh," Joan said, running on. "I really am fine. Just fine. Much better today."

This was too much. She would almost prefer the old mother. At least she could guess at her motives. Then, from somewhere deep inside of her, something rose up and bumped against her consciousness and sense of self.

Ellen smiled, "Sally and the kids said to say hello. I talked to them this morning before I left."

"That's nice," Joan remarked absently. She was trying to analyze what her mother was doing and what was emerging into her own thoughts.

"I miss them," Joan said simply.

Suddenly, words from Dr. Reed, the psychologist she had worked with before her divorce, burst into her mind. *"Your legitimacy as an individual is not drawn from another person, no matter who that person is or what that person means to you."*

"They miss you, too," Ellen said.

With this, Joan sensed a change and braced herself.

"The doctor asked to speak to me before I came in," her mother said curiously.

"Oh really?" Joan replied innocently. "Here it comes," she thought.

"Yes, he did. He said that you had been very sick and had to be in isolation."

Joan waited for more, but that was all she said. That was it. Ellen stopped, waiting for a response. No accusing glances. No remonstrating. She was just waiting for a reply.

"Yes, it was creepy," Joan rattled on nervously. "Everyone had to put on a mask, a full-length gown, rubber gloves, and a hat before they came in. He just took me off the list this morning. Now maybe I can go to the real bathroom instead of having to use this commode they brought in."

"I imagine that will be a relief," her mother stated simply.

"Yes, it will," Joan replied.

She was still astonished at her mother's strange behavior and her own sudden calm.

Joan heard Dr. Reed's gentle voice from afar, *"You have the same right to seek happiness as anyone else on this earth, and no one else has the right to dictate to you the path on which you choose to grow toward happiness."*

"The doctor told me you might be able to go home tomorrow," Ellen said lightly.

"Yes, he told me that, too," Joan replied. "I hope I can. I can't see any reason to stay here. I feel so much better, and he says the infection is basically gone, and I should be able to . . ."

A sudden flash of courage struck Joan, and for some inexplicable reason, she knew without a doubt that she was finally ready to take charge of the situation.

"You know, Mom, I love you very much, and I appreciate your concern about me and the kids, but sometimes I don't think you give me enough credit for knowing what I'm doing. I work very hard to make sure the kids are happy and healthy. I also work very hard at my job, and I think I'm going to be very successful at it. The fact that you got so upset just because you didn't know every little detail of what was going on implies that you don't trust me to do the right thing, and I resent it."

Ellen interrupted, "Well, I can see you're all right. That's what I came to find out. Everyone was being so mysterious, but your Dr. George explained it all to me, so I'll be going along. Maybe I'll see you tomorrow when you get home. Would you like me to pick you up?"

"Oh, no," Joan said firmly. "Ann has already made arrangements to come after me. She's looking forward to a day out of the house. I'll be fine. Thank you, though."

"Well, all right, then," Ellen said, turning to go. "If you want me to visit tomorrow, give me a call," she said and walked out of the door.

Joan almost collapsed with relief.

"You fox, Dr. George," she said aloud. "Whatever did you manufacture to say to her?"

Joan was confounded by disbelief. She flopped back onto the pillow and closed her eyes. Whatever he had said certainly worked. But not just Dr. George—she had helped also. She had been stronger than when she had tried to set her mother straight after the divorce.

Back then, when they would visit her, Ellen would invariably start with, "Oh, you poor fatherless children."

Knowing she had to stop that attitude, Joan had timidly asked her to not to do it. Ellen had cooperated, and nothing much more was said. This time, though, Joan felt she had really stood up to her mother, and her mother had actually backed down and ran.

She felt like a lead weight was lifting itself from her life. The police were apparently letting the whole thing drop, and now her mother had come and gone. The abortion was over with, and she was still alive. She would keep her job and support her family. She wouldn't have to worry about losing her babies, ever again.

All of a sudden, she knew there was only one more thing left to do before she was truly in charge of her life. She had no idea why or how, but in her newfound courage, she knew as surely as if someone had unzipped her brain and dropped the freshly formed, fully developed concept into her head that she had to say good-bye to David.

Chapter 28

Saturday Late Afternoon and Evening

Ann woke her from the nap that had become necessary in order to recover from her mother's visit. The early afternoon sun was streaking venetian blind slats all over the bed as she cranked it up into a sitting position.

"Ray's office had some electrical problems, so they were sent home for the afternoon. I was dying to hear about your mother's visit, so I left him minding Amy and came in."

Ann looked at Joan in anticipation of some juicy gossip. They had always shared a kind of ESP, sometimes beginning to hum the same tune at the same time, in the same key. Whenever one of them was under stress, the other managed to call just at the right time. Joan always knew when it was Ann on the other end of the line. Those things had happened so often that they hardly mentioned it anymore.

"I've been dying to talk to you, too. I'm so glad you came, and there's something else I want to run past you," Joan said.

Joan relished telling Ann about her successful discussion with her mother and how Dr. George had cooperated. They both had a chuckle over the way her mother had turned heel and left.

"I have no idea what Dr. George said to her, but it sure worked!" Joan mused. Then she went on to the most important thing on her mind. "Ann, I don't know where I get the audacity to ask you for another favor after all you've done for me, but it's very important," Joan confided.

"Okay, tell me."

"I don't feel right about discussing it with you before I talk it over with David, but it's really important that I see him before I leave the hospital."

"Well," Ann said. "That will be difficult since being seen by anyone who knows either of you could start all kinds of speculation. Are you sure it can't wait until you get home?"

"Yes, I'm very sure," Joan replied. "When I tell you what's up, you'll understand why it has to be here. It's just so personal that I feel bound to talk to David first."

"Okay, if you say so, but how do you propose to get him in here unseen?"

"I'm not sure," Joan confessed, "I was thinking that if he ran into a friend, maybe he could say he was visiting a family member, and if he ran into a family member, he could be visiting a friend. He could come in through an inconspicuous entrance and then come up the stairs. They let out right beside the elevators outside of my door, don't they?" Suddenly, the proximity to the elevators was an asset.

Ann thought for a moment and then asked, "Do you suppose there is anyone on the staff who could check and see if there is anyone here in the hospital who is from either Camden or Glensville? That would level the playing field a little."

"I have a great idea!" Joan said. "There's a woman in admissions who would be perfect, and from my last conversation with her, I know she'll try to help. Do you have a piece of paper and something to write with?"

Ann rummaged through her purse and found a pen and a small spiral pad she used for grocery reminders. "Here," she said, handing them to Joan.

Joan wrote her request to Mrs. Horn and gave it to Ann. "Take this down to admissions and give it to Mrs. Horn. She's in charge of the department. Let's see what she has to say."

Ann left her waiting apprehensively as she embarked on her mission. Joan heard the elevator door open and close and then waited for an eternity for her to return. When she came back in she was empty-handed.

"What happened?" Joan asked anxiously.

"Nothing yet," she answered. "Mrs. Horn was busy, so she told me to leave it with her and come back in twenty minutes."

"Oh good," Joan said. "Did she read it while you were there?"

"Yes, I think she read it twice. She looked surprised at first and then seemed to understand. She looked as if she intended to do it."

"Wonderful, maybe something will go our way for a change," Joan said enthusiastically.

Ann waited the twenty minutes and then went back. She found out there was no one from either community, and although not everyone included in a particular school district lived within the boundaries of the particular town, they felt the risk was reduced considerably. Now all they had to do was convince David. Joan knew that he would be willing to try, provided he could get away from home.

The nurses cooperated also; although they weren't sure exactly what they were agreeing to, they said they would be glad to relay a phone message from Ann to Joan. They also agreed that if she had a visitor, they would do their best to make sure they weren't interrupted. It was all rather fun and conspiratorial. The staff seemed to be trying to help her all they could, knowing what she had been through. It was women helping women. Joan had never experienced that before except for close friends. She liked it.

Ann left with the promise that she would call the nurses' station with a message as soon as she knew something. Joan felt a little jittery, almost hoping that he couldn't do it but at the same time knowing that it was very important to the rest of her life to carry through with her plan. She also knew that her chances of staying the course that she had decided upon would be infinitely easier here than at home. The impersonal nature of the hospital would be an advantage for her.

The call came two hours later.

"Joan, your friend called and said to expect a flower delivery sometime between seven and eight o'clock," the nurse said under her crisply starched nurses' cap.

"Thanks," Joan replied, bracing her heart and preparing for a very emotional evening.

She was getting tired again and decided that the best thing to do was take a nap. She would need all the strength she could muster in order to do what she knew she had to do. She also knew it would be one of the most difficult things she would ever have to do in her life.

She rested fitfully. She kept going over in her mind what she would say to David. Hurting him was the last thing she wanted to do, but she knew it couldn't be any other way. She hadn't been able to eat much of the dinner they had brought. Broth and Jell-O were about all they offered her, anyway.

After they took the food away, she decided to take a walk. She rang her call bell, and the nurse who responded was glad to help her out of bed and make sure she was strong enough to take a stroll around the hall. It was the first time she'd been out of her room since she was placed in it. She felt surprisingly strong, and when it was obvious that she could continue alone, the nurse excused herself and went back to her station. It felt good to be out of the room and alone. As her confidence grew, so did her conviction that she had made the right decision.

She went back to her room and tried to make herself look presentable. She did the best she could, which wasn't much, but after combing her hair, she climbed back into bed and tried to rest again.

She had just started to nod off when she heard the door next to the elevator open. She turned toward the door with anticipation. When she saw him, he took her breath away. He came quietly into the room and placed a beautiful bouquet of flowers on the nightstand. Then he sat down on the bed and took her into his arms.

It felt so comfortable and welcoming that she wasn't sure she would have the strength to do what she knew she had to do. The emotional roller coaster she had been on for the last several weeks had taken its toll on her, but she resolved to be strong and not succumb to his love. She steeled herself against the flood of warmth that threatened to burst loose in his arms. It would be so easy to escape there for all time, protected from the world of reality, safe in his refuge.

"I love you," he said simply.

It was as if any further attempts to express his true feelings would be utterly inadequate.

"I love you, too," she returned. She knew she had to take control of the situation as she had earlier with her mother.

"There is something that I have to say to you that you are not going to want to hear and that I don't want to have to say," she started.

"Then don't say it," he said quietly, looking down at their entwined hands.

She knew at that moment that what she was trying to say was not a surprise to him.

"You can't throw it all away," he whispered.

"I don't want to throw it away," she said simply. "But I can't keep it, either. You will never know how much you mean to me and how desperately I want to be with you forever, but it can't be."

"If we continue the way we've been, I would still be in danger of losing my girls. If anyone found out about us, it would be just as bad as if the pregnancy had been discovered. You know that's true, David," she said pleadingly.

"This pregnancy almost cost me my life and my children. I can't stay in a relationship that would continue that danger. I live and work in a very small community. It would be very difficult to keep us a secret. It would be a miracle if it didn't get out. I just can't rely on that kind of miracle."

"Sally would have to find out sooner or later, or we would never be able to see one another. What kind of life would that be? We would live lives of deceit, never being able to bring our love into the light of day, forever stuck in the shadows."

"How can you say these things?" he implored. "How can you hurt me like this after all we've been through?"

She lifted his chin so he would have to look her in the eyes. "The only way I can stand to do it is by knowing that I am hurting myself as much as I'm hurting you. But my family is as important to me as yours is to you. We are important to one another, but we can't have it all. It's impossible to have it all. It just won't work. We have to hurt for a while in order to heal, but we are both strong, and we will heal. We just need time."

"I'll need more than time," he said sadly, trying not to let his emotions get the best of him. "I'll never get over you. I don't want to get over you. I want to love you and care for you and protect you from harm. I need you. I need you," he sobbed. "I love you more than I have ever loved anyone in my life. I can't live without you."

"Yes, you can, David," she said, surprised at her own strength. "I know you can. You've been so important to me, but we must move on. I love you too. You have no idea how good I feel when I'm with you. This is not easy for me, either. You made me understand what real love is all about. I never knew before how much I could love a man. You have also helped deepen my love for my children. I hadn't thought that possible, but it happened. Perhaps the very deepening you caused is what is giving me the strength to do this."

She went on softly, "You make me feel complete, as if there had always been a piece of me that was missing, and when you came into my life, I was made whole for the very first time. Life became something to rejoice in instead of trudge through."

"Your love helped me to know that I am worthwhile. You helped give me a confidence in myself that I never had known before. You made me feel important to the world, that I really had something to offer. To have had your love, even for a short time, has given me the courage to face what needs to be done."

"Your love gave me the confidence I needed to dedicate myself to my new high school kids. You made me know I could do it. I would never have had the self-assurance it took to insist on the high school job if it hadn't been for you, and I thank you from the bottom of my heart for that."

"I thank you for standing by me through this. You could have run away, but you didn't. You stayed by my side. You helped me when I had to endure all of those tortuous hours of agony and you gave me the strength to recover".

"Now I need more of that strength to do what we both know needs to be done. We must go our separate ways to our separate families. I will always love you. I will always need you. You are a part of my life that I will cherish until the day I die."

"I want you to go home now and know that our lives are richer for having shared the love we had. There will always be a room in my heart reserved only for you where our love will dwell forever."

His lips silently caressed her fingertips as he gently but deliberately placed her hands in her lap. He stood resolutely and kissed her lovingly on the forehead. Then he turned and walked slowly through the door and out of her life.

Chapter 29

Sunday, October 21, 1965 Afternoon

Puppy-dog barkings. Screen door bangings. Four-year-olds flinging themselves through doors and into her hugs.

"Hi, Mommy! Hi, Mommy! We missed you, Mommy! Duffy missed you too, Mommy!"

Jumpings up and down. Pigtails flying, bouncing into the house. Sheer delight collapsings into the safety of the sofa. Elbows and knees making happy hurts climbing up beside her and all over her.

Tears mixed with marshmallows. Welcome home pictures proudly prancing. Hugs and kisses and touchings of love.

Hot dogs and Oreo eating. Hot chocolate sipping. And happy hominess and hours of togethernesses.

Bundles and bushels of love spilling over and spreading and soaking into every pore.

Sleepiness and coziness and reading nite-nite books. Sitting on beds and good-night hugs and kisses and love, going sleepily . . . exhaustedly into the land of Four-year-old dreams.

And relief . . . blessed, enormous relief.

Epilogue

December 21, 1965

The auditorium was even more crowded than she had expected. There were chairs set up along the back and sides, making it difficult for the first few singers to keep the processional going. As they passed, however, the people who were occupying the chairs did their best to move out of the way. They managed to proceed to the stairs which led up to the stage without too much difficulty.

The air was heavy with the scent of Christmas decorations and seemed thick with expectation as they mounted the stairs. They were doing everything exactly as they rehearsed, moving to their chairs on the risers and standing in front of them. They would sit down after her entrance and remain seated until the end of the first movement, which was a solo.

Joan and her accompanist, Carol, were watching the procession in relative secrecy from behind the red-velvet grand curtain, which was the auditorium's only claim to beauty. They could see well enough to know that the last few singers had begun making their way down the aisles. She wondered where her daughters were sitting. This was a very heavy program for them. She hoped they wouldn't get too fidgety for their grandmother. Joan had to admit to herself that no matter how miserable her mother had been to her while she was growing up, she had always supported her in music. She had also tried to help as much as she could with the twins lately. Right after the divorce, it seemed like they would never have any peace between them, but once the shock wore off, her mother had begun to come around. Last month's episode in the hospital had also helped.

The thought triggered an uninvited realization that if her students knew her secret—and they acted as if they did—so did most of the community. Everyone here could know. Then an even more devastating notion intruded. If they knew, this could be the last Christmas she would be allowed to have with the twins!

Since late November, she had let herself believe that there would be no repercussions, but now, watching her choir so calmly taking their places on the stage with no evident signs of excitement, she had the feeling they were just going through the motions in order to get it over with and get on with their lives. That meant that they *did* know, she was sure of it.

It was almost time for Joan to make her entrance. She had dreaded this part of the concert for a long time, and now it was even worse. It seemed so silly for her to have to wait backstage for all of them to get into place and then have to parade in front of them. She had to go from the wings all the way over to the podium, all by herself, followed by Carol, a few feet behind. It felt like it would be a five-mile walk. She wanted to turn around and run in the other direction. Instead, she looked at Carol, who seemed as nervous as she was.

"I'll be so glad when that fourth movement is over with," she said.

"So will I," Carol agreed. "If we can get through that, we'll be home free!"

They both turned back to watch the choir. They were all in place. She couldn't avoid it any longer. Her palms were cold and clammy. She couldn't do it. What if they really did know? What would they do when she walked out there?

She had heard stories about a school psychologist who was found to be abusing kindergarten boys. The entire town had erupted. There were meetings in school, in the churches, the fire hall, and any place they could find. Tempers flew, and people who didn't even have children in the district joined in the melee. The school board tried to hold informational meetings to try to squelch the bizarre rumors that were tossed about randomly, but they were shouted down time after time. One man threatened to hang the superintendent and his entire family. They finally just gave up in despair. It took months to get the district back to normal.

Anything was possible in a small town like this. They could be so unforgiving. They might even shout nasty things at her as she crossed the stage. Maybe the reason the place was so crowded was that they all came to watch her humiliation.

Unwillingly, her feet began to move. She walked uncertainly out past the last curtain that framed the stage and out into the open, between the choir and the audience. The only other time in her life that she had been that scared was that dreadful night last October which was the basis for all of her fears.

There was a smattering of applause from the audience—as if they were unsure whether they should applaud or whether or not they wanted to. She held her head high and kept on walking. This is where it would happen if anyone intended to shout an accusation at her or mutter some furtive remark.

She was only a few feet from the podium when it happened. She had just begun to think she had made it safely there when from the back of the auditorium, she heard two tiny voices shouting excitedly, "Hi Mommy! Hi Mommy!"

She stopped abruptly and looked out over the sea of faces, which were just beginning to register amusement. She spotted them in the back row on the left, jumping up and down in their seats. Their grandmother was frantically trying to quiet them and make them sit down. Tears came to her eyes, and she found it difficult to keep from laughing, it was so precious in light of the circumstances.

The whole audience began to chuckle, and the kids in the choir started to applaud. Not knowing what on earth to do, Joan turned and bowed her head slightly to the choir, at which point the audience began to applaud, so she turned and bowed slightly to them as well.

She didn't want to risk anything else, so she looked at the chorus and motioned for them to be seated. She glanced at Carol, who was poised, hands over the keyboard. There was nothing to stop them, so she raised her arms and gave the downbeat. Her first high-school concert was underway!

Her mind was swirling with thoughts and emotions as she automatically kept her arms moving in the well-practiced four-four conducting pattern. She wasn't concerned about the *Overture*; Carol knew it almost by heart, so Joan relaxed a little.

"So far, so good," she thought.

As the *Overture* was drawing to a close, she looked over at Steve, the president of the chorus and soloist for the second movement, *Comfort Ye My People*. He smiled back sheepishly, obviously nervous.

He had worked very hard on this piece, and he was beginning to sound really good. She wished for his sake that they had had another week to work on it, but now was no time to be thinking about that. She was sure he could carry his weight.

The *Overture* finished. She nodded appreciatively to Carol and signaled Steve to rise. He made his way downstage to the music stand and clearing his throat quietly, nodded to her. She signaled Carol, and they began. He was to come in on the third bar, after a slow introduction. It took a lot of self-control to stand there, staring out over the heads of the audience while waiting for his entrance. When he did, his tone quality was firm and focused. He made the entrance, crescendoed, and decrescendoed, letting his voice rise and fall over the next phrase as they had practiced. He was doing beautifully and getting more confident with every measure.

She looked up at the chorus. They were staring at him in wonder. It occurred to her then that they hadn't heard him since the auditions. They had been instructed to stay still and not react during the solos, but she could tell by the subtle changes in their expressions that they were surprised.

Then he began the last forte section, which was supposed to be very strong, almost a command to the listener to take action. He did it. He was wonderful.

The voice of him that crieth in the wilderness,
Prepare ye the way of the Lord
Make straight in the desert
A highway for . . . our . . . God!

The audience stirred. He had been so good that it would be difficult for them not to applaud. She had written on the program that in a piece of music like this one, which contained many movements or sections, it was inappropriate to applaud before the final conclusion of the entire work.

She dropped her arms quickly, and when she sensed they were about to begin clapping, she raised them up again just as quickly, stopping the applause. She sighed her relief at the choir, and she knew they understood.

Steve was already back in place with the chorus, and without the audience seeing her, she mouthed her congratulations to him. Then she took a deep breath and signaled the choir to rise.

They rose, all right! They fairly leapt to their collective feet. She looked at them in surprise, and they smiled—They *smiled*!

She couldn't believe her eyes! They were beaming with enthusiasm and pride. Her mind raced. She stood there staring at them, not believing what her eyes were telling her was true. Her mind refused to function logically.

Without making a conscience decision, her arms raised automatically, and she cued the introduction to the first choral movement. The altos had the first line all by themselves. They knew that their entrance would set the tone for the first choral movement and therefore the entire work. At the beginning of the year, they had been a rather weak section, believing they couldn't hit any note above third-space C. Their ability and self-esteem had grown slowly and steadily.

She looked in their direction. They stood with feet firmly spaced for balance and comfort, their music was chest high, one hand supported the spine of the score, the other hand was ready to turn pages, just as they had been taught. They were ready. Every fiber of their beings radiated readiness. She gave them a very firm second-beat cue. They responded in kind. In a rich, resonant tone, their voices sang.

And the glory, the glory of the Lord.

The sopranos, tenor, and basses responded

And the glory, the glory of the Lord

They had never sounded better! They sang with assurance, their voices ringing out on the fast, lively phrases. It was over before she knew it. They sang their last phrase with the exact amount of hearty firmness they had rehearsed. The miracle she had prayed for was forming itself right before her very eyes and ears!

The next movement was a bass solo. The boy who had won the honor of singing it was reluctant at first because his father felt that anything other than sports was too sissy for his son. Joan had almost begged him to sign up for the audition. She knew he was one of the most natural and mature talents she had ever heard at this level, but because of his father, he had never used it. He won the audition, of course, but he had declined. She decided to pour on the psychology, telling him he had a responsibility to the group, to her, to the audience, and yea, even Handel himself. It worked.

He moved into place on her cue and began the slow, sustained, ultramasculine phrases with self-confidence and dignity. She heard his first few phrases and was again struck by his talent.

"Take that, Papa!" she thought to herself. "Let's see if anyone thinks he's a sissy after this performance!"

They obviously didn't. He was so great that one audience member burst into solo applause but was stopped by the surrounding silence. She hoped it had been Daddy!

The real test for the chorus had arrived. Without a doubt, the next number was their most difficult. Even with the simplification of the piece, it was almost beyond their ability. The phrases demanded excellent flexibility, breath support, and accuracy of pitch. They couldn't let down for a second, or it would all collapse, and they would have no choice but to stop and start again, which would be a disgrace. It was unthinkable, but she knew it was possible if they didn't concentrate.

She took another deep breath and cued them to stand. They did so with determination. There was a long introduction, after which the sopranos had a very light and lively dancelike entrance, followed by the tenors and eventually the altos and basses. They began.

For unto us a child is born
Unto us a son is given
Unto us a son is given

They were doing it! They sang the demanding fast pianissimo as easily as if they were frolicking in a field of flowers The tenors answered with the same easy-sounding playfulness that she had tried and failed to get them to do all semester. By the time the altos and basses came in, it was electrifying. They sang as they had never sung before. Their faces were alive with animation as they flew through the difficult phrases with a fiery vitality she had never heard from them before. When they finished, they looked as if they were about to explode from the pure pleasure of their accomplishment.

The next four numbers were very short soprano recitatives followed by the entire group. Janet and Patty had always been excellent sopranos, but just as the rest were performing above their ability, so did they.

The next choral number was the *Glory to God* Joan cued the chorus, and they came in with dynamic forcefulness and a tone quality that sparkled with crisp vigor and strength.

They were sustaining the intensity and finished the movement knowing that they were participating in something so special that it would be difficult to describe to anyone who had not been a part of it. Even though the audience was obviously enjoying it, they—the performers—were in a different existence. Their heightened sense of themselves and one another gave them a feeling of total communion with the rest of the group and with Joan. It was as if they were all individual parts of a whole, which together comprised a spirit that was bright with joy.

They finished the *Glory To God*, and she motioned for them to be seated.

Ellen and Beth sang the last two solos with a quiet gentleness and serene dignity that was all the more impressive for the contrast it provided to the gusto of the previous movement.

"Wow!" she thought to herself. "They have done it!"

They had risen to a place she had not expected them to reach for a very long time, if ever. She realized that she had become so consumed by the music and the performance that she had totally forgotten the fear with which she had started the program. It was the furthest thing from her mind now. There was no question that her secret was safe and her family and job were also.

She was beside herself with relief and bliss. The choir was so excited that she barely had to move to cue them to stand. It was as if an invisible umbilical cord stretched from her to every person on the risers, uniting them all with an ethereal sense of communion with one another and the universe.

It was evident that they couldn't wait to start the finale. *The Hallelujah Chorus* had been their favorite from the very beginning. Once they learned it, there wasn't a rehearsal that went by that they didn't beg to sing it. Even when they were pressed for time, they would stay late to do it.

It started with ten emphatic "Hallelujahs" in a row, each one more powerful than the last, and then went into the body of the piece:

For the Lord God, Omnipotent Reigneth
Hallelujah

Then the sustained:

The kingdom of this world has become
The kingdom of our Lord and of his Christ
And He shall reign forever and ever!

As her eyes swept over them, she could see in their faces an overwhelming exhilaration. Then she saw something else—surprise!

They were stealing glances at the audience and then looking back at Joan. She heard a shuffling sound and turned her head just enough to see out of the corner of her eye. What she saw was one of the most beautiful and welcoming sights she had ever seen. The audience was slowly standing.

With each repetition of the "Forever and ever, Hallelujah, Hallelujah," the intensity and excitement soared. It swelled and multiplied in power and magnificence and swept them up into its celebrated splendor and into the final expansive fortissimo, "HAL-LE-LUJ-AH!" with unmitigated triumph!

Her arms fell to her sides. Her hands shook. She stood looking down at her music, unable to take in all that was happening. Her eyes blurred. She felt weak and shaky. How had it begun? When did it all change and become so beautiful? She was shaking with emotion. Tears welled up, and she didn't even bother to control them. She knew it was useless.

The audience was demanding her attention. She looked up at the chorus, willing them not to begin clapping. She had told them it was improper concert etiquette because the audience was applauding them as well as her. She knitted her eyebrows at them to remind them, wiped her eyes briefly, and then turned.

The entire audience was on its feet, applauding. She stepped down off the podium and, hanging onto the music stand for support, took a bow. They cheered wildly. She bowed again; again they cheered. She walked to the edge of the risers and raised her arm, acknowledging the chorus to the audience. Another cheer went up. Each soloist and accompanist was greeted with the same accolades as she motioned to them individually.

Then she sensed someone standing next to her and turned. It was Steve. He took her hand and led her back onto the podium. She was so stunned by it all that she followed meekly, letting him take control. Standing beside her, he raised his hand to the audience, quieting them down. He placed his arm around her shoulder and addressed the crowd.

"Thank you very much, ladies and gentlemen," he said, glancing back over his shoulder in the direction of the risers.

She tried to turn, but a gentle pressure on her shoulder prevented her from turning far enough to see what he was looking at.

"As you know, Mrs. Winter came to us last fall after Mr. Allen decided to go to Fayetteville to teach. We gave her a pretty hard time at first because we were mad at Mr. Allen for deserting us. She kept at us and didn't let us get away with too much, and we finally realized that she really cared about what happened to the chorus."

Again he craned his neck quickly backward and simultaneously hugged her shoulder a little closer to keep her from turning. She heard a collective but hushed gasp of surprise from the audience as Janet walked out from the wings and handed Steve a bouquet of yellow roses. He took them and turned back quickly as if he were afraid that by removing his hand, he would allow Joan enough time to turn around again.

"We want you to know how much we appreciate everything you have done for us. We could never have sung this beautiful music without you."

He handed her the roses and the audience applauded. "These are from the soloists and Carol."

Then she noticed that some of the audience members were whispering and pointing at the stage. Steve raised his hand again and continued addressing the audience. "She almost caught us talking about our plans right before warm-ups tonight."

"So *that* was all they'd been doing!" Joan thought. Her mind rocketed back to the moment she had walked into the room and they had immediately hushed up. That was all that had been going on. They had been planning the flowers. They were never in a position to have found out about her secret after all. She had almost ruined the concert by letting her imagination run wild. She berated herself for being so foolish.

Steve brought her back to the present as she realized that he was saying something again.

"So here is the real reason we were trying not to let you know what we were doing."

She stood looking at the bouquet and then back at him, not understanding what reason he was talking about—she already had the bouquet. The audience chuckled. She became concerned again.

"As I said, the bouquet you're holding is from the soloists and accompanist. The rest of the chorus got you this."

He turned her around to face the chorus, and she gasped for breath. Her heart tumbled out of her body and stumbled around all over the stage. Every person in the choir stood there, holding a long-stemmed red rose.

It was a sight she could never have imagined seeing, ever in her life. Grateful tears began spilling from her eyes again. Relief, joy, and love twirled around inside of her as the chorus began moving down off the risers.

They filed past her. Each person gave her a hug and a rose and then resumed their places on the risers. After they passed, Steve took each rose from her and carefully placed all sixty-five of them in a wicker rose basket, which had mysteriously appeared next to him on top of the grand piano. When the choir members were back in place, they completely abandoned everything she had taught them and joined the audience in their jubilant ovation. Joan just laughed.

Suddenly a rumble of delight passed through the crowd as something caught her eye on the stairs leading up to the stage. She looked down and saw two little people scrambling up the stairs, hand in hand. They scampered across to where she stood and proudly offered her the last two roses.

She accepted the gifts and knelt down, gathering their precious beings into her grateful arms, knowing at last that they were all safe, happy, and together.

The C. S. C. S. Class of 1954

Nancy Alexander
Helen Ariola
Joyce Baxter
Shirley Bloomer
Charles Blowers
Gerta Brandl
Audrey Brinkman
Neal Brown
Richard Bulson
Beth Burnham
Colleen Carroll
Cathy Clark
Penny Cobb
Arloe Crandall
Gail Crigier
Leta Darling
Carol Davis
Donna Delahunt
Jim Gerow
Ormond Goettle
Barry Goldsmith
Phyllis Greene
George Harris
Donald Hass
Jack Hayden
Reta Hayes
Francis Heistman
Bud Hemmings
Yvonne Herrick
Galin Hill
Ruby Hinman
Eleanor Johnson
Ralph Kelley
Bob Ladd
Joanne Lay
Elaine Lewis
Annette Mahar
Richard Mangus
Sylvia Matthys
Marian Maynard
Bernie Miller
Myrna Moore
Paul Murphy
Nellie Nicotra
Marie Nolan
Paul Pierce
Erkie Porter
Joyce Redhead
Phil Reed
Sam Riccelli
Joe Richardson
Roger Russell
Tom Schill
Dave Sheldon
Lenore Stanton
Ed Tyler
Elet Vollmer
Louise Waldron
Joan Webb
Arena Webb
Joan Weisner
Liz Wojtus
Gene Wolfe
Millard Wood
George Wright